CHILDREN OF LIES

BY
SUSAN LERNER

ISBN 978-0-9752853-8-1

On the Edge Books, New York, NY

ontheedgebooks@gmail.com for ordering information.

"ANY INTELLIGENT FOOL CAN
MAKE THINGS BIGGER, MORE
COMPLEX, AND MORE VIOLENT.
IT TAKES A TOUCH OF GENIUS—
AND A LOT OF COURAGE—TO MOVE
IN THE OPPOSITE DIRECTION."

—ALBERT EINSTEIN

CHAPTER ONE

SEPTEMBER 1970

Michael peered out through a slit in the stone wall, rocking back and forth on his heels, aiming an imaginary gun. His father had left a few days earlier to find them a safer place, and Michael had been up nearly the whole night waiting for him to return. With the light of dawn came the sound of gunfire. "Ommy!" he cried, turning to his mother. She was bent over Hanna, her mouth moving in silent prayer.

His five-year-old sister lay limp on her mat, her brown hair darkened by sweat to the color of mud. She had worsened rapidly, the way a river swells suddenly in a heavy rain, first complaining of stomach pains and vomiting, and then there was only an aching quiet.

"Lay your hand on her forehead," his mother whispered, making room for him to sit beside her. "Heal her."

He closed his eyes tight and imagined Hanna healthy and laughing, her little legs fluttering in the air when he tickled her, the way she looked once when he fit a pebble into her dimple. She was five years younger than he, a tiny plaything he'd adored since she was born.

He'd been the first to notice her symptoms, the pallor and tremors that only her medicine could set right. He'd learned to mix and inject the solution, distracting her with silly faces so she wouldn't be scared. The medicine always restored her; he was awed by its power. He wanted that power more than anything.

It was shocking to see her so weak, without even the strength to cry. His mother seemed almost the same; the panic that had kept her running around the refugee camp, cajoling some and yelling at others, had been replaced by quiet resignation. He didn't know what to do. His helplessness felt like a scratchy blanket of shame that made him uncomfortable in his own skin.

The gunfire drew closer, the air outside grew thick with smoke, and the silky sweet anticipation of battle turned sour in his stomach. His father had warned him this day would come, but he hadn't listened. Instead, he'd snuck across the camp to sit at the feet of Al Akil and the *fedayeen* while they discussed *strategy, movements, weapons, victory*, words that fueled his boy-soldier dreams.

Their feats were celebrated by the people and exulted by radio announcers: explosions in Zionist shopping malls, hijacked airplanes. He saw images of the air rocked with fire. Akil said that was what bravery looked like.

Then the men began saying different words: *blockade* and *dwindling supplies* and *outnumbered*—and the whole mood changed, and it all began to go wrong

His father's arguments and warnings to Akil echoed in his head as if it were an empty chamber: *The Arab nations make promises and fail to keep them…better to negotiate with Jews and have our own country than to be kept in camps …Revenge is not a political philosophy.* Michael stared at the door, muscles tensed, half-expecting Bedouin soldiers to storm through with their guns. But when the door flew open it was his friend, Wadih, his gun slung across his shoulder, his *keffiya* torn and streaked with mud and his eyes watery and bloodshot.

There was no laughter in those eyes, no trace of the easy, lopsided grin he wore when he let Michael follow him around the village like a little brother, playing hide-and-seek while they spread Party leaflets and communiqués. Wadih could make a game of the most mundane chore, and with one look at him, and Michael knew they were lost.

"Akil sent me," he said. "You aren't safe here. You must leave. I will take you."

"Where will we go?" said Michael's mother, her voice a whisper.

"I'll get you to the river and then you can find your way to Ramallah."

She pointed to Hanna. "She's very sick."

He frowned and swept Hanna across his shoulder like a bundle of goods. She moaned and then went silent. Michael and his mother gathered the backpacks they'd prepared and left the house in single file, his mother's hand gripping his shoulder.

They moved through the camp in halting steps, crouching low. There were wails, a keening sound faint amidst the gunfire. A blaze of light erupted in the distance and a tent caught fire. Michael saw someone run out, a figure of panic. Flames, like the tongues of snakes, licked the air. Thick, black smoke burned his lungs and eyes but he struggled to keep them open, bewildered by the changes in the familiar landscape of the camp.

Then Wadih stopped moving and fell to the ground. Where had the shot come from? Were the soldiers on the rooftops? He knelt by his friend and placed his hand over the wound to stanch the flow of blood, but it did nothing. He felt powerless. Ignorant. Useless. Wadih's lips were moving. Michael brought his head close but heard nothing. He sat back, stupid tears rolling down his cheeks. "I'll be back for you," he said, knowing it was a lie. But Wadih only stared, unseeing.

Michael looked to his mother. Her face was drained of all color except for the black dust that had settled into the array of fine lines around her eyes and mouth. She dropped to her knees, murmured a prayer, and kissed Wadih's cheek. Then she rose until she stood straight, taller than her knew her to be, took Hanna, and motioned for him to move on. He was tempted to turn around and bury his head in her dress, just for a moment, but he knew better and kept moving.

He wasn't sure which way to go, but he chose a direction and they walked for what seemed like hours, crouching behind shelled remains of buildings to stay out of sight, hoping to avoid the bullets. They progressed from the edges of the refugee camp into the fields, where others were also attempting to hide. They kept moving until they reached the Jordan River.

It was nearly dry at that point, just a narrow rocky bed with a trickle of water, like the memory of a river. Bedouin soldiers were behind them, bent on revenge against Akil and the *fedayeen* for ignoring the King's laws and attempting to take control of the country.

If Michel didn't get them across the river, the Bedouin soldiers would attack his mother horribly; he'd heard the *fedayeen* speak with anger at the things they did to women. They would kill him and Hanna with one stroke and burn their bodies like firewood.

Zionist soldiers stood on the other side of the river, on the land that once was theirs. Waiting. Their dark green uniforms blended with the greenery along the riverbank. The sun gleamed off the metal of their guns. He heard the rustling of rushes as people crawled through them, and saw *fedayeen* with their hands in the air. They were calling out to the soldiers, "Help! Let us cross! Let us through!" Some begged for water. Red *keffiyas* were scattered on the ground, abandoned.

There was only one choice, only one direction in which to go. He motioned to his mother, still carrying Hanna's almost lifeless body, and they walked toward the river. Michael's hands rose high into the air—a soft breeze pushing them even higher—and he pleaded with the Israelis, Uncle Akil's greatest enemy, to save them.

The soldiers held their fire and watched. One smoked a cigarette, and Michael burned inside, imagining that the man was enjoying his humiliation. But another came toward them repeating, "*B'seder, b'seder, b'seder*," like a chant. He was young, with dark eyes and hair. Except for the uniform, he could have been one of the *fedayeen*. He took a long look at Hanna, his expression one of sadness and concern, and for the briefest, tiniest speck of a moment, Michael wondered if his father could be right, that the Jews were just people and that they could live with them in peace.

But when he saw the fear and hatred on his mother's face, he brushed the thought away.

CHAPTER TWO

BROOKLYN, NEW YORK, 1974

It was May 15th, the day before Rachel Weissman's sixth birthday, and her dad was on his way home from Israel to be with her. Every few minutes she looked at the kitchen clock, announced the time aloud, and asked, "How much longer, Mommy?"

"Soon."

Daddy always brought her presents when he came home from a trip. One time it was a Babushka doll, which was really seven wooden dolls, one inside the other, a secret inside a secret. Another time it was a globe with a miniature city of Jerusalem inside. When she shook it, snowflakes clouded the air. She and Daddy would watch them clear away until the little city reappeared. Her mother thought it was silly, since it didn't snow in Jerusalem. Mommy was very practical.

Daddy was a lot more fun.

Mommy was baking a cake for Rachel's birthday. She moved lightly around the kitchen, like she wanted to dance; she twirled Rachel around as she passed her. "Daddy will be home, soon," she sang.

And then the phone rang.

Rachel ran to get it, but her mother got to it first and said, "Hello!" smiling, but then her expression changed and she shook her head, back and forth. "No, that's not possible. He was supposed to leave hours ago, it can't be him. There must be a mistake."

"What is it, Mommy?" Rachel asked, tugging at her arm, but her mother didn't answer. She put the phone down, pulled her close and patted her head like she was a puppy.

"Was that Daddy?" Rachel asked, but got no answer. Her mother looked like she'd eaten something bad and was getting sicker and sicker. She hugged Rachel so hard it hurt. "Later. Not now. I can't talk about it now."

Daddy never came. Other people did: neighbors, friends, and Uncle Steve, who was a doctor like her dad.

She sat with her mother on the green velvet couch in the living room and Uncle Steve sat beside them. "I'm so sorry, Rivka." He looked at Rachel and then back to her mother.

"I haven't explained it to her," she said. "I don't know how. Mark would know. I want to ask him." She began to laugh, but it turned into a choking sound. "Thank God his parents didn't live to go through this. Nor mine."

"It could have been me," Uncle Steve said. "If I hadn't been asked to fill in at that conference at Yale at the last minute—"

"Thank God for that. It could have been both of you."

They sent Rachel upstairs with a neighbor who babysat her sometimes, and it wasn't until everyone left that her mother told her that Daddy wasn't coming home. Not ever.

Rachel listened carefully. "No, that can't be right."

"It is, honey."

Rachel's eyes clouded over and everything got fuzzy, like the snow globe and Jerusalem, but it didn't clear up. It stayed that way, white flurries in her head, everything blurry.

"He isn't coming home the way you knew him," her mother continued, spinning words together into a rope to pull Rachel back to her. "I mean, you can't sit on his lap or give him a hug. But he's not all gone. His *spirit* is here." She said that word brightly, more enthusiastic than she had been since the phone call.

"What's a spirit?" Rachel asked, suspicious.

"A spirit is all the things he believed and loved, and that is still here. You see? He's in the air and all around us." Her arms lifted and she motioned around the empty living room. "You can still talk to him, Rachel, and he'll listen. He's watching over us. He cares about us so much that he'll never really leave us."

Rachel shrugged, unimpressed. She didn't want a "spirit." It was the worst birthday of her life.

The kids at school acted weird after that, like she had a disease and they didn't want to get too close or they might catch it and lose their fathers, too. Her teacher was too nice to her. She hadn't changed yet, somehow, she was different. And Mommy was a mess. Her eyes were always puffy and her cheeks were an ugly gray.

Rachel didn't bother her much. She played quietly in her room after school and lost herself in fantasies of her father coming back, lifting her in the air over his head, putting her on his shoulders as they walked around town. When her mother asked her what she was thinking about she said, "Nothing."

Her mother talked about Daddy sometimes. She told Rachel how he was born in Germany and left when he was just a little boy, fled with his family, leaving everything behind. He came to this country as Moshe and ended up as Mark, to blend in more easily, and worked hard to be a doctor because he wanted to help people who had lost their homes and had to start again, the way he had done.

CHAPTER THREE

NEW YORK CITY, JANUARY 1988

It was a brisk, clear winter afternoon. The bright sunlight gave an illusion of warmth so convincing that guys were on the lawn in tee shirts and shorts, tossing Frisbees that sailed through the air in mesmerizing arcs to the beat of the Dead blaring from a boom box nearby. The intoxicating music and sun-dappled buildings made Rachel lightheaded and romantic and she thought of Josh.

She wore a short down parka over a black tee shirt, jeans, and Doc Martens boots. It helped to have a simple uniform; one less thing to think about. The only touch of luxury was a delicate vicuna wool scarf. It had been a gift from her mother, a fashion designer with her own label and a workshop in Manhattan.

At first glance the scarf appeared to be solid blue but it was actually woven from a multitude of shades, a study of variations on blue. It reminded her of the Ad Reinhardt paintings at the Guggenheim, entire canvases that looked like simple black squares, but upon careful observation turned out to consist of layers of gradations of black. The detail in the scarf was so fine, and yet easily overlooked. The average person wouldn't notice it. It was a lot like her, Josh had once said—as if only he could see that she was special.

The scarf had brought them together. She'd left it behind on a chair in the student center one day and he ran after her, shouting, "You forgot this!" Her arms were full of books, so he laid the scarf around her. "It's so soft. Be a shame to lose it," he'd said, smiling down at her from his greater height.

He was pre-med at Columbia University when they met, like her but a year ahead, and spoke with comforting authority about courses and professors. They started seeing each other, and when he introduced her to his friends, they became her friends, too. Her future unfolded before her; her ducks marched happily in order. After she finished med school, they would marry and then volunteer at a clinic in a Third World country, an NGO that helped children. Eventually they would run a pediatric clinic and have lots of children of their own—a big family, just as she'd always wanted. The clinic would house a day-care center so she could visit her kids between patients and always have them near.

Rachel stopped in at Java Joe's and scooped some French Roast beans from a bin into a paper bag—Josh's favorite. The aroma escaped into the air; just the smell of it cheered her up on the subway ride uptown to the med school dorm.

As she came out of the subway, a homeless woman with a child at her side held out a cup and asked, plaintively, "Can you help feed my little girl?" Rachel knew immediately that the woman either had mental health issues or was a drug addict or con artist, and a closer look at the woman's eyes and jittery movements made her certain the woman was high. Rachel had been around the city long enough to know the child was probably being used as a prop; kids were sometimes "rented out" for such a purpose. Any sympathy Rachel might have had for the woman was overwhelmed by her revulsion at the way she was treating the child, who was shivering in a flimsy jacket, unsuitable for the weather.

"Can you help her?" The woman held out her cup, again. If Rachel gave her money, she'd use it for herself; and if she gave it to the little girl, the woman would likely take it from her. But she rummaged in her pocket for change and handed it to the little girl anyway, wishing she could do more.

Michael climbed the steps to the Columbia Middle Eastern Studies Center two at a time. His long strides reflected both his natural grace and his natural impatience. His thoughts were on his endocrinology research and his plans for creating a multi-national partnership of doctors and nurses to bring healthcare to children in Palestine. His idea was to outfit and staff mobile clinics to reach underserved areas in remote villages.

He'd been in New York for almost three years, living in the privileged atmosphere of the university, far from the daily indignities of the Occupation. He had little time for the Palestinian cause.

Yusif, an associate professor of poetry who had grown up with Michael, ran the Students for Palestinian Human Rights group (SPHR). He was devoted to the Party and Akil, but he and Michael never spoke of their leader, except to each other. In the eyes of the university administration, they were simply a human rights organization, and that was how Akil wanted it. He had groomed them and paid for their education.

Now they were two outstanding students who had worked their way into respected positions in the community of scholars, living in New York and blending into their surroundings, waiting for the opportunity to strike.

That moment had come.

The *intifada* had begun a few weeks earlier, when an Israeli trucker mowed down four Palestinians in Gaza. A rumor started that it had been deliberate. Within hours, rioting broke out. Then the rebel leadership took control, and the uprising spread and intensified. They barricaded roads, burned tires, and organized general strikes. It wasn't just a disturbance; it was a revolt. The whole world was paying attention. Journalists wrote stories about human rights violations and the heroism of an oppressed people rising in protest. It was as if Akil had written the articles for them, so well did they parrot his thinking.

Like a contagion from Palestine, it led to an explosion of activity at SPHR, and Yusif needed Michael's help in planning a campus demonstration. Michael organized teams of students to distribute flyers and posters announcing the event, and was organizing speakers and a sound system, tables with petitions, a thousand details. An image of all he had to do flashed before him and he saw the tasks in his mind as shapes, sorted in terms of priority. He glanced at his watch, a present from Akil when he graduated med school, and decided he could allot an hour to SPHR before returning to the lab.

Yusif was sorting through photographs when he arrived. Michael sat beside him at the battered wood table and glanced at them. "Where did these come from?"

"Ramallah. Sit down and have a look."

As Michael sifted through the photographs, a pretty girl with a friendly smile came by and sat in the empty chair next to him, moving it a fraction closer as she did so. Her hair was freshly washed and still damp. It smelled nice, like lavender. He riffled through the photographs, ignoring her, and said to Yusif, "They're shooting unarmed children."

Yusif nodded. "The kids throw rocks and they retaliate with rubber bullets and tear gas."

He felt the girl recoil.

He was inured to violence. It was as much a part of the landscape of his childhood as the dirt and the sun. People in New York who knew him as a respected doctor would be shocked if they knew the things he'd done for the Party.

"The demonstration is beginning to come together," Michael said. "There will be mock checkpoints set up in front of the library and near the dorms. We'll have people at each table demanding to see ID's and making people wait in line, so they can get a feel for what it's like to live with roadblocks."

"Has the college administration been notified?"

The girl was getting restless, shifting in her chair. She tapped his arm with two fingers, a little trill.

"Yes. We had to assure them that no emergency exits would be blocked."

A moment of silence. She took the opportunity to speak. "I made a flyer. Want to see it?" She edged her chair even closer. Her plump cheeks were the color of honey. She was Palestinian-American, very pretty, and he was drawn to her.

But he knew she was dangerous for him. Girls like her had fathers who wanted husbands, not boyfriends, and he had no thought of marriage or family.

"It needs a photo. Try this one." He directed her attention to a photograph of small children crouching behind a pile of stones. One child had risen, about to hurl one. Across from him were IDF soldiers aiming their long rifles directly at him.

"That's terrific," she said. An admiring smile. Too bright. The female students thought him exotic, intense, sexy. It would be easy to seduce her; he would just have to play a role and she would do the rest. But it would not be wise. He looked in her eyes with all he had to offer: an acknowledgement of his attraction combined with a regretful rejection. Then he turned away from her, his meaning unmistakable, and she slowly got up and walked from the room.

"Michael, there's something else," Yusif said, closing the door behind her. "Akil was arrested and is in prison in the Negev. He was in a safe house and yet they found him. There is an informant."

The news was a blow. For so long, Akil had evaded capture, moving around, sometimes using disguises. "He has many rivals trying to get control of the Party and they want him out of the way."

The arrest was another rupture in Akil's power. In the ever-changing universe of Palestinian political rivalry, Akil's star was falling. Some said it was because he was Christian, and Islamism was gaining traction. Michael thought it was because he was an idealist who had always been committed to his principles and to the people. He was less skilled in the arts of corruption and exploitation than Arafat, who used bribes and threats effectively, to ensure loyalty.

"Until we can get him out, we'll use a system we worked out a while ago," Yusif said. "He'll send coded messages to Eva. She will pass them on to me, and then she'll send our return messages to certain other prisoners, who will pass them to Akil. Nothing changes for us, unless we hear otherwise."

Eva was Yusif's wife. This plan essentially gave Yusif control of all the communications.

"There should be a backup. Another way to get messages to him. In case one fails or is intercepted," Michael suggested.

"You may be right," Yusif agreed, "but this is all we have for the moment. I will speak for both of us. After all these years, you don't trust me?" He smiled.

"It's not that…I'm just thinking of backups, the way Akil would." He couldn't find a flaw in Yusif's argument, yet it made him uneasy.

CHAPTER FOUR

The door to Josh's suite was open when Rachel arrived and the living room was in artful disarray: empty beer cans arranged in a pyramid on the coffee table, colorful album covers and cassettes piled around the stereo. She'd just put the coffee beans on the kitchen counter when she heard the high-pitched laughter. A girl's laughter. A giggle, really.

And she knew, even before the blur of movement caught her eye and Josh came out of his room with the pretty blonde, her hair held back with a headband. The girl's clothes were in disarray and her expression was blissful. Rachel felt time slow down, as if the room had filled with water, making it hard to move and distorting her vision.

Josh looked from Rachel to the blonde, startled and unsure, but only for a moment. His confidence reasserted itself easily, like that of an actor who knows his lines even though the other player had flubbed his. "Hey, what are you doing here? Have you met Pam?"

Pam smiled a hello and kissed Josh goodbye with a light touch of lips that was somehow very intimate. Her eyes were sparkling and her languid movements owned the space—owned Josh—even as she ambled out the door.

"What's going on here?" Rachel hated the hysterical note in her voice.

"Take it easy. We were studying. She's a friend. Don't overreact."

"So don't lie." It was all falling into place, like random letters forming a word.

"What's the matter with you? I'm the one in med school. I'm the one under pressure here," Josh said.

"Is that your excuse? That you're under pressure?"

He shrugged. "What's that? It smells good." He picked up the bag of coffee beans, opened it and sniffed. "French Roast, my favorite. Thanks, Rach. Sit down, sweetie. I'll make it," he said, as if a gesture of hospitality would solve everything.

"Don't bother. I'm not staying."

"Oh, come on. Don't blow this out of proportion. So, I have friends. What's the big deal? It doesn't change the way I feel about you." His voice lowered, as if he'd adjusted a radio setting. "It's totally different. It's…" He examined the floor as he struggled with his thought. "It's like having a cat," he finally said. "You can pet a cat, but it's nothing like touching a person you care about." He nodded, as if this were a profound thought.

"Josh." It was so absurd she almost laughed. He caught that and smiled.

"Rachel," he murmured. "My Rachel." Something familiar and inviting in his voice made her reflexively relax.

He edged closer to her, his arms reaching out as if to stroke her, and it crossed her mind that he was trying to seduce her. As if she were a complete idiot.

"She's not a cat, Josh. Her name isn't Fluffy or Mittens. It's Pam. She's another woman. Not a cat."

He stepped back to regroup and try another tack, but she caught something in his face at that moment—a flicker of boredom or indifference or amusement—something she couldn't quite place, but it clarified everything.

She grabbed the coffee beans from him, muttered, "Asshole," and threw the open bag at him. The beans clattered as they bounced off his chest and spread around the floor. A few landed on the counter. The delicious aroma of coffee spread through the room, making her heady with incongruous pleasure. Josh stared at her, eyes wide, arms across his chest for protection. She slammed the door behind her as she left, holding the doorknob so tightly her arm shook.

Out on the street, Rachel was paralyzed by confusion. Where to go now? She wanted to be alone but had no private refuge. She'd moved home to save on rent, since she was always with Josh, anyway. Now her home was with her mother, Josh's biggest fan and the last person she wanted to see. There was her best friend, Jill, but she hadn't had a boyfriend in college. Just dated a little. Jill wouldn't understand.

She went back to the 1 train, lulled by the screeching rumble of the wheels as it pulled into the station, standing aside to let passengers out before entering with the small crowd gathered by the open door. People moved past one another with such ease, it might have been choreographed. More people got off than on, so she found a seat, held her head in her hands, closed her eyes and tried to get control.

Beneath her rage was a layer of guilt. For what, she couldn't say, but guilt gnawed through her indignation, and as scenes of their relationship played out in her head, she scrutinized them for evidence that she was at fault. If nothing else she was guilty of bad judgment and of having ignored warning signs, a classic triumph of hope over experience. But in her case, it was the triumph of hope over *lack* of experience. What did she know of men? Her father died when she was so young that she barely remembered him, and her mother was a superlative specimen of overprotective Jewish mother.

When the train got to Riverdale, Rachel got off and headed toward her house. It was only a thirty-minute ride but a world away from Manhattan, a sleepy town with a few restaurants, shops, a food store, and Mother's Bakery, where she used to stand eye-level with the cases of baked goods, pointing to what she wanted, walking out with a white box wrapped with string. Squeezed among small apartment buildings and two-family homes, their small ivy covered Tudor was an aberration and a gem; one of the few single-family homes in the area.

She closed the front door as softly as possible, but the foyer led to the kitchen and Rivka came out before she was out of her jacket. "What are you doing here?"

Rachel felt like she was going to cry.

"What's the matter? Why aren't you at Josh's?"

She wanted to avoid the discussion but lacked the energy for subterfuge. "We broke up. It's finished. Done."

A look of horror crossed her mother's face. It dawned on Rachel that her mother's approval and encouragement had played a role in this disaster of a relationship.

"What happened? You had a fight? Big deal. Don't over-dramatize."

"It wasn't just a fight. He was with someone. I got there early and he was with this girl…" her voice turned shrill and her mother's eyes widened. "It was humiliating. She kissed him right in front of me. He's a jerk, and I can't believe I didn't see it until now. You encouraged it!"

"Come, sit down, Rachel. Come in the kitchen. Have some coffee."

"I want to be alone."

"I know. But sit with me." Her mother put her arm around her and it was so comforting that she had to fight an urge to melt into her arms like a child. She allowed herself to be led into the kitchen and sat at the big oak table. It had heavy legs and a thick top that had aged to a warm golden brown. The oversized, spindle-back captain's chair engulfed her and she leaned back, attempting unsuccessfully to relax.

They sat together in silence, her mother tracing finger circles on the table, deep in thought. Josh was her ideal future son-in-law: good-looking, smart, studying to be a doctor as her husband had been. She was disappointed.

"Maybe it was just something that happened," Rivka finally said, breaking the silence. "Maybe it was that idiot girl's fault. She's probably just a gold-digger. A doctor-digger! She's trying to get him away from you. Don't let her win. Do you know her? What's her story?"

Rachel shrugged, shook her head. The girl wasn't important. It was Josh, and there was no excusing him. She couldn't crawl back into her fantasy of a loving, committed relationship. It was an old comforter that had worn too thin.

"No Mom, don't make excuses for him. It's better to know now and be rid of him."

"Everything is always so black-and-white with you. Did you even give him a chance to explain?"

"Mom, stay out of this. Who are you to give advice? It's been years since Daddy died and you never even date."

"That's completely different. I was married, once. I had you."

"Well I'm all grown up, so why don't you start dating instead of worrying about me? You always thought that because Josh is going to be a doctor, he's just like Daddy. He's not. Daddy loved medicine because he could save lives and help people. Josh just wants to make money."

"What's wrong with making money?"

"Nothing, but that's all it is to him. Medicine is a stepping-stone to a McMansion in Scarsdale. He'll end up in a fancy Park Avenue practice, cheating on his wife and sleeping with the nurse." She had never thought that before, but as soon as she said it, she knew it was true.

Rivka smiled as if it were a joke. "You don't know that. People make mistakes. You can be very unforgiving."

She shouldn't be having this discussion. She wished she hadn't agreed to move home for the year. It dawned on her that now she would be living with her mother full-time, that she couldn't afford to get her own place, and everyone else she knew already had roommates. It wasn't the worst realization of the day, but it was close.

"Maybe I should cancel my trip," Rivka said. "It's a buying trip and I have some appointments, but I don't want to leave you alone—"

"No! That's ridiculous I'm not sick, I don't need you making me chicken soup and fussing over me. The last thing I need is you mixing in."

"Fine. Very nice way to talk to your mother." Her lips tightened into a hard line and Rachel knew she'd gone too far. Now, her mother would probably stop talking to her altogether. It was a weapon she used sparingly: a sudden withdrawal of her love. It had been effective when Rachel was younger. As an adult, she could survive her mother's silence. But it was another pressure she didn't need at that moment.

She went upstairs, lay on her bed and closed her eyes, relieved to finally be alone. Her mother would continue to press her to forgive Josh, but did he even want it? She suspected he didn't, that if the blow-up hadn't happened today, it would have happened some other day. He was marketable and confident, at a top med school, doing well. A lot of girls found him attractive and he wanted the freedom to explore. Well, they were welcome to him.

But, as the days passed, Rachel felt somehow incomplete, like part of her was missing. She missed Josh the way an ex-smoker misses cigarettes, knowing that she had the moral high-ground but longing for the high. She turned on her stereo and drowned her emotions in music. Brubeck's piano jamming with Desmond's alto sax, Keith Jarrett's emoting in *Köln Concert*, Davis's aptly named, *Kind of Blue*. She danced to the soulful music, improvising earthy modern dance moves, comforting in their familiarity after years of modern dance training.

The strain tore at her body in odd little ways. Her hair felt dry and brittle. Her fingernails frayed and she left little scars on the fabric of her sweaters where she touched them. Her lips cracked and blistered. "It's just the cold weather," Jill said, but Rachel knew it was more. She envisioned herself drying out until she was dust and her mother scattering the ashes.

In a bizarre way, her disappointment was familiar, comforting. Men loved, excited, and then disappointed you, whether by intent or accident, and did it make a difference? It was a fact of life she'd understood since she was a six-year-old and the father she adored left on a trip to Israel and never came home. It was etched into her when she held her mother's hand at the memorial service, just the two of them, her other hand flopping by her side, empty. She barely remembered her dad anymore. He was just an outline of a drawing without shading or detail. But she remembered losing him. And now she'd lost Josh.

CHAPTER FIVE

ISRAELI PRISON CAMP NEAR EILAT

Akil sat on the edge of a thin mattress resting on wooden slats. It was positioned in the center of the tent, away from the drafty flaps of the opening. Other cots were crowded together to leave room around his. Such were his privileges as the leader of the People's Revolution Party. When he needed privacy, he had only to nod his head and the others scattered.

Most of the men were outside in the yard—concrete slabs surrounded by high barbed-wire fencing. It was still a comfortable temperature, too early for the daily assault of blinding desert sun. He would have joined them but for the prying eyes of the soldiers. Instead, he stayed inside and a young man, recently arrived, joined him.

Akil was always suspicious of new prisoners and had them repeat their stories multiple times. If someone used the same words each time, it meant they were memorized, evidence of an informer. Some were Jews who'd grown up in Arab countries, physically indistinguishable from Palestinians who spoke perfect Arabic. They were trained spies and more difficult to catch. Others were his own people who had been turned by bribes or threats. He had identified one of them two weeks earlier and sentenced him to death, but the guards got wind of it and transferred him out before the sentence could be carried out.

This young man, still a teen, stood gingerly, like a colt on his own for the first time. He was blinking rapidly.

"When did you last sleep?" Akil asked gently, assuming a grandfatherly demeanor, motioning the boy to sit beside him. "We are all family here, so be at peace. After we talk you may rest."

The boy looked at him gratefully.

"What is your name, son?"

"Dani."

"Why were you arrested?"

"I was out after curfew."

"Doing what?"

"My little sister had wandered off and my mother was beside herself. She sent me out to find her and told me not to come home without her, so I kept looking even after curfew. I stayed in the shadows but they rounded me up and wouldn't listen about my sister. I found out later she'd been hiding in the bushes right by our home. She's only four and thought it was a game."

Dani dropped his head, ashamed.

"It is not your fault. But it is time for things to change so a young man can look for his little sister without being thrown into prison."

Akil quizzed him about his political activity, but aside from throwing stones, he was not active—just a boy who had found himself in the wrong place at the wrong time. He had been trying to help his family get by and stay out of the way, but in their world, that was impossible.

The Israelis did his recruitment work for him, throwing boys like Dani in prison for minor offenses. If they'd left him alone, he'd have pursued his dream of being a mechanic and working alongside his father in their garage. Now, he would devote himself to Akil and the cause.

They spoke until Dani relaxed, and then he went off to his promised rest. Akil also needed rest, now that the heat of the day was seeping into the tent. There were beads of sweat on his wide forehead and he felt lightheaded. His thoughts entered a foggy fugue, another enemy he had to contend with. The strain of prison life took its toll on a man his age. He stretched his arms above his head, took a deep breath, and went outside to speak with Ibrahim.

"Twenty new prisoners have arrived," Ibrahim said. He motioned at the already overcrowded tent. "There is no place to put them."

Akil gave him instructions for reorganizing the space. It was important to keep the new prisoners together to allow for bonding when they were at their most vulnerable, separated from their families, many of them for the first time.

"One man brought news from Ramallah," said Ibrahim. "Rival groups are moving to consolidate power in your absence. They are planning a meeting later this month. A National Council is organizing boycotts to make sure that merchants don't pay the VAT and that no one works at jobs in Israel."

"Civil disobedience? The enemy brings helmets and guns and we hold protest signs! What is wrong with them? They got me out of the way for that?"

"It's worse. They are considering recognizing Israel."

Akil frowned. "Bring this man to me. I will interrogate him myself."

The prisoner was a slight man, his body bent. He had bruises on his arms. He spoke slowly, halting every so often, but Akil didn't hurry him.

"The new council… brought together all the resistance groups…They are putting aside their differences and working together to…to negotiate a peace agreement."

Akil felt the simmering frustration at his incarceration almost boil over. He was considered a revered elder statesman by some, but his influence was waning and his absence from these discussions could prove fatal. New leaders sprang up like weeds. Moderate voices were finding their way to the surface like tiny bubbles in a restless sea.

He asked the man for more details: who said what, the exact words they used. When he was satisfied, he sent the man away.

"It's all a ruse," he told Ibrahim. "Arafat is not a peacemaker in the mold of Sadat. Sadat betrayed us in his heart as well as his words when he forged a peace agreement between Egypt and the Zionists. Arafat speaks from both sides of his mouth. He will never recognize Israel, not in exchange for the return of the West Bank and Gaza, not even for the promise of heaven on earth!" He spit on the ground, for emphasis.

"It's a trick?"

"Of course! As soon as the army has withdrawn and he has gathered sufficient strength, he will find some pretext to accuse Israel of breaching the agreement and use it as an excuse to attack. But words mean something! A peace agreement will create its own reality.

"He should offer no more than a *hudna*—a truce. An actual agreement is a travesty! Saying the words aloud, signing papers with cameras flashing is shameful and stupid."

Akil began composing a message for the leaders of the scattered, splintered revolutionary groups. His arguments would of necessity be distilled from eloquent paragraphs into a few short phrases. He needed to find words that would, like drops of perfume, evoke the memory of the struggle so strongly that it would reach their hearts and cut through their short-term thinking. He needed to regain control of the movement to which he'd devoted his life.

But the words would not come to him.

The prison strangled his thoughts. He struggled against it, but finally gave in to fatigue and lay down for a restless nap. By the time he got up, the sky was dark and the air had cooled. Soon it would be freezing. The desert was a place of extremes.

He went into the prison yard and began to walk, taking measured steps that hugged the farthest perimeter of the yard, pondering all the changes the *intifada* brought about. Others thought they saw opportunity where he saw threat. They were young and impatient and didn't understand that it was a long road to victory; it might not come until the Arab puppet governments, stinking of American oil money, were replaced with revolutionary regimes. They needed to stay the course. Their short-term thinking would be their undoing and it was up to him to remind them of it.

Akil's reputation still held some sway, and outside the walls of the prison, he had loyal followers who would obey his orders. Among them were the boys he helped raise, Yusif and Michael, educated and accomplished and living abroad. It was time to put them to use. He needed a plan, and one began to unfold in his mind with each measured step.

CHAPTER SIX

Rachel and Jill spent the morning at the library, and when they emerged, students were packed on the landing and all the way down the steps, all staring out as if watching a performance. The air outside was still moist from a night of rain, and a slight haze made them squint when they tried to see what had drawn everyone's attention. Spread across the quad below, marchers carried signs written in large block letters: ISRAEL IS A RACIST STATE, ISRAEL IS AN APARTHEID STATE, END THE OPPRESSION.

Demonstrations were a common sight on campus, protests ranged from pressuring the university to divest from companies with ties to South Africa to hiring women on construction crews. But this one, singling out Israel as an oppressor, seemed disturbingly familiar to Rachel, though she couldn't remember having seen anything like it. It was as if she had access to the collective memory of centuries of anti-Semitism, of blaming Jews, hating Jews, being the target of that hatred because she was Jewish.

She tried to make out faces among the protestors but it was all a blur of coats and hoods and red scarves. There were about a hundred people clustered together, standing before a young man with a megaphone. His jacket was carelessly open to the biting wind, his voice hoarse from his efforts.

"Excuse me."

A middle-aged man Rachel recognized as an English professor picked his way through the crowd. He wore a serene expression, as if he were thinking of something pleasant, oblivious to the chaos around him. The crowd magically parted, ejecting him like a foreign body. Rachel had been studying biology all morning. Everything reminded her of cells, even the crowd.

There was a tap on her shoulder and she turned to see her friend Daniel. He wore a blue and white yarmulke that contrasted with his dark red hair. He'd begun wearing it after spending his junior year in Israel where he discovered "how rich and beautiful the Jewish religion is," as he put it. He wore it not because he was religious, but in symbolic solidarity with the Russian *refuseniks*, Jews who were denied permission to leave the Soviet Union and then discriminated against for trying.

"You've got a good view," he said.

"Can you believe this?"

"It doesn't surprise me."

"We've got to get through this crowd," Rachel said. "We're starting the internship today." She and Jill were working three afternoons a week at the pediatric endocrinology clinic run by Dr. Steven Bergman. He was one of the few of her father's colleagues who'd stayed in touch after he died, bringing gifts on her birthday, inviting her and her mother to family events with his wife and kids. He was a link to her father in ways that her mother wasn't. When she was a little girl, she'd sit on his lap, lean her head against his chest, and feel connected to her dad through "Uncle" Steve's heartbeat. She would imagine that all people were connected by their heartbeats, like an orchestra directed by God.

"You may have a problem," Daniel said. "They have tables set up blocking the exits and they're demanding to see IDs and making people wait in line."

"Why?"

"So people can see what it's like to live with roadblocks." He rolled his eyes.

"Are they blowing people up, too? So they know what it's like to live *without* roadblocks?" Jill said.

Daniel smiled mirthlessly. "Yeah, maybe we should pretend to smuggle a fake explosive."

"It's all theater," Rachel said. "And I don't have time to attend the performance. Gotta get out of here."

Daniel followed her as they pushed their way through the crowd—no magical partings for them—and made their way toward the campus gates, where tables were set up and a line of protesters was stretched out to prevent people from exiting.

"Papers! Papers! Take out your papers for inspection!"

Most people were complying, waiting in line and showing their student IDs. Occasionally, they pulled a random person aside and made an "arrest."

Rachel saw someone veer off onto a path that had been cleared by campus security. Everyone could have done that and avoided the delay. They didn't because they wanted to be part of the protest, to pretend to be arrested, like it was a game.

She motioned to Daniel and Jill, and, as they followed her toward the exit, one of the students shouted at Daniel, "Hey, you! Rosenberg! Get back here and see what it's like for the Palestinians you oppress!" Daniel's last name was Weiss. The guy was using "Rosenberg" as an epithet, a name representing all Jews, the way the Nazis called all Jewish men, "Israel."

"You're a racist pig," Daniel said calmly.

What was happening to this campus? Rachel was disgusted, but Daniel seemed deep in thought, the way he looked in class, sometimes. Once they were back out on the avenue, he wished the two women luck and gave Rachel a hug. His strong embrace gave her a sense of comfort that had eluded her lately. When she had first met Daniel, freshman year, she could tell he had a crush on her, but she hadn't been attracted to him. Somehow, they'd finessed their way into a friendship and she was proud of that. Most guys that she rejected as boyfriends wanted nothing to do with her, as if it were all or nothing. Daniel was different. They got along, were in a lot of the same classes, and had a lot in common, so they built a relationship around those things instead of a romance.

Jill was the one who would have liked him as a boyfriend, but it was obvious that he saw her only as a friend. He hugged Jill, too, but Rachel sensed it was obligatory, unlike the way he'd hugged her.

Rachel and Jill ran the rest of the way to the hospital to make up for the delay. Once inside, they walked down a long hallway, past waiting rooms visible through interior windows. It reminded Rachel of walking through the Natural History Museum, looking at exhibits through glass panels.

At the end of the hall, she pushed open the door marked *Pediatric Endocrinology, Dr. Steven Bergman, Director.* The room was painted a cheerful yellow and posters of The Adventures of Gummi Bear, Astroboy, The Care Bears and (her personal favorite) Babar decorated the walls. At the far end, behind a partition, was a desk for the receptionist. Next to that was a door that led to the exam rooms, some offices, and a break room with a coffeemaker and a small table.

Several people were milling around: residents and interns, nurses and lab technicians. The nurses wore oversized shirts decorated with little bears. Doctors wore long white lab coats while the med students wore shorter ones.

"Well, we made it in plenty of time," Jill whispered. "I'm going to the ladies' room."

Left on her own, Rachel scanned the room for a familiar face—but it was an unfamiliar one that caught her attention. He was a tall man, his hair a mass of black curls with some silvery strands shot through that caught the light, making him shine. There were lines around his almond-shaped eyes, as if he'd been squinting against a strong sun. They were a striking blue color, more so since they were set off against an olive complexion. He looked familiar, like a distant cousin she rarely saw.

She heard him speaking to another doctor in what sounded like Hebrew. An Israeli? He looked strong and tough, the way she thought of Israelis. The outlines of his muscles were visible through his lab coat. His sinewy hands gripped a notebook tightly and squeezed it harder as he argued a point.

He swiveled toward her so suddenly that she flinched. "Can I help you?" he demanded harshly, a corporal addressing a private.

"Umm, I thought I heard you speaking Hebrew," she said. "I recognized it. The language."

His expression softened just a shade. "Do you need something?" He looked at her curiously.

"I'm Rachel Weissman. I'm going to be a student-intern here this semester." She smiled.

He nodded, his eyes perusing her, assessing, evaluating, and something more—something electric behind his otherwise calculating eyes.

"We... I..." she stammered, the intensity of his gaze making her flustered, "...almost didn't make it on time. There was a demonstration. A Palestinian group. They weren't letting people through... pretending it was a checkpoint..." She rolled her eyes a little.

His expression changed, surer now, as if he'd figured something out. For a split second he looked at her so deeply that her breath caught in her throat. And then, just as quickly, he turned from her, saying only, "We should be getting started, very soon."

She was left standing there, like a wallflower at the school dance, when the room suddenly shushed and everyone turned toward the source of the silence. The head of the clinic had arrived.

Dr. Bergman nodded to the group of about fifteen people and Rachel felt the room shift and reorganize itself into a hierarchy. It was almost physical, as if the space transformed into a building with a series of staircases leading to the top, where Dr. Bergman stood. He was a man of about fifty, with dark hair cut short and a tall thin frame, except for a little paunch, as if to show the world he was too busy with important things to have time to exercise. He motioned everyone into the conference room.

Jill hurried in, barely making it before the door closed. She whispered an irritated, "Why didn't you get me?" into Rachel's ear.

"I thought you could manage to come back from the ladies room," Rachel whispered back.

Someone shushed them, and the meeting started with a review of patient histories. The conversation was peppered with confusing abbreviations and acronyms and Rachel very quickly lost track, until an intern began describing the condition of a five-year-old patient named Maureen. Her diabetes had gone untreated for too long because she'd been misdiagnosed. When she got to the hospital she was in shock and complications had set in. They tried fluids and injections and exhausted all options, but despite all the advances of modern medicine, they couldn't save her. A wave of sadness washed over the room.

Rachel had first learned about juvenile diabetes in fifth grade, when Emily moved down the block from her. She'd been curious about her condition, and Emily's mom seemed to appreciate her endless questions, gave detailed explanations, showed her how to test for blood sugar and inject insulin. Rachel became alert to signs of trouble: When Emily got pale and jittery, she knew her sugar levels were going awry and cajoled her into eating. It got to where Rachel was the only one Emily's mom trusted to babysit for her.

And then one night Emily was rushed to the hospital, and they almost lost her. It wasn't Rachel's fault, or anyone's fault, but she'd felt guilty all the same, wondering if there was something more she could have done.

She was entering a profession that would be full of moments like that and she didn't know if she'd ever learn to distance herself from the tragedies that awaited her. She noticed the Israeli was listening intently to the intern's description of the patient, and saw pain in the depths of his eyes, otherwise so hard and calculating.

There was some discussion and then Dr. Bergman ended the meeting with announcements. When it broke up, he motioned to Rachel and Jill and when they reached him, said, "Welcome!" He leaned in as if to kiss Rachel, then thought better of it and shook her hand instead. He was clearly trying to be professional in the context of their new mentoring relationship.

"I know most of that was over your head, but you'll pick a lot up just from listening. I always have the interns sit in on these meetings and they thank me for it later, when they realize how much it helped them understand the workings of the clinic.

"You'll mainly be helping out in reception and the waiting room and assisting with intake interviews," he continued. "I've assigned Dr. Jeffrey"—he motioned in the direction of a young doctor, very thin, with wire-rimmed glasses and a short beard—"to oversee your work and help you find a subject for a research project. That's part of the internship as well."

Rachel was dying to ask him about the Israeli doctor, but before she could think of a graceful way to bring him up, Dr. Bergman called him over. "I'd like you to meet someone. Dr. Michael, these are our student interns."

So, his name was Michael.

"We met briefly," he said, speaking slowly, as if accustomed to having people listening to him. By comparison, Rachel felt flighty, like a little bird fighting a losing battle against a strong wind.

"This is Dr. Michael Haddad," Dr. Bergman said. "The kids call him Dr. Michael. He studied in Beirut and is doing some very interesting research on a protein compound that could reverse the mechanism of diabetes." Dr. Bergman had one hand on Michael's shoulder and placed his other on Rachel's as he introduced them. "This is Rachel Weissman and Jill Lazar, our pre-med student interns. Rachel's dad was a wonderful pediatrician. I've known Rachel since before she was born." He gave a little chuckle. "It's their first day. Are you supervising the medical students, today?"

"Yes. We're doing practice physicals."

"How about if the interns sit in?"

Dr. Michael looked thoughtful for a moment. "Why don't they act as patients?"

"Wonderful idea!" Dr. Bergman said. "Dr. Jeffrey!" he called out to the doctor with the short beard. "Take our student interns to an exam room and review some of the symptoms so they can present medical histories." He turned back to Dr. Michael. "Oh, before you get started, I meant to ask you…"

As they walked off, Dr. Michael gave Rachel a brief, parting glance. His eyes searched her face and then flickered over her body before he turned away. She was wearing her usual tee shirt and jeans, but something about the way he looked at her made her wish she had worn something more flattering.

"*Dr. Michael? Dr. Jeffrey?* Why don't they use last names?" Jill said.

"A lot of pediatricians do that with kids."

"Dr. Jill…" Jill said, trying it out. "No way. I'm going to be Dr. Lazar. If I let people call me Jill, they won't take me seriously. They'll treat me like a *girl*, not a doctor. They'll assume I'm a nurse. Or a receptionist."

"No they won't," Rachel said, laughing. "It isn't 1940."

Jill shrugged. "Anyway, I wonder how Dr. Michael ended up here after going to school in Beirut?"

"I thought he was an Israeli," Rachel said. "I heard him speaking Hebrew."

"He's not Israeli," Jill said, definitively. "Unless maybe he's Israeli Arab." She was trying to get into Daniel's orbit, so she'd been learning more about Israel and spoke with some authority. "Either way, he's not a nice Jewish boy, so don't get any ideas. Your mother would never recover if you brought home an Arab boyfriend."

"Boyfriend? That's a leap."

"I saw the way you were looking at him." Jill performed an exaggerated imitation of Rachel's expression: wide-eyed and adoring.

"I was looking at him because he was talking! You were looking at him, too. And what does my mother have to do with anything?"

"Right. Like you don't care what your mother thinks."

It was annoying that Jill knew her so well. They'd known each other since junior high school. Jill had her whole life mapped out and would stay safely within the bounds of family approval all the way. Rachel saw it clearly now, because Josh had taught her an important lesson. Having things like religion and education and family background in common with someone means nothing in the end. She had all that with Josh and yet they'd lacked a real bond. She hadn't understood that at the time, but her awareness of the absence of a mental and spiritual connection made her want it even more—and it had nothing to do with labels.

A few months earlier, she would have seen someone like Michael as interesting but off limits; now she felt open to him. She wanted to get to know him, to let him know her, to explore where that might lead. Her mother would be horrified, but she felt certain that her father would have understood. He'd had his own restless yearnings that led him out of his comfort zone, to travel across the world and work with people that others viewed as enemies.

Dr. Bergman had told her that after the Six-Day War in 1967, there was enormous relief that the country had survived the attempt of five Arab nations to annihilate it. But her dad had been prescient about the difficulties of controlling the hundreds of thousands of hostile Palestinians who were suddenly under Israel's control. The government tried to find ways to appeal to the moderates among the Palestinians, hoping that by creating decent living conditions and better futures for their children, they would find a way to live together that included accepting Israel instead of supporting terrorists.

They worked with local leaders and invested heavily in infrastructure; built hospitals, universities, and roads; and improved the water supply and access to electricity. Her father's Israeli relatives had put him in touch with people in the government, and both he and Dr. Bergman were tapped to work on health clinics for Palestinian children. It was on one of his trips there that he was killed in the car accident.

He'd been something of an adventurer and a reformer and an independent thinker. She liked that role model better than those presented by her over-cautious mother and conventional best friend.

CHAPTER SEVEN

Rachel and Jill went to an exam room with Dr. Jeffrey, where he prepped them to act as new patients: Rachel as the child, Jill as her mother. Three med students and Dr. Michael crowded into the small room with them and Rachel climbed on the examination table, her legs dangling over the edge, feeling like the child-patient she was pretending to be. Dr. Michael began by asking her what was wrong.

"I've been terribly tired," Rachel said, as instructed.

"And hungry, but she doesn't get satisfied when she eats," Jill added.

"What questions would you ask?" He pointed to one of the med students. "Arielle?"

"Any thirst?"

"What else?" he prompted.

"Urination more often than usual?"

"Good, what else?"

"Nausea or vomiting?"

"You," Dr. Michael said, pointing to a young man. Rachel recognized the frantic look of someone under constant pressure to perform.

"Any pain?"

"Rachel?" He indicated she should answer.

"Yes, stomach cramps."

"And what would you do at this point, with a patient presenting these symptoms? Assume they have been referred by their pediatrician, who has ruled out a virus, and that the symptoms are longstanding."

"Urine sample," the frantic-looking one said.

"Blood test."

"Lie down on the table, Rachel." She did as he asked and Dr. Michael pressed points along her abdomen as they discussed the various tests and conclusions they might draw. His hands moved professionally and competently and she was surprised that she felt calm under his touch. Then the students took turns taking her blood pressure, measuring her pulse, and listening to her heart. Arielle had a light touch with the pressure cuff. The frantic intern squeezed too forcefully and Dr. Michael had him do it again, emphasizing that every time you touch a patient, it is a privilege.

He told Rachel to sit up, taking her hand to assist her, but instead of instantly letting it go, he held it for a few unnecessary seconds. The effect on her was electric, as if all her senses were centered on just that one point where his fingers met hers. The room was so silent that she was certain they all knew.

"In a diabetic, the body either doesn't produce any insulin or not enough. Why does that lead to thirst?"

"That's a result of the high blood sugar, or hyperglycemia," Arielle called out. "Without insulin the body is unable to get energy from sugar in the blood and so it sends out signals for more food, but that won't solve the problem. So, the blood sugar rises to high levels, the kidneys are overwhelmed and can't send all the sugar back into circulation, so it spills over into the urine along with water. Fluids are lost, causing thirst."

"Good. What about the lack of energy?"

"Well, without insulin, the cells can't get energy from the blood sugar. It's all part of the same problem," another student responded.

"What would happen if a diabetic couldn't get insulin?" Arielle answered again, as if reciting from a textbook. "That could lead to ketoacidosis. The body is unable to use the sugar in the bloodstream so it turns to its fat stores for energy. This causes acids, ketones, to be produced and accumulate in the blood and spill into the urine. The excess of ketones in the blood combined with the high blood sugar leads to ketoacidosis, and diabetic shock." Dr. Michael seemed to be waiting for more, so she went on, "That would ultimately lead to coma and death."

"What symptoms would precede the coma?" Dr. Michael looked over at the third student who hadn't said anything up until then.

"Nausea, stomach pain, vomiting, chest pain, rapid shallow breathing, and difficulty staying awake… and um…" the student trailed off.

Dr. Michael stared ahead as if debating with himself. "That's correct," he said. "You understand this all intellectually. But you have to feel it viscerally." He tapped his chest with his closed fist. "You need to know that beyond the textbooks there are children who actually die from this condition. If they monitor themselves improperly or run out of insulin and start to go into shock and can't get to a hospital, they die." He looked around at them. "This happens, for example, in Palestine, where there are shortages of medicine and it is very difficult to access medical care, especially in the more rural areas. Closures and checkpoints hold people up for critical hours. In those hours, lives are tragically lost."

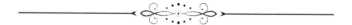

"What was that all about?" Jill said as they walked from the building.

"What as what all about?"

"That doctor. The way he talked about the Palestinians. Why was he injecting politics into the training? Does Bergman know he does that?"

"I have no idea, but I assume so. Maybe he just wants us to feel the urgency of the disease or the real-life consequences of neglect. Bergman has talked about the impact of Israeli policies on Palestinian healthcare."

"There are healthcare problems all over the world. A lot of Americans don't have access to good healthcare. He shouldn't single out Israeli checkpoints, as if their sole purpose is to make people suffer. They are there to protect Israelis from suicide bombers."

"Maybe he knew someone who died on the way to a hospital because they were held up at a checkpoint. He seemed genuinely disturbed when they talked about Maureen." She'd been disturbed by that, too.

"But checkpoints are not some pointless bureaucracy," Jill continued, "People would get killed if they didn't take the time to search. Even ambulances are used to smuggle weapons and explosives. The Red Cross has been complicit." She had her hands on her hips, her head cocked to one side, so sure of herself, as if there was no other way of looking at it. Her cocksureness sometimes worked for Rachel, like the way she totally agreed with Rachel about Josh being a jerk. But now it struck her as narrow-minded.

"It happens, Rachel. Daniel told me. He was there. *Dr.* Michael shouldn't say things like that."

Rachel didn't want to think about Michael as a political caricature. He was a thinking, feeling person. She was still reeling from the way he'd made her feel, the sensation of his hand holding hers—

"And why was he holding your hand like that? What's going on?"

So, Jill had noticed.

"Was that the 'privilege' of touching a patient that he mentioned?" Jill sneered. "It's pretty obvious that he likes you Rachel."

"He doesn't even know me."

"I mean that he's attracted to you."

She felt herself blush.

"Look at you! You're turning beet red!?" Jill looked at her closely. "Forget about it, you're barely over Josh so you're not thinking clearly. He's attractive in his way, something very powerful about him—but he's way too serious. I mean, you need to just relax, to be around happy people. He's got a chip on his shoulder." She lowered her voice, imitating him, "It happens, for example, in the Palestinian territories..."

"Stop it! What's wrong with serious? Life isn't a game for him. I respect him for that. You sound like a spoiled princess."

Jill's eyes widened. "Wow, you're smitten."

CHAPTER EIGHT

Jill dropped out of the internship after the first meeting when one of her professors offered her a position as a research assistant working on skin grafting. "I couldn't very well turn him down. He wrote my recommendations for med school and he knows I want to get into plastic surgery. Pediatrics is your thing, not mine. I really wanted to do it with you, but—"

Rachel put up a hand to stop her. It made perfect sense, and given Jill's attitude toward Michael, it was probably better. Her sarcasm and snide remarks were irritating.

As Rachel continued her internship, Dr. Jeffrey spent time with her, brainstorming ideas for her research project. She learned that, although patient participation in treatment was vital to managing diabetes, there were no tools to help teach young children to manage their care. She decided to write an illustrated children's book to teach them. With their parents' permission, she would work with children at the clinic and then track their progress, to test its effectiveness.

She developed a set of criteria to measure patient involvement and relative outcomes. "This looks fine to me," Jeffrey said, "but you should show it to Dr. Michael before you give it to Bergman for final approval. He's worked with a lot of kids and may have some ideas."

"He's always so busy."

"Just don't bother him when he's in the lab; he'll bite your head off. But you can interrupt him when he's in his office. I think he's there now."

She hesitated. Dr. Bergman had suggested she talk to Dr. Michael about his research, but she rarely saw him and when she did, he barely acknowledged her. When his office door was open, she sometimes glimpsed him at a desk overflowing with paper. He always seemed to be on the phone or reviewing files. His office had a guest chair that no one sat in because it was stacked with journals.

Sometimes she passed him in the corridors and would feel a disturbance in the air and slow her steps. But he never gave her more than a barely perceptible nod and she could never think of an excuse to talk to him. She was beginning to wonder if she'd imagined there was an attraction between them. Or was his distance because she was still a student, too young for him? Or maybe because he sensed that Dr. Bergman was protective of her and didn't want to step over a line?

She wasn't even certain he was single. He didn't wear a ring, but that wasn't conclusive evidence of anything. She couldn't bring herself to ask Uncle Steve. He would guess why and might say something to her mother.

Rachel thought about Dr. Michael a lot, but it was possible it was all one-sided and he wasn't interested in her at all. She chided herself for acting like a star-struck teenager. He worked at the clinic and she needed to ask him something. It was no big deal. She got up, determined to go talk to him, and then wondered how she looked. So, she went down the hall to the ladies' room to check herself out.

It was a regular bathroom like the kind she had at home, not a public one with stalls. A shelf above the toilet held a row of sterile plastic cups with green covers, labeled with handwritten names. They were filled with urine, awaiting analysis in the lab. Dr. Bergman told her that way back in the seventeenth century, doctors tasted urine to determine whether a patient had diabetes. If it tasted sweet, they made the diagnosis—diabetes mellitus, from the Greek word for *honey-sweet*.

She stood by the mirror, running the brush through her hair in even strokes, a soothing rhythm that did little to tame it, but calmed her nerves. She scarcely wore makeup, just some mascara that darkened her naturally thick eyelashes. Her eyes were her best feature, the first thing people noticed, because of their unusual purple-brown color and almond shape. Josh used to say they were haunting and he could stare at them forever. She stared at her reflection in the mirror as if she were observing an interesting stranger. Then she put away her brush and headed down the hall.

Dr. Michael's office door was open. He was ushering out a mother with her little boy, lecturing her so sternly that she looked scared. He didn't raise his voice and he stood the proper distance from her, yet the threat in his stance and manner was unmistakable.

The boy looked up at Rachel with a curious expression and took a step toward her. Then he stopped and edged back to his mother, hiding behind her legs, staring out at Rachel with a mischievous grin. Hide and Seek, the universal language of all children. Rachel averted her eyes, playing along, looking everywhere except at the little boy. When she finally looked back at him, it was with mock surprise. *Oh! There you are!*

The child erupted in laughter; his whole body shook with unselfconscious, pure joy at the simple game. The sound caught Dr. Michael's attention and he looked at the boy, then at Rachel, then back to the mother, dismissing her with, "Make sure you bring him back next week. This cannot happen again." Then he turned to Rachel.

"Yes?"

"You were pretty hard on that woman," she said.

"That isn't your concern." He started to walk past her.

"No, but..." He was right, of course. It was unprofessional of her to comment. He was already halfway down the hall and she had to move quickly to keep up with him. "I came to ask if you'd look over my proposal. If you have time."

"Leave it on my desk," he said. I'll get to it when I can."

The following week, while she wondered whether Dr. Michael would ever get back to her, Rachel spent time greeting patients at the reception desk. One was a nine-year-old boy named Sean. Sometimes you just had to catch someone's eye when they were smiling to feel as if you knew them, and that's how it felt with him.

There were three other children in his family, and getting him to his appointments was difficult for his mother. One afternoon Rachel thought that she looked particularly harried, so she offered to play cards with Sean while they waited. They sat at one of the low children's tables and she asked him what he wanted to play.

"I'm learning solitaire," he said. "You want to see?"

She nodded and moved closer to him as he laid the cards out in neat rows across the table.

Sean was terribly thin—common among diabetics, whose cells can't process the sugar from food and instead try to get energy from the body itself. She knew it was a constant battle to keep his blood sugar stable, but he didn't show any evidence of the strain. He was a typical nine-year-old boy, bright and alert, eager to have fun.

She admired his high spirits, his defiance of his disease. It was impossible not to be moved by him, by all the children who lived with bodies that betrayed them. She tried to think of some comparable struggle in her own childhood but she'd never been tested that way. The only thing that came to mind was losing her father, but that wasn't the same as fighting to stay alive.

Rachel was absorbed in watching Sean sort the cards when she realized that Dr. Michael was standing by the desk, observing them. She looked up, surprised, and he pulled over a small chair and sat with his legs bent awkwardly in front of him. It was such an undignified position she almost laughed. He looked like a kid who'd grown too fast.

"How's it going, my man?" he asked Sean.

"Okay. I'm going to beat these cards. Rachel hasn't helped at all.

"I've been watching, but so far you've gotten everything right," she said.

He kept moving the cards around. "Oh yeah? I made a mistake on purpose and you didn't catch it."

"You did not!"

She gave him a playful punch.

"Oww!" he said, giggling.

Sean's mother glanced over at them, and then looked back at her magazine, but a smile spread across Dr. Michael's face. His entire body relaxed into it, like his whole being was smiling. It was the first time she'd seen any warmth beneath his cool exterior; the first time she could see a way into him. He loved kids, just as she did.

While Sean concentrated on the cards, Dr. Michael spoke to her in a low voice. "I looked over your proposal. It's good, but I have some suggestions. Come by later in the week and we can talk about it."

She nodded and a companionable silence settled over them. Sean continued to flip cards. Michael watched for another minute, but when a nurse called him over with a question, he got up and left with barely a goodbye.

When Yusif stuck his head into Michael's office, Michael motioned him in, sweeping a pile of medical journals from the chair to the floor. The little office was a mess. He kept planning to clean it up but there was never any time, and in some ways, he enjoyed the challenge of keeping track of where everything was in his head.

"I haven't gotten any word from Akil, but we should hear soon," Yusif said.

"No letters from the beautiful Eva?"

"My wife sends many letters. When she signs them 'forever yours' I know they are meant for me alone. Otherwise the key is a poem I wrote for her when I was eleven. You won't find it in any books. We both know it by heart, but it is a challenge to encode from memory."

"You can do that?" Michael asked, impressed. He'd never thought of Yusif as having that kind of mathematical brain.

"No. We jot down bits and pieces and then destroy the paper. She'll send word from him soon. He'll want to disrupt the peace talks. Do you think he'll involve us?"

It had been a long time since Akil had asked anything of him and he was losing the thread of his fervor for the rebellion. These days, he wanted to help his people by fighting a disease that killed more of them than the Israelis—not by carrying out some scheme devised by Akil.

As a kid, Michael had always been ready for action, and was quick to do whatever Akil asked. Part of it was a youthful sense of invincibility that made him a risk-taker. But he had also been desperate to prove himself because he was the son of a traitor. He'd gone to greater lengths than anyone else, volunteering while others were drafted. Fighting had been all he'd thought about as a boy.

He'd been eleven-years-old when Akil allowed him, for the first time, to plant a bomb in a house that the Israeli army had marked to search for weapons. The homes were marked so that civilians knew to evacuate, but the advance warning gave the *fedayeen* the opportunity to plant bombs and kill soldiers. Young and agile, Michael had placed the bomb and then darted away.

When the first soldier entered and the house exploded, tears had come to his eyes.

"You are disturbed?" Akil asked.

At first, he denied it, but Akil persisted until finally he admitted, "That soldier, he was the one with a funny lopsided smile that reminded me of Wadih's. He offered me candy. I never took it, but..."

Akil shook his head. "He was an enemy soldier. You can't make exceptions. Forget the candy." Michael flushed with embarrassment. Akil had a way of making him admit things and then he'd feel stupid. "That soldier arrested our brothers! We are not potted plants, grateful for drops of water. He is an enemy soldier."

Then he motioned Michael to sit closer and whispered a secret in his ear. As often as he made him feel stupid, Akil made him feel special and loved. "When you feel disturbed like this, I'll tell you what to do."

Michael looked at him hopefully, desperate for a way out of the sick feeling in his gut.

"Let the feelings come out, all of them. Let them wash over you. But then, and this is the hard part, separate yourself from them. Put them into a bundle, one by one, like gathering olives into a basket. And when they are all together, attach the bundle to a string and let it go. Watch it drift away and say goodbye. You can do it. You will learn."

Now, years later, he could still picture Akil's eyes—pools of brown, shadow and light, seeing nothing and everything—and that bundle, which had sailed through the air many times since that day.

It was only in last few years, away from Akil, that Michael had experienced the bliss of concentrating fully on his work. He wanted to keep it that way, to immerse himself in medicine and fighting disease instead of killing soldiers.

But the Party wasn't a club one could join and leave at will. The only way to leave was as a martyr. Or a traitor.

CHAPTER NINE

When Rachel left the clinic and turned the corner, Josh was walking toward her, his arm draped around the shoulders of a petite, pretty girl. There was no way to turn back or pretend she hadn't seen them. Josh smiled, and introduced her to the girl. Her name was Allison. "I have to talk to Rachel about something," he said. "I'll meet you in the library in a few, Allie, okay?"

It was okay with Allie, who smiled amiably, even as Rachel protested that she had no time.

"Come on, Rach, just for a minute. It's important. Please?" He touched her arm possessively, as if she still belonged with him. She shook it off.

It couldn't be that important if he'd waited until he just happened to run into her, but she was curious. They began to walk and neither spoke, just caught each other's rhythm. Finally, he said, "You hear from med schools yet?"

She shook her head.

"You'll do fine. I know it."

Mr. Supportive.

"So, how is your mom? Business good?"

"Cut it out, Josh. What do you want?"

He stopped walking, touched her arm again, and gazed into her eyes. "Life is complicated, isn't it?"

"Yes, Josh. So, what's so important?"

"Okay, okay. What I want to say is that I've been thinking about us. I'm in med school, Rach. It's not a good time to be in a serious relationship. All the guys that came here with girlfriends have split up. Marriages are falling apart. It wasn't just us."

"Why are we talking about this?"

His puzzled brown eyes grew misty.

She shook her head. "Stop it, Josh. It's not always about you."

"What does that mean?"

"Figure it out," she said, sharply.

They were silent for a moment, a pause like a curve in the road. Then he said, "I'm thinking of going into plastic surgery."

"What?"

"Plastic surgery. I mean, I could do some good, help kids born with cleft palates and that sort of thing." He paused as if waiting for polite applause. "And the field of cosmetic surgery is growing. I think that's where the big bucks will be. Baby boomers are never going to want to grow old. What do you think?"

All she could think of was how they'd sometimes talked about working in a clinic in a low-income area after they graduated. Who was this person? Had he changed or had he only been nodding in feigned agreement all that time, so she'd think their minds were in tandem? Was it all just foreplay?

As she debated whether to walk away or stay, or what the hell to do, the air around them grew thicker and she felt raindrops, light but annoying. She glanced around, looking for a way out of the conversation. They were on a quiet street outside the main campus.

Then she saw Daniel—his red hair unmistakable—motioning to her from down the street. He wore a brightly colored knitted yarmulke and held a bag with loaves of challah bread; the intoxicating scent wafted toward her as he came walking briskly over. She was reminded of Friday night Sabbath dinners around the mahogany dinner table, her mother lighting candles, her father singing the prayers—practically the only tradition they kept up, and it ended with his death. The image was so strong that her father was suddenly there as the wind kicked up. It wasn't the first time he'd appeared to her in a bracing breeze or the warmth of the sun.

"Hey, Rachel! What are you up to?"

"We're having a conversation," Josh answered for her.

"Right. Hi, Josh."

"What are *you* up to?" Rachel asked him.

"I'm heading over to the Jewish Students Association. Sarah organized a Sabbath dinner for the board members and some friends. Why don't you come?"

She thought of a few different excuses that would allow her to avoid the dinner and still get away from Josh, and was debating which one to use when they all turned toward the sound of a car coming toward them. It was a dark gray sedan that cruised slowly and then came to a halt. Rachel had a bad feeling about it. The darkened windows of the buildings along the street suddenly seemed to be leering at them.

"Hey!" shouted one of the passengers. "What's that beanie? Thought Hitler got all of you." The voice belonged to a guy whose skin had so many scars it looked grated.

"Don't answer," Rachel hissed, and pulled at Daniel's sleeve. His face was flushed, his hazel eyes deeper in the fading light, the color of the sea under a darkening sky. In them, she saw layers of history. He was ready to fight; it was clear from the way he stood erect, shoulders tensed, defying the stereotype of the meek, studious, ineffectual, Jew.

Sounds of laughter erupted from the car. Four guys wearing leather bomber jackets, cigarettes hanging between fingers, stared out. The car reeked of the smoke, which drifted out the window, visible as patches of gray suspended in the cold air. "Hey, don't you own the banks? Come here, honey, I'll make a deposit," one of them said.

"Yeah, we'll all make some deposits," another said. That got them laughing.

The rain finally started to fall in earnest as one of them opened the door, leisurely, as if he were going out for a stroll. Daniel let go of the bag and the challah, soft and warm and fragrant, tumbled out and scattered, as if running away.

Rachel looked around for something she could use as a weapon, and Josh took a step forward to align himself with Daniel, attempting to form a protective wall. She had never seen him fight anyone and he looked scared. The guys in the car might have knives or guns. She knew she could run away and they wouldn't blame her, but she couldn't do it. Perhaps she could throw her chemistry text at them when they got out of the car. She raised it above her head—

Then she saw a jogger running toward them, moving faster with each passing second. Relief washed over her; they weren't alone. The real world existed in the form of this figure, running without panic but with clear intent. As the distance between them began to close, she realized it was Dr. Michael! When he reached the car, he slammed the door so fast the guy barely got his leg back inside. The three of them—Rachel, Josh, and Daniel—stood there wondering why none of them had thought to do that.

"Hey!" the guy screamed.

"Get out of here," Dr. Michael said. He took hold of Rachel's elbow, ignoring the drunks, who drove away, and she had an urge to tuck herself into him, wrap herself in his authority. "Are you alright?" he asked. She felt herself calming under his touch and steady gaze.

"Who were those assholes?" Josh shouted, as the car drove away.

Michael ignored him and stayed focused on Rachel. "I'll see you home if you like," he said.

His words, his accent, the musical way he blended them together, was entrancing.

"Are you okay with that?" Josh asked her, and shook his head as if instructing her to say, "No."

Daniel picked the challahs up from the street, though they were ruined. Rachel lifted her face and closed her eyes for a few seconds, letting the rain wash away the residue of her fright, licking the moisture from her lips. The she looked up at Michael. "Yes, I would, thanks." A moment of awkward silence. "Oh…This is Daniel Weiss, and that's Josh Stein."

"Michael," he responded, shaking hands with each in turn. "Michael Haddad."

"You know each other?" Daniel asked, looking curiously from Michael to Rachel.

Daniel was about Michael's height but that was the only thing they had in common. Daniel's height never gave her any comfort. She'd never wanted to lose herself in it. His pull on her was tentative, weak.

"Dr. Michael works at Bergman's clinic, where I'm interning," she explained.

"Oh." He kept looking back and forth between them puzzled, wary. "You're sure you don't want to come to the JSA for dinner, Rach?"

She nodded, barely glancing at him.

"Okay. Well then, I'll see you later."

"I guess I'll go, too," Josh said, but he just stood there, staring at her.

"You look disoriented, Rachel," Michael said. His voice was low and soothing and concerned, the effect compounded by its contrast with the cold professionalism he exhibited at the clinic. "Why don't we get a coffee?" He made a slight motion with his head as he pulled up his sweatshirt hood and began to walk.

"Doctor's orders?"

He nodded. "There's a luncheonette a few blocks away that I like. Henry's Sweet Shoppe." They began to walk, leaving Josh behind. "Do you know it? It's not too far and we can get out of the rain." He noticed her struggling to keep up with him and slowed his steps as they passed a video arcade.

"I like that place, but it gets a pretty rough crowd," Rachel said. "Kind of like those guys....It ruins it for the rest of us."

He shrugged. "Don't let them bother you. Stand your ground. Live your life. Play Pac-Man."

"I know what you mean, but sometimes you have to walk away; save your energy for important fights." She enjoyed taking an opposing point of view with him, even if it was to argue that she shouldn't always take one.

"On the other hand, if you walk away too often, it becomes a habit."

She considered. "You handled those guys with such... ease. Have you had things with them before?"

"Things?"

She nodded.

"I know the type. Lowlifes. Some of them showed up at a rally, recently."

"What rally?"

"To support the *intifada.*"

"That was your rally?"

"I helped organize it for Students for Palestinian Human Rights, a campus organization. We hold events to educate and encourage discussion."

He defied stereotype. His reference to "checkpoints" during the mock exam showed that he saw things from the perspective of "oppressed" Palestinians. On the other hand, he worked with a Jewish doctor and stood up to the lowlifes who'd hassled yarmulke-clad Daniel.

It didn't put her off that he organized rallies. Protests were a routine event on campus, an accepted way to support a cause. It was a longstanding tradition of American life. Even her mother had protested. She'd seen pictures of her parents marching against the war in Vietnam. She'd even been at one as a child, perched on her father's shoulders wearing a tiny, tie-dyed tee shirt.

Her heart was beating faster, no longer from fear, but from being near Michael. She was safe. Nothing momentous had happened. Nothing except that this man, this intense foreign man—not a boy like Josh—was taking her out for coffee.

Henry's Sweet Shoppe had a retro feel, with gray linoleum floors speckled with faded red and blue dots, worn from years of foot traffic. The glass shelves behind the counter displayed a collection of Russian wooden dolls illuminated by fluorescent lights. Beneath the counter were trays of muffins. The stools were topped with torn red vinyl and Rachel spun one around as she passed it.

It wasn't one of her usual hangouts and she didn't recognize anyone. It was populated with young mothers and kids and babies in high chairs. A few teenagers. A taxi driver holding a takeout coffee chatted with the cashier. Its very ordinariness made it feel special "I like this place," she said.

Michael smiled, as if pleased that she approved of his choice.

They settled into a booth. A child in the booth behind them was on his knees, facing Rachel. He grinned and popped his head up and down. She made a face at him and he giggled.

"Kids like you," Michael said. "You have younger siblings?"

"No, I'm an only child. My dad died when I was young."

"Your mother never remarried?"

"No."

They were having a normal conversation, like friends or people on a first date getting to know each another. She hoped to strike that delicate balance between being open and honest and maintaining some mystery.

"I used to wish she would. I thought that she might get together with Dr. Bergman after his wife passed away a few years ago."

"Oh?"

"But she's not interested. She says she's married to her work."

"What does she do?" He leaned back comfortably, settling in, giving her space. She noticed his accent again, the words clipped, the sound a bit formal.

"She designs women's clothing. She was a designer for Ralph Lauren for a few years, and then struck out on her own and formed her own company. She made a success of it after my dad died. It's supported us all these years."

When Rachel described her mother in conversation it was like she was describing a different woman from the one with whom she fought incessantly.

"A businesswoman."

"Yes, very much so, very strong-willed, talented, and with a good head for numbers."

"You admire her."

"I do. She's accomplished a lot. But I used to wish I had a nurturing mother who built her life around me."

"You didn't have enough attention?" He was teasing her. That was new.

"Nope. Never enough! But seriously, all kids want attention, and I understand that completely. I never get annoyed when they whine and complain. Maybe that's why kids like me."

He nodded, serious again. He was a good listener. "That's interesting."

It wasn't. It was pop psychology. And why was she talking about herself so much? He was the interesting one. The way he spoke, every word meaningful, unlike her frothy chatter. She wanted to turn the conversation around to him and told him she'd thought that he was Israeli when she first met him.

"Why was that?" He didn't seem surprised.

"I heard you speaking Hebrew. Remember?"

"I also speak English."

She smiled. "Yes, that's true. But you look...Michael doesn't even sound like an Arab name."

"It's Christian."

"I thought Arabs were Muslim."

"Most, not all. We're a minority. I'm not religious, though. It's just my family background."

That set her at ease. It was a little bridge to connect them, one easily crossed. She wasn't observant either, and had grown up in a predominantly Christian community. She was familiar with the customs, the holidays. She always thought she had more in common with a non-religious Christian than an Orthodox Jew. She didn't even know how to keep kosher, just a vague notion about not mixing milk and meat.

"What about you?" she asked, "Family back home? Siblings? Wife?"

There. She'd said it.

"No, no one."

She was relieved to learn that he was single, but still couldn't tell if he was interested in her or just being nice, taking the time to make sure that she was all right. He could be so tough and intimidating, but now he was easy company.

She couldn't characterize him. He fell outside her frame of reference.

"So, tell me Rachel, how do you like working at the clinic?"

"I love being with the kids, especially Sean," she said, smiling, remembering how they'd all sat together that day, playing cards.

"He's a great kid."

"He is. They're all so much fun to be with. I mean, some are little monsters, but then it's a challenge."

The waitress, who'd been racing back and forth past their table, finally stopped and asked them what they'd like. "I'm sorry you've been waiting. It's so busy today. Everyone is getting out of the rain, I guess. What can I get for you, doc?"

"Just coffee for me."

"Same," Rachel said.

The waitress didn't bother jotting it down.

"So, where were we? Why did you decide to become a doctor?" he asked. "I can see you as a teacher. Maybe working in a school with young children. Was it because of your father? Did you have a little doctor's bag as a kid and a stethoscope, and pretend to listen to everyone's lungs?"

He was teasing her again but there was some truth in what he described.

"Yes, actually. That was one of my favorite games, pretending to be a doctor. Sometimes a patient."

"That's why you made such a good patient a few weeks ago."

She felt herself blush, recalling her reaction to his touch during the mock exam.

"How about you? How did you end up a doctor?"

"The usual way: med school, internship, residency."

"I mean, what got you interested? Were there doctors in your family?" Absently, she reached for the salt shaker, poured salt onto the paper placemat, and made designs with her finger as they talked. He watched but didn't comment on it.

"My mother used to think I had healing qualities when I was a kid. I suspect it was all in her head, but she was very convincing. And my father's close friend was a doctor. I admired him."

The waitress came over, set coffee cups on the table, and filled them. "Anything else, hon?"

Rachel shook her head, and Michael said, "No, thank you," and asked about her daughter's recent chest cold with a familiarity that suggested they'd discussed it before.

Rachel stared at his profile as he spoke. His nose had a slight Semitic arch, his hair was a mess but somehow perfect; some damp strands curled by his neck. As the waitress moved off to another table, Michael caught her staring and leaned in close. She could sense the clammy warmth of his skin under his damp sweatshirt and had an almost irresistible urge to touch him.

"I saw the power of medicine when I was young. Having access to good medical care was the difference between life and death. I love research, but for me, it's all about helping my people."

She felt his passion and wanted to go deeper, to find ways to keep him with her, so that this would be the first of many conversations and not a onetime thing.

"That's why I found your proposal so interesting," he said. "It's well done as far as it goes, but you can do more with it."

"How do you mean?"

"I'm organizing a group to improve healthcare for Palestinian children. We're raising funds to purchase mobile clinics to reach remote villages with no medical facilities. We'll treat patients with chronic conditions like diabetes, and educate them to manage the disease. Your book project fits in perfectly. We could translate it to use at our clinics."

"For the children?" she said, as if he'd given her a gift. With his vision, her little project grew legs and raced around the globe.

"You seem surprised," he said.

"That's an understatement. You haven't even seen the book."

"We'll make sure the book is good. But there is also the fact that having you on board will help the project as a whole. A Jewish woman working for Palestinian children sends an important message."

She had hoped her project would be of some use, but this went way beyond the simple goal of helping sick children. Michael was turning it into a political statement. She felt a frisson of excitement mixed with fear. Her mother would go through the roof at the thought of Rachel putting her time, effort, and her very identity, in the service of helping Palestinians.

On the other hand, her goal was to help children, and these children were in dire need of help. She'd never before had the opportunity to do something this important; it wasn't just some wild idea that would fizzle out. Michael was an accomplished man who got things done. He'd come from a chaotic, war-torn country and found his way to one of the finest university hospitals in the US, rising past politics to work with a Jewish doctor.

"Maybe you could even go over to help train people," he continued.

Just when she had convinced herself she could handle it, he raised the stakes. "Me? I don't even speak Hebrew, much less Arabic."

"That's not a problem."

"How did you learn Hebrew?" she asked.

"I picked it up along the way. I worked with Israeli doctors and attended conferences with them. We'd put aside our differences for a few days and focus on what we have in common."

"Is that how you met Dr. Bergman?"

He nodded. "I was at an endocrinology conference. It was held in Ramallah, which is on the West Bank. That was the only place most of the Palestinian doctors could get to. Only a few of the other doctors, like Bergman, were willing to travel to us. He recognized that our work in medicine was more important than our nationalities. After all, diseases don't respect borders."

"It's easy to imagine Dr. Bergman doing something like that," Rachel said. "He's very kind—a *mensch*, you know what that means?" Michael nodded. "So you know Yiddish, too?" She was enchanted and he seemed to notice. Reflected in his gaze, she felt pretty.

"Everyone knows what a *mensch* is," he said, as he opened four sugars and put them into his coffee.

She laughed. "Have a little coffee with your sugar."

He looked puzzled for a second and then got it.

"Are you feeling better now?" he asked.

"Yes, much better."

"You should think about learning some self-defense," he advised.

"I thought I handled that textbook pretty expertly."

"Yes, you did," he agreed with a smile. "It was a good instinct. You seem like someone who would stand up for herself, even if it was dangerous. You're a lot more capable than you think."

She held his gaze and felt suddenly lighter. She wanted to know him better, to spend time with him. Working with him on her project, which was now becoming their project, was the perfect opportunity, because, aside from occasional moments—and now this bizarre incident with the hoodlums—she rarely had occasion to talk to him. She knew she wouldn't slip easily into his life the way she had with Josh. He belonged to a Palestinian group that held protests that made her friends cringe, for starters. But that all seemed minor compared to what they had in common and what they could accomplish together.

They sat a few minutes longer, not talking, just digesting the conversation. Then some people walked in, saw Michael, and stopped by their table. There was a man with curly dark hair named Yusif—an Arabic form of Joseph, he explained. A lot of people called him Joe for short, but Rachel knew she wouldn't. She liked the name, it almost sounded like her grandfather's name, Josef, pronounced the European way. He was smaller and thinner than Michael, his skin darker. Another Palestinian, he taught poetry in the English department.

With him was a pretty girl named Amira, a junior at Barnard, with hair that flowed down her back, shiny and almost black. She gave Rachel a warm smile and when she reached out to shake her hand, the movement was organic, arising from her core. Rachel wasn't sure if it was training or natural grace, but she guessed that Amira had studied dance. They began talking about a Students for Palestinian Human Rights meeting to be held later that night. "Why don't you come?" Michael said to her. "It's open to everyone."

"Me? No, I have a paper due tomorrow and I haven't finished it yet."

"The meeting's not till nine o'clock. You'll have plenty of time to work on your paper. You should come. It'll give you a better idea of what's happening, and that will help you with the project we're talking about. Just come and listen," he said. His voice turned softer, as if he were weaving sentences together into a cushion against her misgivings. "We're discussing plans for a symposium where we'll present different points of view on the *intifada*. It will give you background for your project, help you decide for sure."

It was as good a reason as any, and the meeting would provide an excuse to see him again. Yusif and Amira waited patiently, politely indifferent, yet she felt pressure in their silence. At the same time, she could almost feel her mother, like a physical presence, pulling at her to get her away from these people. She imagined Jill reacting with disgust and Daniel with disappointment. But none of it had any effect on her at that moment. With the slightest movement of her head, she agreed to go.

CHAPTER TEN

Yusif was buzzing from the sugar and caffeine high, a side effect of the childish cravings he'd satisfied at Henry's Sweet Shoppe with an espresso, a wedge of lemon meringue pie, and a dose of Amira's charm. He was lightheaded all the way downtown on the subway, but he forced himself to focus. There was no reason to suspect anyone was following him, but when your guard was down bad things happened. Justifiable paranoia was how he thought of it.

He exited the subway at 23rd Street, entered Madison Square Park, and circled the perimeter. No shadows lurked. He noticed a homeless man lying on a bench, covered with blankets and surrounded by black garbage bags that served as suitcases. The whole area reeked of urine. He shook the man's shoulder lightly to rouse him. "Here, take this buddy. Buy yourself something." He handed him a five-dollar bill.

"Thanks, man," the guy mumbled, clutching the bill and sitting up. He had a matted beard and watery eyes.

Yusif kept walking, sidestepping the used syringes and a condom that littered the dirt. Out of the corner of his eye he saw his contact, Ari, wearing a blue-gray sweatshirt and jeans that faded into the dusk. He looked like a college kid but was older than Yusif by a few years. He designed computer software in his spare time and hardly ever slept. *He'll be a millionaire before he's forty,* Yusif mused. The gleam of a blue-and-white pin on Ari's sweatshirt caught his eye. The Israeli flag. He was proud of his heritage.

As Ari sauntered past him, Yusif felt him lift the paper from his pocket. His action was so smooth that Yusif wasn't entirely sure it had happened until he reached inside the pocket and found it empty. They didn't need to speak. It was an oddly intimate relationship that required absolute trust in a stranger and former enemy.

Yusif had had nothing of consequence to report in a while. It was blissfully boring until the *intifada* started in December. Suddenly messages were flowing back and forth between Ramallah and New York. The Israelis wanted details, however unimportant they might seem to him. And he gave them what they wanted because they had a hold on him.

It had begun when shots were fired from his neighborhood. He'd been home reading, but that didn't matter; he was arrested as a suspect. The interrogations went on for days. Like doctors they probed for his weak spots and then they sent Ari, his Israeli counterpart. Intense and intelligent, Ari had even written poetry. They'd rapped for hours, smoking cigarettes, drinking coffee, Ari convincing him that he was uniquely positioned to make a difference. He could help end the cycle of violence and bring peace. And they sweetened the deal. They would help him and his family with money and travel documents so he could study in New York. He just needed to tell them what Akil was up to. If he didn't, Ari insinuated, he would be considered an accomplice to any further acts of terrorism.

He didn't need the threats. It was as if he'd found the words to a tune that had been playing in his head for years. Yusif had never forgiven the Party for Black September. Akil and the *fedayeen* had brought the wrath of the Jordanian king down on all of them and Yusif had lost his parents in that battle. Akil blamed the king, the Jews, the Americans for supporting the Jews, always someone else, never themselves. But he'd been inexcusably careless with their lives. He'd protected "honor" as if it were a living breathing being.

It took Yusif years to reach this point; years of listening blindly to Akil's speeches, convincing himself that he believed in the charismatic leader. But, after a while, it made no sense to him. He had only to look around to see the wasteland created by the violence and corruption among his own people. The photos of the bruised and burned victims of their terrorism sickened him. He wasn't built for it. He knew he was different, but he kept it to himself, for there was grave danger if anyone suspected. Even Eva didn't know. It was better, living over there, that she had no doubts about his loyalty to the cause. Only Ari knew, and, in a strange way, it made him feel closer to him than anyone.

He looked at his watch, a gift from Akil, as he headed back to the subway. Seven o'clock. He should have had a meal at Henry's instead of sugar and caffeine. There would be no time for dinner if he wanted to get to the meeting on time.

The subway was infuriatingly slow; each stop seemed like an eternity, with people shuffling on and off, the door attempting to close and getting stuck before finally closing for real. When it finally reached Riverdale, Rachel raced up the stairs and walked briskly home. She sat at her desk for an hour, working on her paper, then showered, and searched her closet for something to wear to the meeting. She imagined each outfit through Michael's eyes as she studied herself in the mirror, but in the end she kept it simple, with a variation on her "uniform": stone-washed black jeans and a long-sleeved white, V-neck tee shirt edged with embroidery. *Down-to-earth with a touch of femininity.*

The door slammed. She groaned when her mother shouted, "Rachel? You home?

"Yes, but I'm leaving again," she shouted back.

The sound of footsteps coming up the stairs was followed by her door opening. She clenched her teeth, not wanting to argue about privacy—or anything else—at that moment.

"You're going out?"

"Umm hmm."

"Where?"

"To a lecture."

"My studious daughter. What's the subject?" Her mother examined her, patting a stray hair behind her ear.

"It's about a children's health clinic. Might be useful for my project for Bergman."

"It's dark out."

"I know, Mom. It's nighttime. I go out at night. You're going to have to get used to it."

"Why, what's so important? Who's speaking?"

"A Palestinian group." As soon as she said it she regretted it. She was rushing, not thinking straight. Sometimes she had urges to be truthful with her mother, instead of relying on obfuscation and outright lies to keep the peace. But she knew that honest, open communication would result in continual arguments instead of respectful disagreement. "I'm just going to listen."

"Since when do you spend time with Palestinians?"

"It's about kids who need better medical treatment. It's nothing to do with politics."

Her mother sighed. "You should worry about kids here who need help. Arabs don't value life."

"Mom! How can you say that? We're talking about little kids."

"Yes, I know it's a terrible situation, but don't get in the middle of it. Don't you have anything better to do? How in the world did you get mixed up with them, anyway?"

"I'm not mixed up with them. There's a doctor in Uncle Steven's clinic. He's very nice."

"Steven. That figures."

"Honestly, Mom."

"Fine. Do you what you want," she said, meaning exactly the opposite.

"Thank you. Besides, Uncle Steven—"

"He's not your uncle and you're old enough to stop calling him that. Listen to me. The Palestinians are dangerous."

There was a familiar note of terror in her mother's voice and Rachel felt the need, the responsibility, to calm her. Her mother got nervous whenever there was a terrorist act in Israel. Her face would transform into something familiar but unfamiliar—normal, but not quite, like a child's toothless smile.

Rachel had felt more threatened by the drunken creeps in the car than by Michael and his friends, who were intellectual, serious, and academic. She didn't tell her mother that, though. It was tricky, picking topics with her mother. The woman worried about her constantly and still tried to tell her what to do, even though she was nearly twenty-one years old. Whenever her mother said, in a wistful voice, "You'll always be my baby," Rachel wanted to break away and get as far from her mother as she could go—but she wasn't sure it would ever be far enough.

Rachel left the house without saying goodbye and returned to campus. It was raining again, and the mist rising from the pavement could give rise to angels or devils, depending on your state of mind. She was leaning toward the dark side. The haze of streetlights spoke to her of dangerous secrets. As cars passed, their tires seemed to growl on the wet pavement. She kept a brisk pace, anxious to get to the library, but the conversation with her mother had dampened her enthusiasm.

Much as she willed herself to be independent, it was impossible to blithely dismiss Rivka. For so many years it was just the two of them; they were entwined in ways as deep as their shared loss of her father and as shallow as her mom paying her way through college. Her legs began to drag. It was as if Rivka's caution was pulling her back while her desire to break away pulled her forward. If this continued, as she knew it would, she would have to let go of one before she was split in two.

If she were still with Josh, she'd never be going to this meeting. But there was a grayness to her life, lately. The only color was in her work with the kids...and Michael. If she refused to be a part of this aspect of his life, he would shut her out—she knew that without him ever saying it.

"Rachel?"

The voice was so soft it sounded like it came from inside her head. She spun around and Daniel came up beside her. Did he follow her around? Sometimes it seemed that way, although she knew he wasn't a stalker. They all made the same orbits around campus.

He leaned toward her with a shy smile, like he wanted to hug her but was restraining himself.

"You okay?" he asked.

"Yes, fine. It's spooky out here, though, isn't it? Or is it just me?"

"No, it is spooky." As if on cue, some tires screeched as a taxi barely avoided a drunk pedestrian weaving his way across the middle of the street.

"Let's get out of there. I'm on my way to the library. Walk with me," she said.

"Okay. How come you don't have any books?"

"You're observant."

He waited a beat.

"I finished my paper. There's a meeting in the library about the protests," she explained.

"No there's not....Oh, you mean the Palestinian group?"

"Yes."

"Why go to their meeting? They just bash Israel."

"No, they don't," she said, automatically, even though they did. "Anyway, that's their right. It's part of democracy. My parents took me on protest marches before I could walk."

"A rebel baby. Cute. I can just picture you."

She smiled. "Anyway, I'm not going because of politics. I have an opportunity to do some work for Palestinian children's health care."

He rolled his eyes. "Rachel, Rachel, Rachel."

"Yes?"

"Why not work for Israeli children's health care? They need you, too. And they would appreciate it more."

"Daniel, Daniel, Daniel. Kids are kids. And the truth is, it means a lot when Jewish people show they care for Palestinians. It's important." She was parroting Michael, but it sounded right.

Daniel started to say something and then seemed to reconsider. "That guy Michael...he walked you home...?"

"Yeah."

"Oh, I see. Well, good luck with that."

"With what?"

"Never mind." He paused. "You look nice."

"Thanks."

He seemed to be grasping for a new topic. "It was pretty strange with those guys, today. But you know, in a way, it was interesting."

"Fascinating."

"No, really. I've been thinking lately that I might specialize in psychiatry. Did I tell you that? They'd make an interesting case study about anti-Semitism and low self-esteem. You know what I mean? They lashed out at us because they feel worthless."

"Daniel," she laughed, "every day you think of studying something else."

"Yeah, I know. I can't help it. I'm also thinking of applying to med school in Israel. Maybe first doing a stint in the IDF and then going to school over there."

"And then stay there? Live there? Make *aliyah*?"

He nodded.

She wasn't surprised. Daniel came from a Jewish family, though they weren't at all religious and he grew up in a mostly Catholic neighborhood. He'd told her stories of being picked on, called names, and beaten up because he was Jewish. So, when he went to Israel and saw that the soldiers, the firemen—all the professions that were stereotypically dominated by non-Jews in the States—were filled with Jewish men and women, he got a bug that nothing would cure. Zionism was his religion, his response to the bullies of the world, a tribute to his Russian grandfather who'd fled the pogroms.

"Things like what happened today make me think about it more. Even here, in America, we aren't people; we're Jews."

They were standing near the curb and a passing car splashed them. Daniel's arm rose protectively and he stepped to block her from the spray. Rachel felt something inside of her melt a little at his gesture. She would miss him if he moved to Israel. He'd been a good friend. She knew he still wanted more than just friendship, but she didn't feel that way about him. He was cute in his way, and very sweet, but he lacked an edge, the indefinable something that would draw her over the invisible line from friendship to romance.

"I've been thinking about it a lot," he continued. "I feel like a fraud, talking about my commitment to Israel yet living over here, all safe and comfortable. Of course, my parents want me to go to med school here."

"Don't listen to your parents," Rachel said.

He looked at her with surprise.

"Oh, don't mind me. I'm just sick of my mother interfering in my life." She glanced at her watch. It was a few minutes past nine. She was late. "Look, I've got to go."

His face fell. "Okay."

"Later," she said.

"G'night." Before they separated, he touched her arm and gave her the old, confident Daniel smile that always warmed her heart.

The library, alive with light and people, was a welcome refuge from the streets. Whispered voices, rustling papers, and shoes tapping on the marble floor all set her at ease. She walked past students seated on spindle-back wooden chairs, their textbooks and loose-leaf binders spread over shared tables, to the stairway that led to the conference room on the second floor.

The meeting had started and Yusif was speaking to a group of around thirty people who sat on metal folding chairs. Michael was beside him. When he saw her, he motioned her in but she wasn't sure where to sit until Amira touched her arm and slid over to make room for her. She felt the cool metal of Amira's bangles contrast with her soft touch and the breath of her whispered welcome.

When Yusif finished, he introduced Michael and the room got measurably quieter.

"Thank you for coming, tonight," he began. He was looking out at the group, but Rachel felt as if he were speaking directly to her. I know we've been asking a lot of you lately, because the *intifada* presents us with an opportunity that may never come again. Life has its 'moments' and this is one of them for those of us who care about the children—the future of our people and the forgotten victims of this decades-old conflict—languishing in refugee camps, hungry, homeless, oppressed."

He's like an anchor on the evening news, she thought. *People trust him.* He didn't shout or rant or rave. He was an academic fused with a street fighter; there was a toughness underlying every word. To think that such a powerful man might be interested in her...it was a heady feeling.

After a while, Rachel became mesmerized by the timbre of Michael's voice and the expressions on his face as he spoke. But even only half-listening, it was clear that everything he said pointed at the Israeli army and the ever-expanding reach of the government in the form of settlements, as the cause of all their suffering. And with that as the premise, it was only logical that they should rebel and throw stones at the Israeli soldiers.

"We all know people who have suffered because of the occupation. I lost my entire family. But finally, a beautiful flower has emerged out of the rubble that is Palestine. Young children, teenage boys, mothers, all are saying, 'I have had enough. I will shake you off me, you and all your military might.' And some unknown young hero picked up a stone—the only weapon at his disposal—and hurled it at an Israeli soldier. Others followed and it has spread like wildfire. *Intifada*—the shaking off."

Rachel wanted to argue. Retorts flew into her mind but she stifled them. What did she know of these people's lives?

Michael took a sip of water. The crowd waited silently for him to continue.

"We are far from the squalid refugee camps that have sprung up in desperation, marring the natural beauty, the rolling hills, vineyards, and farms of Palestine. We are removed from the frustration and hopelessness that hangs over the land. But we can make the world aware of what these brave young people are saying. We can be their voice to the world outside when they feel that no one is listening. They have thrown their stones and with our help, the impact will be felt all over the world."

He looked directly at Rachel, as if the next words were meant for her. "Let me be clear. This is not a movement against the Jewish people. They, too, have suffered from injustices. But the remedy for that injustice is not to take our land. We protest the policies of the Israeli government and welcome all people of all faiths to join us. Stand with us on Friday, at three pm, for the sake of the children."

The room dimmed and a projector clicked to a slide of a young boy, his frail body rising in motion, hurling a stone at a fully attired IDF soldier with his rifle raised. The next slide showed the boy sprawled on the road, perhaps dead, perhaps wounded. Rachel glanced at Amira, who was totally absorbed, biting her lip, her eyes moist with emotion. She had a round face and long neck. Her black hair fell in cascading waves down her back. She sat perfectly straight, perched at the edge of her chair so effortlessly, as if she might float away. Her expression reminded Rachel a little of Daniel, the layers of history in her eyes, the refusal to accept victimhood. On her, it was beautiful.

Wristbands with symbolic stones attached appeared in bowls like candy at a party and were passed around. People grabbed them and put them on their wrists. A raucous atmosphere was developing, as when exams are finally done and school is out.

Michael went on to describe the plans for the "*Intifada In-Depth*" conference, which was officially sponsored by the Middle Eastern Studies Department and designed to educate. Possible speakers ranged from a Middle-Eastern History professor to the parents of a slain Palestinian teenager, to Michael, who would speak about health care. Yusif was heading a subcommittee responsible for printing the agenda and coordinating refreshments, layout, reception, and other details. After Michael concluded his remarks, he set out sign-up sheets. People congregated at the table to add their names.

Amira placed her hand on Rachel's arm and there was a slight tremor in the delicate touch. "I'm very glad you came. I spend all my time either at SPHR or classes or home, always the same people. It's nice to make a new friend."

Rachel knew exactly what she meant.

"You know Michael from his work?"

"Yes, I met him at the clinic. I'm doing an internship."

"Michael is so intelligent. I'm not smart that way. I study dance."

"I knew it!"

"You did?"

"I used to study modern dance in high school. I could tell you were a dancer. I wish I had time for it, but haven't taken class since I started college."

They looked at each other with new interest. It felt to Rachel like freshman year, when she'd formed instant friendships with other students, all of them swimming in unfamiliar waters, relying on one another for support and camaraderie. That, along with whatever alchemy causes people to become friends, had led to closeness with strangers unlike anything she'd ever experienced before.

Then Michael was beside her. He began to introduce her to Amira, then realized they'd already met.

"That's right," Amira said. "It's so nice to see her again!" Then she turned abruptly to another student, a little too obviously leaving Rachel alone with Michael.

"Come, have something to eat." He took hold of her arm and ushered her to the back of the room, where there were sodas and cookies spread out on a table.

"Would you like a coke?" He took a plastic cup and poured it for her.

"That was a good speech," she said.

"Thank you. So, will you help me out wcoith the symposium?"

She was in a good mood and wanted to say yes, to go with the flow, to take the proverbial extended hand. "Help you how?"

"How about working with me on the speech I'll be giving about the children's clinics? I could give you some background material and you could write an outline or a draft. I'll work it out with Bergman so it's part of your internship. It won't take extra time, and we can work together."

That sounded good.

She reached for a cookie and bit into it. A chunk of chocolate momentarily distracted her; she was starving. He lingered by her side. A couple of people came over to say hello to him, and, as Yusif pulled him away, Michael turned back to her and said, "Agreed?"

She nodded. At that moment, she couldn't think of one reason not to.

CHAPTER ELEVEN

Now that they were working together, it was natural that he would stop and talk to Rachel when she was on duty at the clinic. Sometimes she stopped by his office with an idea or a question and he would enjoy the cozy intimacy of sharing his small space with her. She would make herself comfortable in the chair across from his desk, her legs stretched in front of her, biting her lip while she thought through a problem.

He wanted more, but it didn't feel right to ask her on a date. At least not yet. This had to unfold naturally, he thought, so he waited.

One afternoon, he was with Yusif at SPHR headquarters, sorting through photographs, eating pizza from an open box, trying not to get food on the photos. "You're coming by tonight, right?" he asked his friend.

Yusif nodded. "I have to fill out some permit applications this afternoon but that shouldn't take too long."

"Don't we have undergrads that can do that kind of thing?"

"I wish. I'd have to spend so much time explaining it that it's simpler to do it myself. On top of which, they're unreliable. I train them and then they change their mind and join some other organization that they think will look better on their resume."

"Hard to find good help these days."

Yusif rolled his eyes. Palestinians always had the shit jobs. They *were* the help.

"Eva says they've identified collaborators over in Ramallah," Yusif said. "Remember old Yassim, the one who always sat outside the café?"

"Him?"

Yusif nodded.

"Hard to believe," Michael said, and wondered if it were true. He knew that people sometimes accused others of collaborating purely for personal revenge, and Yassim was a waspish man with many enemies. The truth was rarely revealed in these cases. There were no trials; an accusation was enough. If the Israelis did that kind of thing, there would be protests from all over the world, but somehow the same people ignored it when it was the Palestinians.

"Then the employees of Ramallah's Civil Administration were accused of collaboration because it was originally organized by Israel. They were found guilty and executed. Every single one of them." Yusif took a sip of coffee, black, cold, and bitter, more punishment than refreshment. "Afterwards, the Party reviewed their cases and decided four of them had been arrested mistakenly, so they declared them martyrs."

"Martyrs," Michael repeated.

Yusif nodded. "The families will be compensated."

"That will take care of it," he said, with just the slightest edge of sarcasm. They regarded one another, two men whose childhoods were a wild ride in a fractured land. They knew better than to criticize Party decisions aloud, even to each other, but sometimes a look passed between them that recognized the ruinous consequences of the unending conflict, an expression that spoke of their longing for a better way.

"Are you making any progress on the health clinics? It will be harder to organize them now," Yusif said.

"I know. But the student intern at the lab, Rachel, the girl you met—"

"The one who came to the meeting?"

"Yes, I've gotten her involved. It will help to have some American Jews on board. She'll be an asset, especially if I get her to travel over there."

"What do you know about her?"

Michael hesitated. "Not much. She knows Bergman well; he's a family friend. She is interested in helping children."

"Has she ever been politically active before?"

"Not that I'm aware of."

"I'll let Akil know about her."

They never knew what Akil would do with information, only that he had to know everything. He was like the CEO of a company. Information was an asset along with guns and territory. Michael began to regret mentioning Rachel at all, but Yusif had already met her, so it would have seemed odd to leave her out.

"How is Eva?" Michael asked. "She said that soldiers came to our neighbor's house last month. They walked in like they owned it and arrested the father on some trumped-up charge, and now the family is struggling. I hate that Eva is living through all this while I'm here. I've tried to persuade her to come over, but she insists that her parents need her."

"She's right."

"I need her, too. She's my wife. She should be by my side."

For many men, loneliness or restlessness would have been excuse enough to stray. Not Yusif, though, with his dark good looks, he probably wouldn't have any trouble. He'd been with Eva since he was a kid and never looked elsewhere. She'd been there for him after his parents were killed; her family had brought him into their fold. Their marriage had just formalized a bond that had existed between them their entire lives.

It was different for Michael. When he lost his mother, Akil had convinced him that the occupation had caused her death and that revenge against the Zionists was the only possible response. At first, Michael didn't get it. His mother hadn't been killed by the Zionists. She'd gotten a simple chest cold that progressed to pneumonia.

Akil explained that she'd succumbed to illness because she'd lost the will to live after Hanna's death, which was the result of having been driven from their land by the Zionists, stranded in a refugee camp in Jordan, and subjected to King Hussein. This was tortured logic at best, but it gave Michael an outlet for his grief: hatred of the Zionists.

Losing his mother was the worst thing that had ever happened to him and it shaped his relationships with women to this day. He was determined never to be that vulnerable again. In those rare moments when he felt himself respond with tenderness to a woman, he immediately put his guard up and pushed the woman away. He turned instead to his female counterparts: women in the movement who had something to prove and wanted uncomplicated relationships. Or he got involved with wealthy, beautiful women who wanted to rebel against their parents and viewed romance with him as an adventure. They were fun, exciting, and easy to ditch once the moment passed.

Rachel was another version of them; there was no possibility of a future with her, so he was free to indulge his attraction. She was beautiful, but not dramatically gorgeous like that Lebanese model he'd dated in Beirut. When he saw her at the clinic with her hair pulled back, she seemed serious and intelligent and older than her years. When she let it down, it tumbled over her neck in waves, reminding him of shadows on the sand cast by the wings of birds. Her eyes were a violet color, quite unlike anything he'd ever seen. He'd never been with a Jewish woman and felt like a teenager, fantasizing about her.

He and Yusif stopped talking at the sound of footsteps in the hall. It was Rachel, his daydream made real. She brought in wintry, cold air as she breezed into the room.

"Oh good, I found the right place! I wanted to drop off these drawings..." She glanced at the table and noticed the pictures. Her smile crumbled and was replaced by a mixture of alarm and horror. "Oh my God. What are these?"

One of the photographs showed Israeli soldiers pointing their guns at a group of women and children. Another showed a young boy, apparently injured, lying in rubble, his eyes closed.

"They just came in from Ramallah. The situation is getting worse. The soldiers are there to crush us and they don't know anything but military tactics. Children are suffering," Michael said, although he suspected the particular shot had been set-up for the camera, because he recognized the boy and would have heard if anything had happened to him. It didn't matter. Children were suffering. That much was true.

"This is terrible," Rachel whispered.

Headlines from the college paper and from *The New York Times* peeked out among the pictures: "11 More Hurt in the West Bank and Gaza"; and "Israelis Put Total of Rioting Arrests at 1000"; and "Ex-Israeli Officers Say a Deal for Peace is Needed." Rachel took them in at a glance, then picked up the article that reported that the IDF had shut down universities because they were considered "hotbeds of insurrection."

"I've been reading a lot of about all this, but seeing this all together drives it home," she said.

It was a small shift in her attitude, a widening of the lens through which she viewed the situation—and it warmed Michael. He liked the idea of her by his side, genuinely sharing in the struggle. It seemed like a good moment to ask more of her. "I'm going to put up posters for the symposium. Want to help?"

"Now?"

He nodded. "I invited some friends to come by my place later for drinks and music. Why don't you join us?"

She touched her hair as if wondering if she looked all right. It was a typical female gesture, yet seemed quite unlike her. Maybe it was the influence of her fashion-designer mother.

"It's just some friends, very informal..." He waited a beat, and then began putting on his coat. "So, are you coming?" He grabbed some tacks and a small hammer, gave her an encouraging smile, and it seemed to do the trick.

If she had any reluctance about putting up inflammatory posters against Israel, it wasn't enough stop her. She began helping him with the pile of posters. There was a new bounce in her step as they walked from the room.

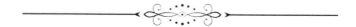

Michael and Rachel walked around campus discussing where to put the posters for best effect. One showed young children crouching as an Israeli soldier aimed his long gun at them. FREE PALESTINE was emblazoned across the top, along with information about Students for Palestinian Human Rights and the date and time of the symposium. She stared at it, biting her lip. Michael put his arm around her shoulder. "It's good, isn't it?" he said.

"It certainly gets your attention. But I have friends who would be pretty upset with me for spreading this message, and I don't even want to start to think about what my mother would say."

"This is what is going on. Ignoring it doesn't change the facts. Pictures are just a way of bringing attention to it."

If that picture was even remotely accurate, then her father's fears about Israel being unable to control hundreds of thousands of hostile people were prescient. Michael's arm tightened around her for a moment and she thought, not for the first time, that the way they were working together was a model for the future. It was as if she were carrying out her father's legacy. Tears came to her eyes as it struck her that she was destined to be with Michael in this moment; that greater forces were at work than she could comprehend.

They continued walking, putting the posters up in places like entrances to classroom buildings and cafeterias. Then Rachel suggested putting one outside the campus, on a kiosk that held notices for residents as well as students. "Great idea!" he said.

On their way back to campus, they passed the local Methodist church, which had a small graveyard by its side.

"I've always wondered who's buried here," she said, stopping for a moment and peering through the fence.

"People from another era. I've seen kids taking grave rubbings and art students sketching here. When it gets dark, the atmosphere is kind of otherworldly."

"I've only been to a cemetery in the daytime, visiting my father's grave."

"Where is it?"

"In Westchester." A pigeon landed on top of one of the headstones but, in the half-light of dusk, it reminded her of a crow buzzing around a dead body.

"Is it far?"

"No. Less than an hour from the city. I go with my mom a couple of times a year."

She leaned against the gate at the entrance to the graveyard.

"I haven't been to my father's grave in many years," he said.

"Over in Palestine? Does someone else in your family go?"

"There is no one else."

"Oh. I'm so sorry."

"It was a long time ago. Save your sympathy for the kids over there now. Would you like to look at these headstones? They're interesting."

He was like a multi-faceted stone, she thought, as they walked down the narrow paths of the graveyard. She was reminded of her mother's tiny but always polished diamond engagement ring. She used to hold her mother's hand up to the window on sunny days to reflect the light onto the walls. The stone cast beautiful rainbows they would admire together. Once, her mother had been so enchanted by the play of light that she said, under her breath, "Let's show Daddy." Rachel had been startled by this. Had her mother forgotten he was dead? This had happened at odd and unexpected moments throughout Rachel's childhood. Her mother would express an impulse to share something with her father, realize what she'd said, and her expression would change from excitement to grief—as if he'd died all over again, and she'd just found out.

"I don't think my mother has ever gotten over my father's death," Rachel said. "She still gets hysterical when we visit his grave. It makes it so difficult. It would be much easier to experience it on my own, without having to worry about her. Even so, I go with her because I feel as though he appreciates it."

She hesitated for a moment and then the words slipped out. "He comes to visit me afterwards. It happens every time." She held her breath, wondering if she'd be ridiculed, but Michael was nodding, deep in thought. He seemed to be listening with such intensity and respect that she was drawn to move closer to him as she spoke. "I don't talk to him, exactly, but I sense him and I always have some kind of insight afterwards, as if he's spoken to me."

Michael nodded and gazed at the headstones as if they held some secret.

"When did your father die?" she asked.

"A long time ago."

"How old were you?"

"Twelve."

His answers were terse but he didn't change the subject. They sat down on the steps of the church and gazed out over the graveyard. "What happened?" she asked. He seemed suddenly younger, more vulnerable than he ever had—like a child who acts tough to mask his fear. He sat one step lower than her. She rested a hand lightly on his shoulder and felt him relax.

"What happened to him, Michael?" she asked again. Her voice had a new resonance: deeper, soothing. It fit the dusk and secrets.

"A long time ago, my father's family lost everything— their home, their land—everything. It became his life's mission to get it back. But when it happened again twenty years later, something snapped. He stopped wanting everything back the way it was. He just wanted peace. He was a lawyer and knew his way around and he contacted the Israelis."

"That's amazing!"

Michael shook his head with an expression that said she didn't have a clue. "He became a pariah in our village. There were threats on his life. Even over the radio, they tried to intimidate him, naming him with all the other 'traitors.' He became secretive about his movements. People we'd known for years began avoiding us as if we had a disease they might catch."

"No one else agreed with him?"

"No, not even my mother. She would say that she married a rebel and was living with a coward."

"What about you?"

"I wasn't even ten years old and I was much closer to my mother. She said he was cowardly to give up his dream and I believed her, although when I think of it now, he was brave to fight the tide the way he did.

"But he had been so convincing about supporting the resistance and the importance of fighting for our land, until then. The complexity of the logic that led him to reverse his thinking was beyond me. I was just a kid. It seemed like he'd given up."

"Negotiating isn't giving up."

"Yes and no. It's complicated."

"So, what happened?"

"He kept meeting with the Israelis even though it was dangerous. He tried to recruit others. And then one night he didn't come home. He was found murdered. We never found out who did it."

She was speechless. Michael's father was murdered because he was negotiating? That was sick. How did Michael manage to grow into such a rational, intelligent man, coming from such violent surroundings? Maybe he got his rationality from his father? "But you realized he was right as you got older," she said, more as a statement than a question.

He hesitated for a moment. "Yes…but it's complicated."

It occurred to her that both of their fathers had died too soon. Perhaps because of this she could understand him in a way that few others could. She reached out and placed her hand on his shoulder again, and saw the edges of his lips turn up slightly. They sat that way for a few minutes as the sky darkened and the wind picked up a little.

"Come, Rachel." He stood and reached out for her hand. "I want to show you some of the inscriptions. This cemetery goes back over a hundred years. And then we should go. I've got to set up the food before everyone arrives at my place."

"Let's leave something," she said. "I always leave a stone on my father's headstone."

"I'd like to go with you sometime."

"Where?"

"To visit your father. I could take you. I have a car I share with some friends. You could visit without your mom. See what it feels like."

The man never stopped surprising her.

Michael's apartment was only a few blocks from the little cemetery, on the second floor of an old brownstone that had an air of genteel poverty. There were high ceilings and dentil moldings, dark parquet floors and a marble entry foyer, but everything was in a state of mild disrepair, the wood scratched, the floor yellowed and cracked. It was furnished with a beat-up brown leather chair and a couch covered with a red-and-gold throw in a zigzag pattern.

He took her jacket and put it in what appeared to be a small room furnished with a desk and armchair. He gave her a beer and declined her offer of help, while he busied himself bringing out food from the kitchen: hummus, pita bread, olives, tabouli, and a yogurt dip.

She sipped the beer and noticed a beautiful drum nestled in the corner. It was ceramic with an iridescent black glaze. "Do you play the drum?"

"Yes. When I have time."

"I wouldn't have taken you for a drummer."

"No? Well, it's a private pleasure."

"Why private?"

"Why are things private?" he repeated, as if giving himself time to think about his answer. "Maybe because it takes me completely away from myself. It's hard to explain." He stopped working for a moment. "A drum mirrors your emotions and then carries them away."

"I can see that. Or it creates a mood. When I hear a drum, it energizes me."

"That's happens, too," he agreed. "Sometimes when I'm tired, I play an upbeat, fast rhythm and it energizes me. When I want to relax, I play something slow. When I was young, I could play for hours and hours." A trancelike expression veiled his eyes. "My friend, the doctor I told you about, gave me this drum when I turned thirteen. It was the perfect gift. I've kept it with me ever since."

"Are you still in touch with him?" she asked.

"Yes, he's a good friend and a kind of mentor."

"Your guardian angel."

"Kind of. He was close to my father for many years, but they had very different personalities. The doctor is very warm, a people person. Everyone loves and respects him. I think of him like an uncle. He always made time for me. Not only me. He was good to a lot of kids, but I felt especially close to him."

She wished she had known Michael as a kid. He was seven or eight years older than she was and if they'd been neighbors he'd have been like a big brother. She might have been a little pest trying to get his attention, or maybe she would have idolized him and been too scared even to talk in his presence.

"He helped me make decisions about my career, where to study, the fellowship..." he continued.

"Sounds a little like me and Dr. Bergman. He always encouraged my interest in medicine and steered me toward endocrinology."

They were interrupted by the sound of loud voices and laughter. The unlocked door flew open and people streamed in one after another: Yusif and Amira, then some of the other students Rachel had seen at the offices of the Students for Palestinian Human Rights.

While they were talking, laughing, and taking off their coats, Rachel's eyes wandered around the room and rested on one of the few pictures that hung on the wall. It was of a man with piercing black eyes and graying hair dressed in an open shirt and dark trousers. He was seated at a desk, looking up from some papers, as if he'd been interrupted while lost in thought and was in the process of refocusing. He looked like someone she knew, or would want to know.

"Rachel! You were the first to arrive!" Amira put her arm around Rachel's shoulder and leaned in close as if they were co-conspirators. "I'm supposed to be visiting with

Maryam, so if you ever meet my cousins and they ask, make sure that's what you say." She giggled, and Rachel suspected she'd already had a drink. "I love these little gatherings at Michael's, but my parents are very strict."

"Your secret's safe with me," Rachel said.

"I brought some baklava. Try some. It's delicious!"

Gifts piled up on the table: sweet pastries, a lamb dish made with rice, a meat pie—Rachel smelled turmeric and cumin and garlic—cucumber salad, boxes of tea, and bottles of wine. It reminded her a little of informal gatherings at Josh's dorm, when one person would drop by and then another, everyone looking for something to do, and they'd end up ordering a pizza and blasting music. Sometimes someone passed around a joint. Occasionally, she took a few hits and it made everything—the music, her thoughts, her feelings for Josh—much sharper. In those moments, she was free from the constant striving that drove her so relentlessly that she rarely completely relaxed. She was content just being among her friends, leaning comfortably into Josh, listening to his voice over the competing sound of Springsteen's "Born in the USA." She missed those gatherings and had found nothing to replace them, nowhere to hang out except at the Student Center with Jill and Daniel. Until now.

People drifted in and out of the apartment over the course of the evening, sitting and talking in evolving clusters like bubbles forming and popping and reforming. She drank a few beers, sipping slowly but not keeping track, and at one point found herself in an armchair with Amira squeezed next to her, her long hair draping over Rachel's arm. "Ah, this is the life," Amira said, giggling.

"You're drunk," Rachel said. "I'd like to see you dance, now."

"Oh, I can always dance. Even better when I drink. But not now. I'm too comfortable." She sank further into the chair, and gazed up at Rachel. "You're nice," she said.

"In vino veritas," Rachel said, laughing. "So you like me?"

"Yes. You're one of the good ones."

"Well, thanks...I think."

"Not like the others," Amira muttered, her mood darkening. "I shouldn't be laughing when my cousins are suffering."

Rachel's enjoyment at being squeezed into a chair with Amira vanished and she just felt cramped.

"I've never met them but I've seen so many pictures that I feel like I know them—you know what I mean?" said Amira, looking directly into Rachel's eyes.

"Honestly, no, I don't."

"My cousin Minnah, she's four years old. The other day she was playing outside when a crowd of teenagers started throwing stones at the soldiers. The soldiers threw tear gas and Minnah got caught in the middle of it. Only she started choking. It was too much for a little girl! Don't they know that? Can't they control themselves?"

Rachel stared at her.

"A neighbor tried to take her to a hospital but they were delayed by closures."

"Is she alright?"

"They got her there eventually and she's okay physically. But she's terrified, doesn't sleep well, and has nightmares. It's so sad."

"Wow." *What else could she say?*

They sat quietly for a minute, then Amira turned to her again. "I know it's not all...I mean...I know that there are two sides to this conflict. Jews have always been persecuted, the Holocaust... if Jewish people hadn't been shut out of Palestine and the US and pretty much everywhere, so many more would have lived. There was nowhere for them to go. People say it should have been somewhere else, not Palestine, but I think there could be room for everyone. Only it has gotten very bad there now. I pray that the *intifada* will force everyone to the table and that something good will come from it, so people can go on and live their lives."

Rachel was impressed at Amira's effort to see both sides. Maybe it was because she was raised in America and went to school with people from different backgrounds so she was more open-minded. Or maybe it was just who she was. There was so much Rachel wanted to say to her, but a guy named James had been eyeing Amira for a while, and he came over and sat on the arm of the chair and gave her a shy smile. Amira gave her a long, hard hug and then turned her attention to James.

Continuing to sip beer steadily throughout the evening, Rachel was lightheaded by midnight, when people began to drift away and head home. When the last person had left and Michael offered to walk her home, she held up one hand and walked toward the photograph on the wall.

"Who is this? I've been curious."

"That's Dr. Waseem. The man we spoke of earlier."

"The one who gave you the drum?"

"Exactly."

"He reminds me of Dr. Bergman," she said. "Do they know each other?"

"No, they've never met."

The drum was sitting near the photograph and Rachel lightly fingered the top. It was covered with some kind of skin and her fingers accidentally produced a sound. "Can I hear you play before I go?"

He considered. Everything seemed to be a calculation for Michael.

"Or not," she said carelessly, and started toward the door.

"Sure, I'd like to play," he said. She felt a mild surge of pleasure at having manipulated him. He sat down on a hard stool, put the drum between his legs, and began tapping lightly, as if warming up. She sat opposite him on the couch but he shook his head.

"No. Move."

She looked at him uncertainly.

"You said you used to dance," he said, as he trilled on the drum. "I sometimes play for Amira and her dancers. Just move, wherever the beat takes you."

He wasn't even looking at her anymore; a serene expression crossed his face like a cloud that turns the air around it into hazy fog. Rachel felt self-conscious but decided it would be okay. She could explore the unknown with impunity; no one, not her mother, not Jill or Daniel, would ever know.

She saw Michael's legs tremble slightly and her desire to move became irresistible. It wasn't because he'd told her to; the drumbeat gave its own command. As he played, Michael was there but not there. It felt to Rachel like praying next to someone in a church or synagogue: they were together but separate, each in his own world, connected only by the beat.

She'd never heard anything quite like this drum, or perhaps it was only that she'd never listened in quite the same way. Michael's fingers moved lovingly across the skin of the drum, then every once in a while, he scooped up some of the ribbons with jangles that hung from the side as an accent, a spice added to the dish. His fingers tapped faster and then he used his whole hand, slapping the head in punishment, then stroking it reassuringly, then seeming to plead with it.

The slapping sounds washed over her, infusing her body with its spirit. She had an urge to leap across the floor, but was restrained by the limitations of the space, so instead she took vertical jumps, her legs kicking as if she were swimming in air, her arms lifting until she almost touched the ceiling. The drumbeat kept up with her and then became more furious and she found herself twirling like a Sufi, slowly at first, then freely, endlessly, in the center of the vortex of her own movement. She slowed down but was still moving, breathing hard, sweaty, when all at once he stopped. He was watching her with approval.

She was very aware that she was alone with him. He'd always been circumspect with her, but now it was as if some barrier was breached. Her confidence wavered. Who had manipulated whom? He put down the drum and then he was beside her, an arm wrapped around her waist, a hand touching her cheek, guiding her face toward his. She felt his strong fingers pressing on her lower back, pulling her closer, and a throbbing inside her lower abdomen that only intensified when he whispered in her ear, "You're stunning."

This is what she had wanted. She'd felt it building all

day. And yet, for a tiny, terrible moment she hesitated. Another man would have ignored her ambivalence, would have persisted through it, might not even have noticed it. But Michael reacted to her moment of indecision by loosening his grip instantly. Then everything reversed itself, leading to a cascade of miscues, until her hesitation evaporated and her desire took charge. He responded to that as well, and she felt his hands moving and exploring her as their kisses intensified.

Being in his arms felt somehow familiar and yet thrillingly new. She'd always dismissed girls who were attracted to "hunks" as shallow, and yet part of the thrill was his strength. His chest was muscular, his neck was thick and solid, and she had the notion that she could squeeze him with all her might and not hurt him—that she was free to do anything, to be anything she wanted in his arms. It made her feel delicate and feminine and desired, which was anti-feminist and yet oh so pleasurable.

They explored one another with their hands and mouths until their clothing began to get in the way. It had to progress or stop and she didn't know how to stop, but she needed time to process it all, and he seemed to understand.

He looked into her eyes and said again, "You're stunning." Then he kissed her neck and pulled her down to the couch, settled her next to him and held her until her breathing returned to normal. After a little while she got up and whispered that she needed a minute, and pulled herself together in the privacy of his bedroom,.

"You ready?" he asked, when she came back into the room.

She smiled a yes, and kissed his cheek and he hugged her again and sighed. His car was parked nearby, so he drove her up to Riverdale and parked a few blocks from her house when he saw an empty space. The streets were quiet and dark and empty, silent in ways Manhattan never was, as he walked her to the door of her home.

"I can take you to your father's cemetery a week from Sunday. Is that good for you?" he whispered in her ear. She felt his lips brush her neck lightly and a shiver went down her spine.

Yes. It was good.

CHAPTER TWELVE

Akil circled the prison yard, taking slow measured steps to get a rhythm. As always, steady movement calmed him and helped him think.

"My friend," Ahmed, called out, startling him. Ahmed smiled an apology, showing spaces in his mouth where teeth had once been. "This is for you," he said. He placed an object in his leader's hand, and they instinctively glanced at the barbed wire fence. A passing soldier regarded them curiously for a moment and continued walking.

The gift was a rock in the shape of Palestine. A streak of blue dye showed the flow of the Jordan River through their land.

"Many thanks, my friend. This is a treasure, a fine symbol of our struggle."

"It is nothing. You deserve much more," Ahmed responded, the first link in the chain of obligatory flattery.

"It is you who deserve more," Akil said, "Your wisdom and bravery are well known."

"I will never stop, even if I die in this filthy prison," Ahmed said.

Akil looked at him with compassion. "If that happens, others will continue the fight until our victory. May we all live to see the day!" He gripped the rock and put out his hand. "For Palestine!" Ahmed placed his hand atop his and they stood that way, looking out at the monotonous landscape, united in respect for the moment of giving and receiving and the land they loved.

They continued walking, side by side. "You and I understand our history and goals," said Akil. "But the people are losing their way."

"You must remind them with something spectacular, like the old days."

The sound of an airplane roared overhead, as if on cue. They looked up, but their vision was briefly obscured by a black cloud of smoke rising from the water heaters.

"Yes, the old days," Akil said, with longing. "We had some great success, but there were mistakes. You remember Karim? Handsome? Educated as an engineer?"

Ahmed nodded. "Yes, of course."

"When he was living in Sweden he got a Swedish girl pregnant and promised to marry her. He sent her ahead to Palestine, supposedly for the wedding. He packed her bags and took her to the airport, but when the Israelis questioned her, they were suspicious of her story. Pregnant women didn't usually travel alone. There was no hotel reservation. They searched and found the bomb." He paused. "The idea was right, but Karim didn't think things through thoroughly and the girl was wrong. We need to find someone the Israelis would never suspect, someone above reproach."

They sat in silence, thinking. They scratched gray whiskers and gradually drew themselves up straighter, trying to fulfill the memory of the soldiers they once had been.

"What about Michael? He is in New York. Many Jews live there," Ahmed said.

"If only they all did," Akil said, wistfully. "Michael works for one—a physician. And he has a young Jewish woman working for him."

"Ah, yes?"

"She's been helping them with their protests."

They were silent for a moment, thinking.

"She has no history in anti-government activity?"

"No."

"What is his interest in her? Does he have a plan?"

"He thinks she will be useful for getting funding for his clinics. Michael is obsessed with them, and it clouds his judgment. Clinics are like Band-Aids," Akil said, dismissive. "They are not a solution. There is a better use for her."

Ahmed smiled. "The plan you tried with Karim?"

"With this girl, we will do it right—and Michael is more competent than Karim was. He will make sure no detail is overlooked."

Ahmed nodded agreement.

"'She'll sail through airport security like…" He blew a piece of dust off his finger and watched it fly in the air, and they began to discuss details.

Michael picked up Rachel in Riverdale. She saw him leaning against his Mazda sports car from her bedroom window. The top was down, despite the chilly air. She ran downstairs and out the door and kissed him as he held car the door for her. Amira had said that he'd been a playboy over in Lebanon, when he was a student at the American University of

Beirut. He'd had money to spend and girlfriends—supposedly a former Miss Lebanon among them, a tall, leggy, dark-haired beauty.

He sat behind the wheel in his dark brown leather jacket, filling the seat perfectly, as if the car were built around him. Sitting so close to him in the small, sexy car made her breathless and a little off-balance. She settled into the worn leather seat, the stick shift on her left and the windshield low in front of her. Her hair was braided so it wouldn't fly madly around and she wore Dior sunglasses, a gift from her mother.

Michael edged out of the parking space, drove through Manhattan and over the Triborough Bridge. He was a confident driver, and she felt safe with him. They didn't talk much, except to establish directions to the cemetery. The noise of the car and the open air made conversation nearly impossible.

It took almost an hour to get to Elmwood Cemetery. It was vast—acres of burial ground intersected by roads and paths. They parked and walked for a while, until they found the pale gray marble headstone etched in large letters: WEISSMAN. Resting on the ground beneath it was a marker, indicating where her father's casket lay buried. "Mark Weissman, MD, beloved husband, father and son. Healer of the sick and injured. Rest in peace, my beloved." They stood in silence before the grave and Rachel took a small prayer book that she always brought to the cemetery and began to read:

Man is like a breath; His days are like a passing shadow; He flourishes and grows in the morning; He fades and withers in the evening, O teach us how to number our days, that we may attain a heart of wisdom. Mark the innocent, look upon the upright; for there is a future for the man of peace.

She loved that passage because that was how she thought of her father, as a man of peace. She knelt and picked up a few stones before choosing just the right one. Michael followed her lead, kneeling beside her to search for his own stone. He took his time finding one, and finally chose a long, white rock gleaming with mica, mottled with dark streaks.

They put them atop the headstone. Then Rachel kissed her fingers and placed them on the stones. A cool breeze kicked up—a message from her father perhaps, showing he approved of Michael? Standing beside him, it was as if someone had plucked a guitar string and they'd both resolved to the same pitch. He took her hand in his and they walked back to the car.

On the way back to the city, they exited the highway and found a diner. It was that in-between time, not lunch nor dinner, so the place was nearly empty except for a young mother and her two small children. The kids sat at the counter eating ice cream, their legs dangling from the stool, the spoons too big for their hands. They approached every spoonful with intense concentration.

Rachel smiled and nodded toward the kids. It was nice in the diner, quiet and peaceful. Easy to talk after the noise of the car.

"Thanks for bringing me here today," she said.

"It was my pleasure."

She ordered a glass of milk and pound cake from a dark-haired waitress wearing a black polyester skirt and crisp white shirt puffed up with shoulder pads. The whole outfit seemed rather uncomfortable for someone hustling back and forth between the kitchen and tables.

"It was different coming up here without my mother. It was easier to feel him. It doesn't make sense, since he isn't really there. But I feel as though I communicate with him." She paused. "Does your father ever speak to you?"

He looked confused.

"You know, not literally, but don't you still feel a connection with him?"

"Oh, that's right. Your father speaks to you. He must have been young when he died. You were just a child."

He hadn't answered her question, but she didn't push him. "Dad was in his mid-thirties. I'd just turned six. I don't know all that much because my mother doesn't like to talk about it. Sometimes I think she's hiding things from me but maybe it's just her sadness. She is very protective. Over-protective."

"When exactly was it that he died?"

"May of 1974."

"You said it was a car accident?"

She nodded. "He was on his way to the airport to come home for my birthday. Maybe he was rushing. Sometimes I think that it was kind of my fault."

Michael looked at her with surprise. "It wasn't your fault," he said. He was staring at something behind her, as if his attention had drifted, and she felt a loss. Had talking about her father triggered it? Josh used to act aloof at times, but with him, it was a way to manipulate her, to keep her off balance. With Michael, it was something else.

She couldn't figure him out. He was like a puzzle with missing pieces; no matter how hard she tried, it was incomplete. Settling back on the soft, torn plastic seat in the booth, staring out the window, she yearned to know where he went in the moments he withdrew from her and to follow him there.

"I saw that picture of the doctor in your apartment, but none of your dad. Do you have any?" she asked.

"Oh, sure, somewhere. How about you? You have pictures of your dad?"

"I have one in my room. My mom has them all over our house. She gave me some of his books, too. She was cleaning and throwing things out and she came across this beautiful picture book of Israel that a friend of theirs edited and gave to my father. It has an inscription in Hebrew, but it has no vowels and I can't read it."

"I can translate it if you want."

"Oh, that's right, you read Hebrew. You know more Hebrew than I do."

"Necessity."

"Why necessity?"

Instead of answering, he signaled the waitress for the check. She ripped it from her pad and gave it to him and he took out a few dollars, which he handed to her. Then he got up to leave and motioned to Rachel, leaving her question unanswered. It was starting to get annoying. When she got up, she punched him in the arm. "Answer a question once in a while. It's called conversation."

Instead, he responded to the punch, pinning her arms against her body as he grabbed her in a bear hug and lifted her off the ground. "No punching," he admonished.

It was funny, really, and fun to be scooped up in his powerful arms. She forgot her question.

When they got back to Riverdale and pulled up in front of her house, they sat for a few minutes enjoying the peaceful silence of the car.

"My mom is in the city today," she said. "She usually doesn't come home from work until after seven."

He nodded. "Let's have a look at that book."

She unlocked the door, nervous at his presence in her house, a place fraught with such meaning; it was where she'd spent almost her entire life. What would he think? It was modest by the standards of Riverdale and the mansions of nearby Fieldston, but neat and pretty and well located, walking distance to town and the train. Her mother's fine taste showed in the décor, the delicate patterns on the upholstery contrasting with the fine cashmere throws.

She took his hand and led him upstairs to her room, the only part of the house that was truly hers. Her bedroom faced a quiet side street. The only sounds were an occasional car, a dog barking, kids laughing. It was so ordinary in contrast with the extraordinary man beside her. *He is like the land where he was raised,* she thought: *complicated, shaped by nature and history, struggling to survive, and yet triumphing over it all.*

She couldn't believe he was there with her. It seemed like a magical mix-up of some kind, made possible by being in a country where everyone somehow manages to live together despite their differences and a Jewish girl can work side-by-side with a Palestinian man.

Her bed, wedged into the far corner of the room, was strewn with books and papers and a radio remote. She sometimes kept the news on in the background while she worked, lounging against the loud, brightly colored pillows she had collected. She liked to lie among them, lose her papers in them. Sometimes she punched them when she was angry after an argument with her mother.

He looked around curiously. She loved the way his eyes scanned the room, resting on objects of interest; the periodic table poster that had been her father's, her family photo in a silver frame, a stereo, the charts on her desk.

She found the book and opened it. "It's over here, Michael."

Her voice sounded different to her own ears. It was coming from somewhere outside herself, from another more confident, more seductive woman. She liked this woman and didn't want to lose her, so, she fought the feelings of nervousness that thrashed about, trying to surface.

"Here, Michael," she said again, and waited until he was ready to turn the lens of his curiosity on her. He didn't smile or try to comply with the social mores she'd been raised with. He operated on his own timetable, and when he was ready, he came over and sat beside her on the bed, leaning over her shoulder to read the inscription in the book.

"Read it aloud," she demanded, and he did. His fluency and accent were remarkable. He could be Israeli. She stared at him, astonished. He put his finger to her lips, which were slightly apart in surprise.

"*Al ma at choshevet.* Rachel?"

"Was I right to begin with?" she responded. "Are you an Israeli masquerading as a Palestinian?"

A half-smile softened his expression, but she could only guess at what he found amusing. He reached out and put his hand on her cheek and she instinctively leaned into it. His touch was gentle. When his finger brushed across her mouth, her lips vibrated like the strings of a violin awakened by a bow.

"*Ken*—yes—an Israeli," he said, but it was a lie. He was her lovely lie. "Is that what it would take, Rachel?" he asked, his voice teasing, as he gently leaned her back against the pillows. Then he gripped her neck and for a moment she thought he could strangle her and there would be nothing she could do, no one to hear. But his hand just drifted down and traced a line down the middle of her chest, and the odd thought crossed her mind: *I am a target and he is locating where to put the bullet.*

"I learned Hebrew in an Israeli jail, Rachel."

She lay very still.

Her breathing was so light and shallow that she felt as though she was floating, with no will of her own. The force of his presence, everything about him compelled her to stillness. She was almost overwhelmed by the power of his wanting her, and at the same time, she felt her own, extraordinary power. She was temptation. She was irresistible to him, just as his hand on her chest and his dark presence looming over her made him irresistible to her. Here, in her mother's house, she was behaving in a way that was contrary to everything her mother believed, breaking boundaries, and the notion intensified her feelings.

She sensed danger. Not imminent physical danger, but something else. The residue of Jill and Daniel's disapproval, and her mother's, briefly sullied the moment, but the compulsion to be near Michael quieted any doubts. He was an individual, not some placard with anti-Jewish sentiment. They were beyond all that, alone in her room. She looked up at him and saw that his expression had softened, his features relaxed. He was aroused but cautious and so beautiful.

Images floated through her head of places she'd visited, and villages in the furthest reaches of the desert that she hoped someday to see. Yusif had described Ramallah as desolate and boring, but Michael described a town situated on a hilltop overlooking the rolling hills of Palestine, where on a clear day you could see the Dome of the Al-Asqa Mosque in Jerusalem. Perhaps it depended upon whose eyes were seeing it. Someday she would see for herself.

She was content for the moment to just lie in his arms and watch the colorful images pass in her mind's eye, but he wanted more. She sensed his restlessness and was drawn into it, moved in response to him, until the momentum took over and she was lost in the feel of his hair on her cheek and his hands moving under her clothes and over her body. Each touch evoked some new feeling and she heard his breath come from way deep inside him and she herself made little sounds, but they didn't speak and she realized that she was, for the moment, inside his remote silence from which she had always been excluded.

And finally, they gave in to all that had been building over the weeks and she had to have him, would not let him go. She heard a car and not even the thought of her mother walking in would have stopped her. Nothing could have stopped her, then. If she'd known he would abandon her afterwards, she wouldn't have cared, she was too far gone. When he hesitated, asked her if she was sure, she laughed at his naiveté. She was more than sure. She was desperate and insistent and in control.

Hours later she made him coffee and couldn't stop smiling. Not even the thought of having to face her mother could dampen her spirits. She didn't want him to leave but he couldn't stay. Going home with him would have been too much too soon. So, she kissed his now familiar mouth again and whispered goodbye.

He reached for her hand and held it for a moment, running his thumb in little circles on her fleshy part of her palm, as if making his signature.

Then he left.

Michael learned of Akil's plan a few days later. Tucked into Eva's handwritten words of endearment and gossip about the village was a message for him to find an excuse to send Rachel on a plane to Israel and plant an explosive in her luggage, set to detonate at takeoff. The Party would take credit, weakening the rival parties, disrupting their negotiations.

Michael knew that something like this might be coming, but it had been so many years—not since before he'd come to New York—that it felt a shock. Al Akil hadn't asked much of him in years, had encouraged him to develop a reputation as a moderate, academic Palestinian for just such a purpose. He'd done it so successfully that he'd forgotten why he was doing it.

There was no question in his mind that he could manipulate Rachel. He could easily convince her to travel to

Israel to work on the clinic. The seed for that idea had already been planted. Getting her to agree to a trip, hiding a device in her luggage, was all very doable.

The scientist/engineer in Michael, the man who'd analyzed Karim's failed attempt, was briefly intrigued by the technical challenge of constructing a device that would be undetectable by security. He knew of a method of encasing a bomb in plastic to get past metal detectors. He thought about how to construct such a device and ways to hide it in her luggage.

But it was all a mental exercise because he wouldn't do it. He felt an overwhelming revulsion at the whole idea, especially since it involved Rachel. Did Akil suspect he had feelings for her? Was this a test?

Al Akil wasn't thinking straight and Michael understood why. He was stuck in a prison camp, frustrated that moderate groups were considering recognizing Israel. He wanted to disrupt the negotiations however he could because negotiation was anathema to him. Akil would never change. That was the problem.

When he was younger, Michael had always assumed Akil knew best, but now he was a grown man and he knew better. Rachel would be better off alive and working alongside him, not as a human sacrifice. He wanted to protect her. Was that love? Was it atonement? Whatever it was, he would have no part of this plan.

Still, the thought of disobeying Akil brought back long-buried torments, the other times he'd resisted the man's orders but ultimately followed through. Did he have the strength to go against his mentor?

Akil needed him, needed this plan, and Michael was bound by an oath of loyalty he'd made long ago. Others might desert the man, but everything important in his life was made possible by Akil, and he loved him as he had loved few people. He didn't want to disappoint him. But not this. Not Rachel.

She did unexpected things that made him smile, throwing up her hands in mock frustration when he was distracted, beating him on the chest with her fists like a tiny hurricane. She had a sense of fun and he'd had so little in his life, such a short childhood, just a few scattered memories of teasing Hanna and playing hide-and-seek around the village with his friend Wadih, spreading Party leaflets around, carelessly giddy, vying with each other to come up with ever more outrageous places: the top of a flagpole or just out of reach of the flames of a fire. The *fedayeen* were dead serious, but to him and Wadih, it was all a game.

The game ended on Black September, destroyed in the carnage that killed Wadih as they escaped the refugee camp. He'd lost Wadih and Hanna and then his mother. His father was murdered. There was only Akil, the one person who'd always believed in him, who'd encouraged his dream of becoming a doctor, paid for his schooling, loved and supported him through the long years of darkness after his family was gone.

His priorities came back to him in a swift rush of gratitude. Michael had committed many acts willingly to prove himself to Akil; this would not be the worst. Memories rose in his gut and threatened to overwhelm him.

He felt, again, the weight of the bomb that he'd placed in the house all those years ago, when he was still a child, the dust kicking up from his feet as he ran to safety, to watch from afar, hiding behind a rock just an instant before the bang, the soldier's body flying like a doll, one minute alive and smiling, the next minute dead. And then the soldier was Rachel, her body breaking apart, and he closed his eyes but couldn't erase the image. He knew he had to find a way out. A way to satisfy Akil without killing Rachel.

It didn't have to be her. She was chosen because she could get through security with a minimum of scrutiny. Maybe there was someone else, an older woman, perhaps. There were women in the clinic, but they didn't travel much. Who did he know who travelled?

Rachel said her mother often travelled abroad for business. She was going somewhere soon. He could meet her and figure out how to get the device in her bag. He would have to get to work creating it. He had an image of Rachel turning to him for solace, sobbing in his arms. He would comfort her, gather her in his arms and kiss her hair, her cheeks, her lips... he would hold her in her sorrow, for he, too, knew what it was like to lose a mother.

CHAPTER THIRTEEN

The next day, Michael was waiting for her outside the library, just before four o'clock. She hadn't expected him and her throat went dry. She barely managed to say hello.

He smiled.

"I felt lightheaded all day," she told him. "I couldn't concentrate."

His face looked softer, like someone had erased the hard edges. There was a light behind his eyes. "All day, I couldn't wait to see you," he told her with such simple honesty that she wanted to cry. It was like being in an hourglass with silky sand flowing around her. It felt wonderful, but there was a sad certainty it would come to an end.

He pulled her into a stone alcove separating two classroom buildings. It was damp and dark and he leaned her against the cold, hard wall and kissed her there. His tongue explored her mouth, the curve of its roof, the smoothness and hard edges of her teeth. She made herself available, let him take the lead. His hand traced the line of her body with a light touch as he kissed her. She felt little sparks everywhere he touched her. She wanted the pressure of his body against her and pulled him close, but all at once he stopped, looked into her eyes until she focused. They laughed and separated.

"I'll see you later at the conference?" he asked.

She nodded and they parted.

The "*Intifada* In-Depth Conference" would begin at 4 pm. She'd done research for his speech and understood more about his plans for mobile clinics. When she thought about them working together, achieving more than either of them could alone, it seemed almost like a spiritual calling.

But her moral clarity began to cloud as she looked at the sobering images lining the hallway leading to the conference: an endless line of cars at a checkpoint, homes reduced to rubble, a lone burning tire in a barren field. A group of SPHR members, none of whom she recognized, stood at the entrance to the building with gags stuffed loosely in their mouths and their hands tied, symbolizing "the suffering of the Palestinians."

How things had changed. Daniel had once shown her a *Life* magazine cover from right after the Six-Day war. It showed a handsome young Israeli soldier, his eyes shining and his dark curls gleaming like a halo. "The Astounding War" the caption said. The Israelis were heroes then, flotsam from a decimated, ruined people that rose up and conquered the great Arab Empires. Theirs was a story of redemption, David victorious over Goliath. But now it was reversed. It wasn't the great Arab Empires against tiny Israel; it was mighty Israel against a bunch of kids.

She hesitated. Michael's talk would be apolitical, a vision of how the mobile clinics would operate, the need to raise funds, and a little about advances in diabetes treatment. But these pictures told a different story. Rational arguments were boring. They wanted to incite people with propaganda.

Yusif motioned her over. "So, you made it," he said. "Michael is inside."

"What's going on out there, with the gags and handcuffs? I thought this was a symposium with speakers."

"It is. This just sets the tone. Sometimes education is best accomplished with a measure of theatre. It speaks to the truth. There are checkpoints where people wait for hours."

"They're not gagged, Yusif. That's over the top."

"The gags represent the curfews, the strangling regulations, and the constant presence of the soldiers. The handcuffs are for when you are arrested."

"Yes, but..." This wasn't her area of expertise. "What about the bigger picture? The reasons for the occupation? Shouldn't a symposium show all sides?"

"Go," he said, motioning her toward the seats. "Sit and listen and then see what you think."

She did as she was told.

The program went on into the early evening, the start of the Sabbath. It was not a day she normally honored. Her life went on in one uninterrupted stream and Saturday was an errand and study day. But the incongruity of her presence at that conference in those moments when the sun went down and the time for Jewish prayers began suddenly made her nostalgic for something she'd never had.

She'd had that feeling in Riverdale, too, when she was younger. On Friday afternoons, women with scarves on their heads and children in tow shopped at *Mothers*, the local kosher bakery, for Challah bread and pound cakes. A flurry of activity around preparations for the Sabbath went on from the late morning into the afternoon, and as daylight faded to darkness, the neighborhood went quiet. Families gathered in their homes, lighting candles, eating roast chicken. Not at her house, though, where it was just another dinner with her mom.

The memory was oddly dissonant from the discussion in front of her, which had nothing to do with religion, except to the extent that religion reflects moral values. Photographs of a family with seven beautiful children lined up in a row, their thin, tired parents behind them, were projected on a screen as a Palestinian man spoke about how he was imprisoned for protesting. Other photographs, some of which she'd seen on the table at SPHR, had been enlarged and stared down at her from the walls, the worn faces of Palestinians contrasting with soldiers in the background. There were no handsome, joyful Israeli soldiers with haloes of dark hair. These were helmeted monsters.

Someone tapped her shoulder and asked her to move down and she was surprised to see Daniel. He wore a baseball cap, which she assumed was functioning as his head covering, instead of a *kipah*.

"What are you doing here?" she whispered.

"Jill told me you'd be here and then I saw the signs and thought I'd hear what they have to say. There are a lot of protestors outside, you know." She heard the reproach in his voice and felt guilty despite herself.

He settled back in his seat and began to concentrate with the intent expression he wore in classes. Daniel was one of those kids who learned by listening and always got top grades even though he studied less than she did. He questioned everything—it was part of what made him such a good student—and sitting next to him, she began to listen with more skepticism.

But when Michael came out and began describing the Children's Healthcare Initiative, the need for it given the current situation, the dismal and scanty healthcare services, and how it was especially hard for children with chronic illnesses like diabetes, she felt good that she could help. He articulated his vision for a series of clinics serving the more remote villages, making the same treatments available to them that were available to children in Israel. He used words that she had written and it was as if they were acting in concert: his voice, her words. When he described it as a multi-national effort that would help bring together all sides of the conflict, it was as if he were talking about the two of them.

But Daniel got restless, started shifting in his seat. "You want to go?" he asked, and she could tell from his voice that he expected her to jump at the chance, but she shook her head. "Well I can't listen to this anymore. I'll wait for you outside."

When it was over and people began filing out of the auditorium, Amira caught up to Rachel and they walked out together. Daniel was sitting on a bench, reading and waiting for her. Amira was talking about how inspiring Michael's talk had been, her eyes sparkling. She looked beautiful and Rachel felt a kind of pride in being her friend.

"This is my friend, Daniel. This is Amira," Rachel said.

Daniel smiled and said, "Hi." An odd image flashed through Rachel's mind, of the two of them getting together.

"You two have plans?" Amira asked.

"We're just getting some coffee," said Rachel. "We have to catch up on some things. I'll see you later?"

"Sure. Thanks for coming today." Amira kissed her goodbye and gave Daniel a warm smile.

"All these new friends," he said when Amira was out of earshot. "I see why you've been too busy to come to JSA activities."

"Come on, Daniel, be fair. I hardly ever went to JSA activities. Not my thing."

"But helping spread anti-Israel propaganda is your *thing*?"

"That's not what I'm doing—"

"Of course it is. You give them credibility, a Jewish girl who takes their side."

"Do you really want to get into this? Can't we just relax and talk? There's no 'our' side and 'their' side. Michael talked about children's healthcare at the symposium."

"Michael runs the group that organized that thing, doesn't he? Doesn't it bother you that they're trying to get everyone all stirred up against Israel? It's all caricature. Israeli soldiers are grotesquely evil, and the Palestinians are all innocent, adorable children."

"Oh, come on—"

"Why do you have to hang around with them?"

"I know you don't get it, but that's your problem. They're not a 'them.' You sound like my mother."

"She may be right, sometimes. Even just statistically, she's got to be right some of the time." He smiled.

"Okay, Daniel, okay. How about we get some coffee? I know a place nearby that you've probably never been to." She led him to Henry's Sweet Shoppe, which had become one of her favorite hangouts.

"Isn't this place great?" she said when they walked in.

He examined the shelves behind the counter and pointed to the Russian wooden dolls. "My sister used to have dolls like that. When you open them up, there's always a littler one inside."

"I had those, too. My dad got them for me on one of his trips."

They flopped into a booth and stared at each other.

"So?" Rachel said.

Before he could answer, the waitress came over to take their order. They agreed, with barely a word, to split a tuna sandwich on rye and a side of fries. Daniel ordered a milkshake to go with it. They had eaten so many lunches together over the years that it felt easy and familiar. With most guys, she was self-conscious about how much she ate or whether her manners were correct, but not with him.

They were silent for a minute, until Daniel said, "You know, you're just getting one side of the story and you don't even seem to realize it. So, I'm going to tell you what happened to me when I lived in Israel last year. I don't like to talk about it... but I think I have to."

She waited.

"I mean, they were criticizing checkpoints as if they had no other purpose than to harass and demean people. The truth is that Israel wouldn't have checkpoints and searches if the Palestinians didn't harbor terrorists."

"But they go overboard," Rachel said.

"You say that because you're safe. What about if you lived there and you had to take the bus..." his voice broke a little.

"What bus?" she asked.

He shook his head.

"What is it? Tell me." Daniel could be a wise guy, funny sometimes, strident sometimes, but at that moment he looked genuinely vulnerable.

"It happened a few months after I arrived in Jerusalem. I was waiting for a bus, the Number 19. I took it every day so I knew the bus driver, Moshe. He was typical of the way I think of Israelis, stocky and gruff but soft inside. That's what a sabra is, you know, tough on the outside and sweet on the inside."

She nodded.

"He kept up a running conversation with the passengers, with me when I was there. He liked to practice his English with me. He'd come from Russia originally. We used to joke around when the bus was empty. He told me about his daughter. She lives in New York. His wife works in a bakery.

"So, anyway, this one day I'm waiting at the bus stop for my friend Benny. Moshe comes by, but I wave him on because Benny was late. A few other people got on at the stop; a soldier on his way home for a leave, a mother with a baby in a stroller and two other kids at her heels. Moshe stopped an extra minute to do me a favor and an Orthodox woman, all wrapped up in a headscarf, got on, and then he drove off. I still remember him waving to me, looking in the rearview window. Five minutes later, I heard the explosion.

He looked down at the floor. "Ten people were killed, including the mother with the kids. And Moshe. I could've been one of them. I ran over to see if I could help, but it was all cordoned off by the time I got there. They're very efficient at taking care of these things in Jerusalem."

"Did they find who did it?"

"I heard later that the bomber was dressed as an Orthodox woman. He left a bundle and got off. Someone noticed it, but before they could get rid of it, it exploded. It may have been the woman who got on while Moshe waited for me. I keep thinking that if he hadn't waited—for me—he'd still be alive."

"Omigod. I can't believe you were so close to getting killed!"

"That's not the point. It's not that I was almost killed; it's that every day Israelis can be killed. They're vulnerable and they must defend themselves, and then people criticize them for doing a good job of it. Should the army just lay down their guns and let people get killed so Israel gets sympathy from the press?"

He looked at her as if waiting for an answer, so she shook her head, no.

"Exactly. They must defend themselves. Sometimes that means getting rough and treating everyone as a suspect. The Palestinians are honoring suicide bombers and recruiting women. They're using children. Where is the uproar over that?"

"There are a lot of decent people who are suffering. And you can't blame children."

"No, I blame the Palestinians for blaming Israel. If they want peace they could help Israel crack down on the terrorists. They could force their leaders to negotiate and to stand up against the terrorism. Instead, they go along with them. They insist we have no right to be there, to be anywhere in that part of the world. In all these years, they've never recognized that Israel even exists. They don't want peace and this is the consequence. They could change it, but they don't."

"Maybe their leaders don't want to change it. But if the soldiers treated people differently, their attitude might change."

"Don't be naïve. If the soldiers are nice, they're seen as weak. The problem is the Palestinian leadership. They're corrupt and evil, and kill people who try to stand up against them. Protest *them*, not the Israeli soldiers who are protecting their families."

Rachel took a sip of her coffee and then stirred it with a spoon to cool it, watching the swirls. Thinking. "But Palestinian children are innocent victims. Especially kids with chronic illnesses. They need help, and it seems that I'm able to help them. I'm working on a book to teach diabetic children to manage their condition."

"Oh?" He sounded skeptical. "Be careful, Rachel. A guy may be good-looking and kind of cool, and dress like a hip college professor, but that doesn't mean he's just a regular guy."

"Are you talking about Michael? You met him for, like, three minutes."

"I know. But there's something off about him."

"You have absolutely no basis for saying that," she said, although she knew what he meant. Michael made people a little uneasy, but that was part of his attraction. "Anyway, let's talk about something else. I'm nervous about med school. Do you think we'll end up at the same place?"

"Hope so," he said, and they started talking about schools and specialties, pre-med student shop talk. When she started to tell him stories about the kids at the clinic, he put on a kind of amused smile and got a slightly glazed look in his eyes, which meant that he'd stopped listening. That was the look he got when she'd done something he found sexy. Maybe it was the faces she made, imitating the kids. Maybe because they were having a discussion and he liked talking to her. She didn't quite get it, and neither of them acted on it.

CHAPTER FOURTEEN

A few days later, Rachel ran into Yusif while she was waiting on line at Gristedes Market. She had chocolate; he had a soda and a bag of nuts. As they left together, the sidewalk was so crowded that they were shoulder to shoulder. Yusif was around her height; when she turned her head, they were face to face, and she saw the web of creases around his bleary eyes.

"What's the matter, Yusif? You look tired."

He shrugged. "Did you ever try to pick apart a chain that was all knotted up and you couldn't figure out where to even start?"

She nodded.

"That's how I feel."

She wasn't sure if he meant the *intifada*, life in general, or some personal problem.

"I miss my wife," he said.

"It must be hard to be separated. Will she come here soon?"

"She can't leave right now," he said.

Rachel was curious and waited for more, but instead he said, "Why do you bother with us, Rachel?"

"What do you mean?"

He opened the bag of nuts and held it out for her. She took one.

"Well, you have a nice life, plenty to occupy you, med school to think about. Why get involved in this mess?" It sounded like a warning, something in his voice.

"You, too?"

"What do you mean?"

She shrugged.

He kept passing the bag back to her. The nuts were salty and somehow better for being eaten outside.

"It feels right to me. And I'm learning so much from Michael."

He nodded. "He's a brilliant guy. He could have done anything with his life, but he's driven to help kids with diabetes because of his sister."

"She was diabetic?"

"You didn't know?"

"I knew she died, but—"

"Michael doesn't like to talk about it."

"Did you know her?"

"Sure, I remember her. She was always toddling around after him. He would pretend to be annoyed but it was obvious he adored her. She was like a little Palestinian Shirley Temple, always smiling."

They were nearing Central Park and Yusif motioned to one of the benches that lined its perimeter. As they sat down, a little girl, thin and athletic, broke from her mother and did a cartwheel in front of them. Rachel was charmed and even Yusif smiled. They watched the girl for a minute, eating the nuts, like an old couple with nothing to do but watch the day pass by.

"Sometimes I think he still blames himself for her death, even though it wasn't his fault that there wasn't medicine. They had to leave when the fighting started."

"Leave where? "

The bag of nuts was empty now. He crumpled it in his hand, held it tightly.

"Jordan."

"What exactly happened?"

"The Cliff Notes version is that we were living in the refugee camps in Jordan. King Hussein wanted us to abide by his laws but our leaders wanted independence, so they ignored him and his laws and edicts. They clashed, and finally Hussein sent his soldiers to throw us out.

"It turned into a massacre. You never want to be in the path of Bedouin soldiers when they are on the warpath. Hussein killed more of us in a single month in 1970 than the Israelis did in the two decades we'd been under their control. We call it Black September."

Rachel shuddered at the thought of a young Michael and little Hanna caught in the middle of a deadly war. But she had assumed the enemy was always Israel and was astonished that it was Jordan.

"But you were out already? Before it started?"

"Yes, I was out. My parents stayed behind and were killed in the fighting."

"I'm sorry," she said.

He nodded, acknowledging her condolence. "Hanna was in bad shape. They had run out of insulin even before they left. They crossed into Israel and the soldiers took her to the hospital."

"Israeli soldiers took care of her?" She felt proud of Israel, and Yusif sensed it.

"Yes, maybe because they realized who her father was. But in any case, it was too late. She didn't survive. I think that the time Michael spent in the hospital with Hanna inspired him to study medicine. He learned something about her disease from the doctors there."

They rose from the bench at the same time and walked toward the campus. Amira was waiting by the gate. "Right on time," Yusif said.

She smiled at Rachel, "Hi."

"Hi."

"Yusif is coming to watch my dance performance," she explained.

"Michael told me he plays for you sometimes," Rachel said. For a moment, when she mentioned Michael, she thought she saw a flash of distaste cross Amira's face. But it passed, almost as if she'd willed it away, or perhaps she'd only imagined it. "Is something wrong?" Rachel asked.

"No, no. I was just thinking. Why don't you come, too?"

"Now?"

"It's very informal. There won't be many people. Come!"

"Yes, come," Yusif said. "They're very good."

She hesitated. "I was just on my way to the library. Maybe another time?"

"Oh," Amira's smile faded. "We don't have performances very often. The whole thing will take less than an hour. I'd like to introduce you to the other dancers. You'll enjoy it."

Amira was easy to like, in part because she was so attractive: her posture beautifully straight but not rigid, her every movement graceful. She was friendly but not overbearing. Rachel felt close to her after the talk they'd had at Michael's apartment. The idea of seeing her dance was appealing.

"Well..."

"You can't work all the time. Dance will tap into the other side of your brain. You'll work better afterwards. And Michael told me you used to study dance. I'd like your thoughts on the performance. It would be very helpful."

Michael had talked about her? That was interesting. She decided that she could spare an hour. "Yes, sure. I'd love to."

"Great! Let's go."

They walked to the basement of the student center, where a small audience had already gathered on the floor in front of an area cleared for a stage. Rachel took a handwritten, photocopied program from a pile on a table. It explained that the dance recounted the story of a woman mourning her husband who was killed in the revolution and dreaming of revenge.

After a while, someone turned out all the lights except for a lone spotlight and Amira came onto the stage wearing loose pants and an embroidered shirt. Her hair was tied back in a high ponytail that bounced as she jumped in light steps, kicking her legs in graceful but unstructured movements, not like ballet, but spirited and organic. After a brief solo, four other dancers came out and formed a circle around her. The lyrics were in Arabic and the audience clapped to a beat kept steady by a tambourine. Rachel had an urge to join them; the dance resembled a hora, and at times another Israeli folk dance, the Miserlu, which she'd learned at summer camp. It told the story of a line of women dancing off a cliff rather than submitting to conquering forces.

Breathless and flushed, Amira greeted the audience as they gathered for refreshments at the conclusion of the performance. Yusif hugged her. "You were wonderful!" he said.

She turned to Rachel. "I'm so glad you came." She kissed Rachel's cheek and grasped her shoulders with warm, sweaty hands. "Did you enjoy it?"

"Yes! You're terrific. And it reminded me of folk dances I learned at summer camp."

"Would you like to come to our practice next week? We're going to work on some new pieces, so it's a good moment to start."

"Oh, no. I haven't danced in years. I can't..."

"It's very low-pressure and we have a lot of fun. Think about it."

Yusif excused himself, and Amira brought her over to the other dancers and introduced her to them. They recognized her name, making her feel like a celebrity.

"Come next week," Amira urged. "Do it instead of the gym. I'm sure you'll enjoy it."

It was funny, the way Amira coaxed her like a Jewish grandma. Rachel smiled.

Amira was right; it would be a break from her routine. She could at least give it a try. She agreed to join them.

The dance group met a few days later at a local studio that had recently been painted; careless splashes of paint spotted the wood floor. A ballet barre was attached to a wall of mirrors, and the smell of old sweat lingered faintly in the air. Five women dressed in harem-style pants and loose shirts were chatting, the sound of their laughter like chimes in the wind. They were spread around the room like dancers in a Degas painting, some sitting or lying on the floor as they warmed up, others at the barre.

Amira looked at Rachel's jeans and tee shirt and frowned. "That's not right. Here, I have extra outfits." She picked up a gauzy shirt with embroidery and loose harem-style pants from a pile on the floor, "Try these. They're perfect."

"No, no, I'm fine, I'll just watch," Rachel said, setting off a flurry of refusals and soon she was surrounded by a flock of girls.

"Don't be silly, you'll join us. You've studied dance so it'll come easy to you," Amira assured her, as light hands worked to pull Rachel's shirt over her head and brought down the other. It was soft, billowy, light, made for dancing.

Rachel gave in to the pressure of the women hovering around her and the unexpected pleasure of their delicate hands and laughter. She followed their lead as they formed lines behind Amira, who explained they were working on the same dance she'd performed the week before. One girl sat alongside and shook a tambourine with ribbons attached near the jingles, and the ribbons danced along with the beat as Amira led them through the steps

They began in a line, holding one another's hands, and then formed a circle, let go and raised their arms above their heads, bare feet keeping the beat. The movements were unstructured and she found herself lifting higher into the air as her arms swept upwards, adding to the momentum, and the steady beat of the tambourine keeping her in motion. They practiced the steps over and over, until they were all sweaty.

They took a break and someone brought a pitcher of water and poured it into little cups. Rachel threw some on her head, setting off peals of laughter. When the group finally broke up, she said she'd return the clothes after she washed them and Amira said she could drop them by the SPHR offices in the Middle Eastern Studies building.

She left feeling pleasantly exhausted, loose and tranquil. A dance troupe was like a family and she felt at home with these women, sharing the common language of movement. It was so different from her friendship with Jill, which existed on a soft cushion of security. The biggest dramas they shared had to do with grades and boyfriends, goals, and ambitions. These women were different. They expressed their passions through movement. Mind, body, and spirit unified when they danced, and the pressures of school and grades and expectations disappeared. When Amira invited her to join them to learn another dance over the weekend—adding that Michael would be accompanying them on the drum—she agreed once again to join them.

On Saturday, Rachel and Michael walked over to the studio together. Her eyes were moist from the cold air and the pleasure of having him by her side. He squeezed her hand before he went to the corner and sat with a drum—not his black one, but it would do to keep the beat. She felt a jab of concern when the women greeted him with hugs and kisses. They were dressed in black leotards with loose colorful skirts made from a similar soft, stretchy material that moved with them; together they were like a string of jewels and she didn't like sharing him with these attractive women, his compatriots, but she forgot her jealousy as she followed Amira through the steps of her dance.

Maryam explained that the dance was their interpretation of the *dabke*, a Palestinian dance of solidarity. The central dancer is like a tree, with arms in the air and a proud upright trunk but feet that stomp the earth to show their connection to the land.

Most choreographers created dances that best suited the idiosyncrasies of their own bodies. Amira had an exceptional ability to move her arms and legs in different rhythm, and when she brought her head in with a third rhythm it was impossible for the rest of them to follow. Somehow, Michael captured it with a shifting beat. Rachel and the others looked on helplessly until finally they decided to let Amira do a solo as they danced variations of it around her, like different sections of an orchestra, each contributing to the whole.

Michael's hair had grown longer and he shook his head to keep it from his eyes as he focused on his role as accompanist. Rachel was tempted to go over to him and brush it back, the way one might turn the pages of a score for a pianist. But she continued to dance and, after a while, she felt completely at one with the other dancers as they moved together, sharing the rhythm. At the end Amira hugged her, kissed both her cheeks, and looked at her in a new way—as if she'd found a treasured object where she least expected.

Then she asked Rachel to lead them in a hora.

"I know that dance," Maryam said. She was one of the clumsier dancers, but she had a lot of energy. "That's a Palestinian dance."

"Yes," Nina said, "I learned it from my mother. The Jews learned it from us and now they've appropriated it."

The room grew very silent. Michael stopped tapping the drum. The women looked at each other like they were holding their breath under water, waiting for the moment when they could break the surface and breathe deeply again. Rachel wanted to cry. She was too emotional. It was the thing with Michael.

"Maybe this wasn't such a good idea," Rachel said, her voice flat. She was like a cork in their bottle; they wanted her out so they could enjoy the wine. She was Jewish and they fought Jews for everything—even ownership of a dance. She was sick of it; always walking on eggshells, being rational, straining to see both sides of every little issue.

It was far easier to bluster and yell and protest and believe unequivocally that you were right and morally superior, then to listen and question and probe. It required hard work to bridge gaps among people who thought that theirs was the only truth. One needed a willing partner. She wasn't made to be a diplomat. She longed for the simplicity of a formula with verifiable postulates, of a math problem with a clear solution. Mainly she wanted to be alone with Michael, away from these women and their stupid politics.

"They're all Middle-Eastern dances," Amira said, breaking the silence. "The program will just list them by name, not by country. It's okay, Rachel. I think I heard the hora originated in Romania anyway. Nothing to do with any of us." Amira rubbed Rachel's neck, making little circles with her fingers. "You're being ridiculous," she said sharply to Nina. "We'll do four dances with a two-minute break in between. It'll be fun."

They were all looking at Rachel expectantly so she smiled and shrugged it off. Michael's expression was sympathetic but there was something cold in Maryam's eyes. Did she really believe that the Jews had not only stolen their land, but their culture? That there was no end to what the Jews would take? It was unbelievable.

She would get through the performance and then take a break from the dancers. Not from Michael, but from them. He'd understand. She felt like kicking herself for being pulled in this far, but when you dip you toe in the water, sometimes you end up getting drenched.

CHAPTER FIFTEEN

Amira said she understood when Rachel told her she had too much work to dance, although she made some joking references to the "hora dispute" and encouraged her to come back when she had more time. In fact, Rachel did need to spend time putting the finishing touches on her book. She hadn't yet come up with a name for it, but it read like a storybook, with colorful illustrations of children of different nationalities and races. It followed the case of a child with diabetes, taking him through a typical day, with explanations of his diet and insulin injections. He started out young and in each section, he aged a few years and the explanations were a bit more sophisticated—though still in the voice of a friendly child. She asked Michael what to name him.

"Khalid or Ahmed or Osama or Jim or Joe or George. Whatever you want. How about Michael?"

"You want to be immortalized in great literature?"

He ignored that. "This is a good proposal. Go over it with Dr. Bergman. And talk to him about fundraising for the conference while you're at it. He likes you. Soften him up and then I'll talk to him."

"Okay."

"And another thing. Why don't you come for the conference?"

"Really?"

He nodded.

It was as simple as that.

Rachel set up a meeting with Dr. Bergman and brought a draft of the book and her storyboards. He seemed pleased with them, so she brought up the Children's Healthcare Initiative. "Michael wants to bring everyone together: physicians, social workers, and nurses from Palestine, Israel, and America," she explained. "We would hold a conference in either Ramallah or Tel Aviv, depending on the political situation and travel restrictions. It's the most efficient way to organize the Initiative and get it going."

"It's a good idea. Those kinds of gatherings, where you can speak informally over a breakfast or in the elevator, are invaluable. The personal relationships are what lead to results. You can look people in the eye, and that is often more meaningful than what is said."

"I knew you would support it! After all, you went to that conference in Ramallah where you met Michael and look at how well that's worked out. That was courageous of you."

"Courageous? Nah."

"But it was dangerous, wasn't it? Going into the territories?" she said.

"The way I see it, there's always something to be afraid of, so I don't let fear rule my life." He paused, and then his voice went deeper. "You've been spending quite a bit of time with Michael, haven't you?"

She felt herself flush. "He asked me to talk to you about whether you could help in getting clearances for the Palestinians doctors to travel to Israel. I won't have a problem, even though I'm less important. They love Americans in Israel, don't they?"

"You? I thought you were just doing the book. You mean you'll be going over there?"

"Yes! I have the summer off and no plans, and it'll be a great experience."

He looked down at his desk and when he looked up he was Uncle Steve again. "Rachel, have you mentioned this all to your mother?"

"No, not yet."

"She won't want you going. She asked me about the work you are doing with Michael. She's upset about your association with him. I think she blames me for it."

"That's ridiculous."

"Not really. It's always been difficult for her that I continued the work your father and I started, so you need to make her comfortable about this. She has legitimate concerns, and you need to address them. Don't fight with her. Talk to her. She worries about you."

"That's an understatement."

He smiled.

"Maybe *you* can talk to her?" she said. "Tell her that there's nothing to worry about?"

"I can't do that. There is a rational basis for concern. Don't delude yourself, Rachel. It is dangerous there. That doesn't mean you shouldn't go, but you do have to be careful."

"Oh," she said, disappointed that she hadn't been able to

convince him to take the burden of Rivka from her shoulders. She wished she could make decisions about her life and have someone else explain, cajole and convince her mother.

"Rachel, explaining this to your mother is a good way to test your convictions. Talk to her."

"Okay," she said, without enthusiasm. And decided to put it off for as long as possible.

Later that night, Rachel was in bed with Michael, listening to U2's *The Joshua Tree*. He was reading the *Times* and she was snuggled under his arm, skimming the page. The headline said, *Israeli Soldiers Arrest Protesters. Prisons Overcrowded.*

"What was it like?" she asked.

"What?"

"The Israeli jail."

He looked at her. "It was a depressing place. Over-crowded and dirty. Not the side of Israel you'll ever see." He lay the paper down and drew her closer. "But I wouldn't have missed it for anything."

"Seriously?"

"Seriously," he said, mock solemnly.

"Why?"

"It was a rite of passage."

"Huh? How old were you?"

"Seventeen. My first year at the university. The American University of Beirut."

She snuggled up under his arm, both of them staring out in the same direction as if watching his story play out on an invisible screen in front of them.

"It was the late seventies and Beirut was torn up, but parts were still untouched." He stroked her arm absently as he spoke. "The university was on a hill on Bliss Street. Isn't that a beautiful name? There were rolling lawns and little wooden benches set between huge cedar trees that overlooked the Mediterranean Sea."

"It sounds spectacular."

"Yes, well, it was also very political if you were a Palestinian. I remember being tempted, just briefly, to pretend I was Syrian or Jordanian or something else. To be invisible, irresponsible."

"You've always had so much responsibility. You never had a childhood."

"Of course I did! But sometimes I thought about what it would be like to have been born in a different time and place. Anyway, I was asked to volunteer as a teacher at a Palestinian Refugee Camp in the West Bank one summer. I went with a group of other students and we were arrested."

"What was the charge?"

"Charge?" He laughed. "Spreading dissent, nationalism, membership in a seditious organization. Take your pick. Or maybe it was just administrative detention, where they put people in prison and decide the charge later. That was a leftover from the British Mandate period. They used it against the Zionists and now the Zionists use it against us."

"You say Zionist like it's a bad word."

"No, it's just a word. It's what they call themselves. If I sound angry it's because it didn't make sense to me to be arrested for building schools, teaching, and distributing food and medical supplies."

"They wouldn't arrest you for that," Rachel said.

"They did, because we were sponsored by a political organization that advocated for a Palestinian State. They let me go after a few months."

She pictured Michael in a sea of *keffiyas*. She'd seen a picture like that in the paper, once, a mass of dark angry faces, eyes burning with rage. In her mind, though, Michael was set apart from the rest, more an observer than a participant.

"So that's where you learned Hebrew?" she asked.

"There wasn't much to do in prison and they let some of us follow the Hebrew course they used for Jewish immigrants from foreign countries. I already spoke a little. My father had taught me; he was fluent. As I got more proficient, I ended up translating for the guards, since only a few of them spoke Arabic. I even got friendly with one of them, though it seemed perverse, considering the circumstances. He was an American who'd made Aliyah and was learning Hebrew also. We helped each other learn."

"So, you would study? And talk to the Israelis?" She stretched and got up, strolled over to the window and looked out at the nearly empty street. Michael had a slight accent. Sometimes she forgot about it, but now it sounded almost British, the way he sculpted his words.

"There wasn't much else to do. The prison was near the Lebanese border. I didn't get any visitors, but I had friends and we stuck close together, organized lectures and study sessions and we entertained each other. They had us all crowded together. It was ironic because they forbade us from congregating on the outside, but when they sent us to prison, they forced us to congregate."

It was all beginning to seem otherworldly, like walking in a seedy area late at night, the kind of place she'd always avoided in the past. She retraced the steps that had led her into this room with this man, talking about prisons and revolutionary groups. She thought back to Michael touching her during the mock exam, to sitting with him and Sean at the clinic, to the meetings at SPHR—but all the images seemed distant, like scenes from another person's life. She realized she was twisting a strand of hair so tightly it hurt. Michael was looking at her curiously.

"Come here, Rachel," he said, his voice soft and friendly and familiar, "Make *aliyah* to the bed."

She smiled and went to him, let him wrap himself around her, and he stroked her until she fell asleep.

She was curled up against him, soft and warm and heavy with sleepiness. Her skin felt smooth and smelled faintly of flowers, the residue of an expensive soap that her mother brought her from France.

He enjoyed telling her about his life, watching her eyes grow wide with fascination. He rarely spoke of these things to other Palestinians, who had their own stories of hardship, pain, and unjust treatment. They would sit glassy-eyed at the familiar litany of refugee problems. But Rachel was enraptured, so he seduced her with tales of his childhood antics and tragedies. He spun a fine web of facts and innuendo around her until she was caught.

He knew he could never marry Rachel or have a family with her, but that somehow made her even more perfect for him. She didn't look at him with visions of the future in her eyes. The two of them existed for the moment, a romance without complications. Its limitations were liberating.

In the darkness, listening to her breath, his thoughts roamed through the memories their discussion had provoked: prison, Beirut, the children in the refugee camps, and inevitably he thought of his mother and Hanna. His father lurked unwanted in his mind, a shadowy figure haunting him. *Leave me be.*

He turned to Rachel and began to stroke her neck, his thumb pressing against small knots he found there, then down her back, gently kneading, his hands wandering over her until she was semi-awake and aroused, but too muddled to think or have any inhibitions. His lips found hers and she responded, and then he moved down, brushing his lips past her neck. The room was so dark it was only their nearness that made her visible. He loved her when she was like this.

Afterwards she said, "I love you."

"It was wonderful," he responded.

"So you think it's just physical? Not love?"

"I'm not capable of love. Loyalty, not love."

"Why do you say that?" He heard her disappointment. He was being too honest. Sometimes he had that impulse with her, wanted no barriers between them. At moments like this, when the world seemed distant and unreal and all that existed was the two of them, he wanted her to know all he'd done and to love him for it. In spite of it.

"Everyone I loved died," he said, sounding pathetic to himself, but unable to stop. It was as if the words were coming from someone else and he was just a vessel repeating them. "My mother, Hanna. Much too young, both of them."

Rachel turned to him and he saw himself reflected in her eyes. "Those were terrible times," she said, "but now you're making it possible for kids like Hanna to live. Think of all you're doing. Hanna's death will mean something because of you."

"It wasn't diabetes that killed her. It was the war. The endless fighting. We couldn't get her insulin. She might still be alive. I think of who she would have been, sometimes." He felt her listening, taking it all in.

"Tell me about her."

He did. He spoke about Hanna, things he'd kept inside himself, buried so deep that he'd almost forgotten them: her silly antics that had made him laugh in ways he hadn't laughed since, her truncated childhood, the tragic loss of the woman she would have become.

"Let's name it for her," Rachel said.

"What?"

"The health clinics. The whole thing. Let's name it for her. The Children's Healthcare Initiative, In Memory of Hanna Haddad."

It was the perfect thing to do. How had she known? Tears came to his eyes. He didn't want her to see so he crushed her against him. She rubbed his back, her touch mystically, magically soothing and whispered, "It's okay." It was a little like the way she talked to kids sometimes, except her tone was right, appropriate for an adult. For a man.

"They'll be remembered and honored by all you're doing."

Would they? Hanna had died too young to understand about honor. And his father would never have forgiven him. He wished he could have that forgiveness, that it was as simple as naming a clinic in his honor.

"Your father's spirit watches over you, Rachel. Mine haunts me."

She turned to him, clearly puzzled, but didn't ask for clarification. Instead she said, "I will always love you. No matter what happens. So, know that if I die before you, my spirit will be sending you loving vibes."

If she hadn't been so serious he would have laughed, but instead he let himself sink into a sea of Rachel, let her close in on him. His always-calculating mind ceased its machinations and he felt a surge of something he hadn't felt in years: a sense of belonging, of being where he was supposed to be, where he could relax, let down his guard. And for the first time since he was a child, he allowed himself cry.

CHAPTER SIXTEEN

By the beginning of April, had letters started to arrive from medical schools. Jill had been accepted at Columbia and so had Daniel. Rachel checked her mailbox obsessively and when the one from Columbia appeared, the envelope felt too light and she knew before she opened it that she'd been rejected.

She had already gotten into her safety school, a state school that would cost less than Columbia, but still it felt demoralizing. All her hard work hadn't paid off. Her friends would have more prestigious credentials. For the rest of her life, people would be asking her where she'd gone to med school and she would feel second-class. This had never happened to her before. She'd always risen to the top.

She felt like curling up on her bed with a pint of ice cream, but Michael had invited her to a working dinner along with Yusif and Amira to discuss their project, so she pulled herself together and went to his apartment. When she saw him in the kitchen and smelled the wonderful aroma of a chicken stew with tomatoes and onions, she gave him a hug.

"You really can cook!" she said.

"My mom taught me a few things."

"You're full of surprises."

He smiled and then saw something in her expression. "What's wrong?"

She told him about her rejection and he shrugged as if it were no more significant than spilling coffee on a white shirt. "It's not important. There are many good schools in this country. And you'll do well wherever you go. It's the person, not the school."

"That's the kind of thing Dr. Bergman would say."

"And, you know…it could even be a blessing."

"What do you mean?"

"Or maybe it's a *sign*." He looked heavenward and she realized he was teasing her about the way she saw signs in everything from the wind in her hair to matters of consequence in her life.

"A *sign*, Michael?" she said. "Are you saying you believe in them, too?" When he gave a half-smile, she punched at him, and he caught her arm.

"Maybe I'm beginning to believe in them, too," he said. "Because, don't you see? It's the perfect reason to take a year off. Reapply next year and you'll get into Columbia or wherever. But this way, you can spend the year in Israel working with me. It's the perfect excuse and, on top of that, it will look good on your application."

"Wow. Take a year off and work with you in Israel?" Her head was spinning. Yet it felt unreal, not the kind of thing she'd ever done in her predictable life. How would she explain it to her mother? And how would she support herself for a year if her mother was against it? She had no money of her own. She wasn't a trust fund baby; her dad had died too young to accumulate any wealth. Except for some odd jobs to pay for extra expenses, her mother paid for everything. It had never been an issue because they'd always been aligned in their goals for her and she expected to make a good living once she got her medical degree. She'd pay her mother back. But she couldn't take a year off and essentially volunteer for the Health Initiative without her mother's financial support.

She knew that Michael's fellowship was almost done and he'd be returning to Palestine in June, but she hadn't focused on it. She was unwilling to deal with their impending separation until it was absolutely necessary. The idea of putting it off for another year was very appealing.

"Seriously, Rachel, it's a once in a lifetime opportunity. You could be training nurses and social workers, getting to know people of another culture, and there might be opportunities to do medical procedures that med students in the US could only dream about."

"Spend a year in Israel?"

"Yes. And live with me."

Her eyes widened. Was he serious? "Where would we live?" she asked, in a tone that could either be playful, like she knew he was kidding, or serious.

"How about a seaside apartment in Yaffa?"

"Umm. Romantic."

He took her hand in his. "Close your eyes."

She did.

"Hear the waves crashing. Feel the heat, broken only by the whisper of a breeze. It blows the curtain on the open window."

"The room is dark," she said, "lit only by paper lanterns. The floor is tiled and cool. We always walk barefoot."

Her disappointment at her rejection floated away. It *was* a blessing in disguise.

The doorbell rang and she opened it to Amira, who was smiling and holding a salad with almonds and raisins mixed in. Yusif arrived a few minutes later with a bottle of red wine. They settled in and chatted about nothing in particular as they laid the food on the table and began to eat.

"We have news. Rachel is going to spend the year in Israel after she graduates," Michael announced.

"Michael! It's not for sure!"

"Aren't you supposed to go to medical school next year?" Amira said.

"Yes, that's the problem. Among other things."

"Your mother won't want you interrupting your studies," Amira guessed. "Even my mother wouldn't like that. Well, maybe for Palestine. But your mother will want you to go to med school straight away."

"Working for a year isn't uncommon," Michael interjected. "Your mother has her own passion for her business. Show her your passion for the Children's Health Initiative and she'll support you. You can handle your mother."

"You say that because you've never met her," Rachel said.

"But I want to. I think she should visit Israel before we go. We can have her meet some of the doctors we'll be working with, and she'll see how valuable the work is, and that it's safe."

"Maybe you can talk her into going to Israel. I never could."

"Maybe I can."

After desert and a strong cinnamon tea, they began discussing the wording to use to solicit funds for the Children's Healthcare Initiative. As a non-profit, everything would depend on donations. They came up with a description that was one page long and so vague as to exactly where and for whom the money would be used that it was almost meaningless. Rachel was beginning to understand that ambiguity was an art in the Palestinian world, and thought it had to do with pride. They were powerless in many ways and yet, like Michael, they were fiercely independent. They didn't ask for help, they explained why they were entitled to it. Sometimes she felt like she'd discovered the key to peace in the Middle East: play up to Arab pride.

"I've been in touch with two excellent Palestinian physicians who can speak at the conference in Tel Aviv," Michael said. "And we need to book hotel rooms for the middle of June. Rachel, you should contact some hospitals in Israel and identify which doctors to invite. Dr. Bergman can help you with that. Amira, you can help with the hotel and travel arrangements."

Rachel dreaded telling her mother about her rejection. Her mother took her disappointments harder than she did. She decided to talk to Dr. Bergman first, and get his opinion about taking a year off.

He responded just as she'd expected, assuring her that where she went to school wasn't important and her mother would be proud of her.

But when she explained about taking a year off, he shook his head and wished her luck with her mother.

"I know," she groaned. "She's going to say no and then we'll fight. That's why I wanted to ask if you would consider talking to her about it first. I never even spoke to her about going there for the summer. This is going to be even harder. It would be better coming from you!"

"*Me?* I can't do it for you, Rachel."

"What about if we tell her together, then, like over dinner or something? Can we do that? Have dinner and tell her then?"

"Dinner? Yes, sure. I haven't seen Rivka in a while. I'm not promising to fight for this idea until I understand it better, but I'll call Rivka and set it up."

That night, Rivka came home late. Rachel was at the kitchen table working on the children's book, and her mother sat down beside her.

"Steven called and we set up a dinner for tomorrow. I offered to cook something, but he insisted we go out." She paused. "He told me about Columbia. I don't understand why you couldn't tell me yourself. I don't care where you go. In fact, I'm glad you'll go to a SUNY school. It's much less expensive, much less of a strain."

"You never said you were worried about that."

"Honestly, it's nothing to be ashamed of. Your dad went to a state school and he did fine."

"Yes, but..."

"I know it's hard for you because Jill got in. You've always been so competitive."

"That's not it, Mother. Maybe I am competitive—and that's not necessarily a bad thing—but I'm not looking at it that way. Maybe it's an opportunity."

"What do you mean?"

"Just some things I've been thinking about. We can talk about it tomorrow. At dinner."

"What's going on?"

"Nothing! We'll talk about it tomorrow," Rachel said with finality.

"Tomorrow, fine," Rivka said. "Can't wait."

Her mother examined her with familiar dismay when she came downstairs dressed for dinner. She wore black pants and a white, embroidered, peasant-style shirt, an attempt to please her mother, but she could tell from Rivka's expression that her attempt had failed.

She could see her mother biting back clothes criticism— as if she knew that there were bigger battles on the evening's agenda. Then she handed Rachel a small quilted Chanel black bag with a thick gold chain. "For getting into med school."

"Thanks, Mom. This is beautiful."

"It's vintage. An exclusive from Rivka's closet."

It was an old joke between them. When she was a little girl, Rachel loved to rummage around her in mother's closet to find things to wear. It was full of the sample dresses her company designed. Her mother wore them around the house to see how they felt as well as how they looked, and when

Rachel was tall enough, she modeled them. Some ended up being one-of-a-kind, since they didn't all go into production.

Rivka's charm bracelet glinted under the light as she rested her hands on Rachel's shoulders and kissed her cheeks. "You'll be moving out of here next year. It won't be the same. I'll miss you."

"I'll miss you, too, Mom. But I may not…well, we'll talk later."

"May not what? Let's talk now. You don't need Steven as a buffer. I don't bite."

"Okay, okay." She took a deep breath. "It's just that I've been thinking that going to med school straight out of college may not be the best idea." She saw a flicker of horror behind her mother's steady gaze as she explained about taking a year off to live in the real world, first. "So, that's what I'm thinking. I'd defer for just a year. I can do it. They'll still take me next year. I asked."

"You already asked? Without even talking to me?"

"I just asked about it, I didn't commit to it. And the other thing is, I'd like to reapply to Columbia and some of the other top-tier schools. Some real-world experience would look great on my application. It would totally be worth it."

"How can you even think of something like that? What's gotten into you?"

She didn't respond.

"What, may I ask, do you intend to do for a year?"

"That's the thing. It has to do with health care in Pales… the territories"

"Palestine?"

Rachel nodded. "Let's talk about it at dinner."

"Why bother? It sounds like you've already made up your mind. What is it? Is your father's spirit talking to you again? Telling you to sacrifice yourself to Israel like he did? Sometimes I think he hated me."

"Mom—"

"Don't 'Mom' me. It's true. He took chances with his life and he had no right to do that. And now you're going to do the same thing? After I've worked myself to the bone so that I could afford to send you to this exclusive college? That's what you learned there? That's who you met? Palestinians?" She practically shrieked the last word. Rachel wondered if people outside could hear her through the open window. "I didn't send you to this fancy school so you could work for Arabs! Are you out of your mind?"

"Why shouldn't I help them? They're people! Children!" Her heart was racing and a pounding started in her head. She forced herself to take a few breaths. "Look...I appreciate that you paid for my education, Mom, I really do. A lot of my friends are drowning in debt. But I'm Daddy's daughter too, and he would have approved of doing something to help the children over there. I haven't explained it well. Let's wait until dinner. Please, Mom."

Her mother just shook her head. "You don't take after me at all."

An American Place had high ceilings and glass cube light fixtures hung from wires over the tables. The bulbs were dimmed to create a pleasing golden glow. The maître d' was a young woman in a long black dress, who led them to a round table set a little apart from the other tables, in a private corner. As they crossed the room, Rachel noticed some diners throw admiring glances at her mother.

"Rivka, you look wonderful, as always," Dr. Bergman said. "Someday you'll have to teach me about fashion so you won't be embarrassed to be out with me."

"You look fine. Although…perhaps a new suit occasionally would be a good idea." She smiled. "But you get more distinguished as you age."

Rivka had on a bright print dress that narrowed at the waist. Its hemline ran just to her knees, and a slit revealed even more of her slim legs. Rachel felt unattractive compared to her mother. She didn't have her knack for putting an outfit together, wearing a touch of blue to bring out the color of her eyes, or draping a scarf at just the right angle. Her mother knew how to wear clothes—swaying to show the movement of a flared shirt, gathering up a shawl so it fell just right.

By contrast, Dr. Bergman was the absent-minded professor in his frumpy gray suit of no discernible style. He was smart, her mother was beautiful and sexy, and Rachel fell somewhere in the middle. Sometimes she wished she had an intelligent but homely mother—a lawyer or judge or accountant who would encourage her in her intellectual pursuits and to hell with how she looked. Instead she had Rivka.

"Steven, Rachel wanted you to be here before she would tell me more about her plans for next year. I was wondering why you hadn't mentioned anything to me about all this before."

Dr. Bergman shifted around in his seat as if he couldn't get comfortable. Rachel knew he hated arguing with her mother and felt bad that she'd put him in an awkward position. "I only learned about it myself the other day," he said, evenly. "That's why we are here. To discuss it."

"I don't see why she's even considering taking time off," Rivka continued. "She should stay on track for med school. She's already been accepted. Why muck around with it?"

"There's nothing wrong with taking a year off to get some real-world experience," Dr. Bergman said, using his doctor-in-charge tone, then waving his hand to dispel any objections. He had long, graceful fingers, one of his best features. "She won't be the first. It's not unusual at all and will help distinguish her when she looks for residencies. She'll be meeting doctors and administrators, making contacts, getting experience. It's a good idea."

Rachel could have kissed him.

"So let her take a year off and work in New York! Why is she going *there*? I don't recall you encouraging your own son to go half way around the world and work for Palestinians. As I recall, he went straight to medical school. In fact, is there anyone else who was accepted into medical school and not going? Who came up with this brilliant idea?"

"I did," Rachel said.

"All by yourself?"

A waiter appeared. "Excuse me for interrupting, but how are you all doing tonight? I'm Tim, and I'll be your waiter this evening." He coughed into his hand, and Rachel saw her mother cringe.

"May I tell you the specials?"

Her mother was about to say no, but Rachel stopped her, happy for the interruption. "Yes, please," she said.

He reeled off a few additional menu items, an appetizer of baked asparagus with cheese, an entree of Mediterranean bass, and a ravioli pasta dish. "Well, I'll give you a few minutes to think about it," he concluded with a bright smile, and backed away from the table.

"Where were we?" Rivka said.

"I was just about to remind you that Mark would have supported Rachel in this," Dr. Bergman said.

"Mark worked with the Israelis, not the Palestinians."

"It's a joint group, Mom."

"How many other Jewish students are involved?" her mother asked.

"I'm the first because we are just getting started. I'm in on the start of a new enterprise. It's a unique position, a rare opportunity."

Rivka dismissed that with a shrug and turned back to Dr. Bergman. "You don't know how Mark would feel about this. You don't even know how the Palestinians would feel. Even back then, many of them didn't take kindly to getting help from Jews."

"It's true that there were Palestinians who thought that accepting help from Israel was tantamount to accepting the occupation." He began playing with his wedding band, twisting it around his finger. He'd been widowed for four years and still wore it. "I remember after the war, one town refused to hook up to the Israeli water system even though it would have made their lives easier. I think the women there still carry water in buckets from an ancient well. They'd rather do that than accept Israel's water. But of course, that's the radical view."

Rivka threw up her hands. "It's not just the radicals and you know it! All of this fighting over a few miles of sand? It's insane and I don't want my daughter risking her life for it. She should be go straight to medical school and get her degree."

"Oh, she'll go to medical school. I'm certain of it. I know some of the people in the group she's gotten involved with. It's organized by a young man named Michael Haddad who is a fellow at my clinic."

Rachel blushed at the mention of his name, and her mother gave her a sharp look.

"He's doing groundbreaking research as well as organizing these health clinics. Rachel has been working with him; it's important work. She's not planning to be a beach bum! It's a fine opportunity for her and will be as asset for her medical training."

"Don't be ridiculous. Medical school is what she needs for medical training. Not some *meshuganuh* group, and—"

"So! Have you decided?" It was the waiter again. His eyes were watery but he wasn't sneezing or coughing anymore; he must have taken something. "What can I get for you? Will you start with an appetizer?"

"Give us a few minutes, more," Steven said, "In fact, we'll let you know."

The three of them looked at one another, united in opposition to the waiter, even as they were at odds with one another. It always helped to have a common enemy. The waiter frowned and went on to another table.

"Rivka, they're going to help kids. It's a perfectly respectable organization, not *meshuganuh*. It's exactly what

Mark wanted. Even that last trip he made, the one where…
well, he'd just met with some people in the government to
discuss the logistics of medical care in connection with
transferring the territories to Jordan. That idea was alive even
then."

"That's probably why they killed him," Rivka muttered.

Rachel was confused. "Killed who?"

Rivka looked at Steven and something familiar passed
between them; some bond that Rachel had noticed before but
chalked up to "an adult thing" and ignored. Now that she, too,
was an adult, she wanted to share in it.

"What is it, Mom?"

Now it was Rivka shifting in her seat like she couldn't
get comfortable. She took a sip of water and held the glass in
her hands a few extra moments as if to steady herself. The
waiter came over and looked at them hopefully, but when no
one said anything, he left for greener pastures.

"She should know, Rivka," Dr. Bergman said.

"There was never a time…"

Rachel wondered what secret it was they held between
them, a package so tightly wrapped she'd never even thought
about trying to open it. She knew about her mother's visits to a
psychiatrist when she was in high school. The doctor had sent
her a change-of-address notice and Rachel had looked him up,
but that seemed okay; it wasn't such a big deal.

For a minute, Rachel thought her mother was going to
leave it to Dr. Bergman to reveal whatever it was, but then
Rivka turned to her with an expression stark and naked, one
unlike any that Rachel had ever seen cross her mother's face.

"I've always told you that Daddy died in a car accident.
You were very young when it happened, and for years

afterwards you were still just a child. And then it just became its own reality. But I wasn't completely honest."

Rachel's lips parted a bit but she didn't make a sound.

"We moved when you were seven, do you remember? And you started a new school and no one knew or remembered; there was no one to even hint to you that the story wasn't completely true."

Rachel's mind was working feverishly. Why was this coming up now? "He didn't die in a car accident in Israel?"

"Not exactly. No. He didn't. It's true that he was about to fly back from Israel to be home for your birthday. But that last night, he stayed with a colleague, Yaacov Levi, a doctor who lived in a town in Northern Israel, near Lebanon. It was part of Israel proper, within the original 1948 boundaries, not a settlement, nothing like that. In fact, it was right next to an Arab village and the two towns had merged into one and they got along well."

Rachel sat forward in her seat, her elbows on the table, transfixed.

"Yaacov had asked him to stay with him so they could visit and catch up. He had a five-year-old daughter, Miriam, and his wife, Dafna, was four months pregnant. That night... that was the night... that Palestinian terrorists from a group called the People's Revolution Party snuck across the border from Lebanon and went on a shooting spree. The town was near the border, you see."

Rachel nodded as it dawned on her where this was going.

"They wore Israeli army uniforms. They stopped a bus and shot a group of Arab women who were on their way home from work. Then, later that night, they started knocking on doors of the houses in town. There was a lot of commotion and Mark opened the door to see what was happening. And they shot him. Just like that."

"Shot him?"

Rivka nodded. "Yaacov's wife tried to run and they shot her in the back…and then they shot their young daughter. Only Yaakov survived."

Rivka's face was twisted; her red lipstick looked like a gash in her delicate beauty. Rachel had a sick feeling in her stomach.

"It changed Yaakov forever, like it did the rest of us. 'Such animals,' he told us. 'But cunning. They wore those army uniforms and carried explosives and guns.'"

She seemed unable to go on; her mouth opened once or twice but no words came out, so Dr. Bergman picked up the story.

"After that, they went to the elementary school. There was a group of high school students and their teachers who were visiting from Safed and sleeping in the school. They took them all hostage and demanded that Israel release a group of prisoners—imprisoned terrorists, people who'd committed terrible atrocities. They gave the Israeli government a deadline. The government asked for more time. They refused. Instead they began killing the students. An elite Israeli Special Forces group stormed the building. In the end, the terrorists shot twenty-two high school students before they were killed themselves. Scores more were wounded."

"But why? Why did they do it?"

"Why?" Her mother said, incredulous. "Do you think they need a rational reason? It was around the time of Israel's Independence Day and that was their protest. They wanted to free their fellow terrorists. They're irrational. They're animals. That's what I've been trying to tell you."

"I can't believe this."

"What your mother is saying is that there is no room between black and white for some people. You are safer here than you realize. Don't give that up lightly."

"I can't believe that you've both been keeping this secret from me for all these years. He was my father!" Rachel's voice was uncontrollably loud. People at nearby tables stopped talking and stared at her.

Dr. Bergman leaned forward. "Your mother did what she thought was best. You were very young. It was a difficult time. You can't judge from hindsight."

"Somehow a car accident made more sense," Rivka said. She was staring out, her face rigid, holding back tears.

"That's what you thought? I was terrified of being in a car for years! How could you make something like that up? How could you lie to me about my own father? You always act like he was yours alone, like he only mattered to you. You can have other husbands. I'll only ever have one father!"

"I know that Rachel. And I meant to tell you when you were older." Now, her mother was speaking slowly and carefully, pausing every few words. "But there never seemed to be a good time and then the fib became its own reality. I thought of telling you when you were a teenager, but you were so volatile in those years. We argued all the time. I couldn't find a moment. I decided to wait until you were in college, except that was a tough time for you, too. So now, well…now you know. I knew the time would come."

"Yes, this is a good time, isn't it?" Rachel sneered. "It's a good way to stop me from working with Michael. That's why you told me, isn't it? You only want to control me. That's all you ever wanted."

Rivka cringed and shook her head. "No. That's not why. Not to stop you." She started to speak more quickly and her eyes became moist. As tears finally spilled out, she wiped them away with a napkin. "I see so much of your father in you, and here you are talking about Palestinians the way he did. You're both blind to reality because you want so much to believe that the good in people will overcome the bad. You look so much like him—doesn't she Steven? Don't you see Mark when you look at her, especially at this age?"

He nodded.

"There is one other thing that I should tell you, Rachel. I spoke to Yaacov after it happened. He was a broken man. He'd lost his whole family and I think he had survivor's guilt." She was speaking more calmly now; talking about Yaacov was easier than talking about herself. "He was shot too, but only wounded. The terrorists thought he was dead, that's the only reason he lived. But he managed to crawl over to Mark. Your father stayed alive for several hours. In that time, he asked Yaacov to tell us that he loved us and that you shouldn't grow up hating because of what happened to him; that you should love and be happy and believe in the best in people."

"He did? You're not making that up?"

"No, it's the truth. His last words, or the last anyone heard, were for you. And I took it as a message to me, on your behalf. I've tried to raise you as he wished me to. But I don't want to lose you the way I lost him!" At that, she let out a sound, like a broken cry. Dr. Bergman reached over and stroked her arm.

"I can't believe I never knew any of this. I feel so stupid. I could've gone to the library and looked at the old newspapers on microfiche. But it never occurred to me that you'd lie to me about something so…important."

At the word *lie,* her mother flinched.

"That you'd made up a story to protect me? Is that better? But it was a lie, Mom. You should have told me. I should have known. He was my father."

Her mother looked down at the table. "I wanted you to know and to hate them as I did. We could have been united in grief and hatred. But I kept it from you because you were too young and also because I knew that wasn't what he wanted. I lied to you because it was the only way to honor your father's wishes. He was gone; I couldn't bring him back. But I could protect you from hating. I guess I've done it too well."

"So. Now you know," Dr. Bergman said. "It was tougher on your mother than anyone, keeping this from you. Cut her some slack. Your grandparents had already passed away. She had to bear it alone, raise you alone. She was right not to raise you to be fearful and hateful."

Rachel stared at Rivka and saw the woman she must have all those years ago: a fragile young widow. Always, there had been a hint of trauma in her mother's eyes, and now Rachel understood its origins. It wasn't just losing a husband. It was losing him to violence. No wonder she shuddered when there was news of a terrorist attack. Suddenly, she felt sorry for her mother—but also for herself. Anger at the lies warred with compassion for the loss.

"First, get your education, Rachel. If what you say is true, you can help more if you're trained. Steven helps because he can offer something. So did your dad. He wouldn't have approved of your doing this now, before you even have your degree. You have no skills. What can you offer?"

It was a good question. Was her mother right? If she didn't go to med school, if she veered from the established path, would she ever find her way back?

They sat in silence for a while, staring at the silverware, the untouched basket of rolls in the center of the table.

The waiter reappeared. "You folks ready yet?"

CHAPTER SEVENTEEN

Rachel couldn't sleep well in the days after learning the truth about her father. It was like he'd died all over again and she was in mourning. She stared at the periodic table poster on the wall and remembered them reading it together: *hydrogen, helium, lithium, beryllium…* touching the boxes, laughing when she made a mistake. His mock anger inevitably led to a mock punishment and she'd be on the floor, rolling with laughter, the elements forgotten. After he died, she'd memorized the whole chart for him and would whisper it as she went to sleep, like counting sheep.

Emotional memories, deeply buried, were dislodged and floated to the surface: her confusion at all the commotion after they found out he died; people in and out of the house with platters of food; her mother's face, filled with grief, and Rachel's need to comfort her. She hadn't understood that she, too, needed comfort. It didn't penetrate in those early days that she would never see her daddy again.

The fact that her mother had lied about something so crucial made her wonder about everything and anything she'd ever been told. What other deceptions had Rivka perpetrated in the name of protecting her? The ground no longer felt stable beneath her feet.

There were moments when Rachel wanted to get back at her mother, to spend the year working in the territories, living out her mother's nightmare, punishing her for her lies. But she knew she wouldn't do it. Whatever their arguments, their fights and disagreements, it had always been just the two of them. Good or bad, her mother was part of her and she needed that relationship strong.

The room began swirling around her. She drifted into a restless sleep sitting up in her chair, dreamed that she was alongside her father when the terrorists came knocking.

She peered out the window, saw them, and pulled her father back just as he was about to open the door. He and Yaacov shot the attackers in the arms and legs, so they were disabled but not dead. The IDF swept in and captured them. It led to negotiations. The negotiations brought compromise, and compromise brought peace.

But that's not how it happened. Her father was long dead and still the terrorists worked their black magic. It saddened her anew, and she tried to feel her father's spirit around her, as she sometimes did. But now that presence was disturbing; not fatherly and invincible but vulnerable and frightened. Sleep only led to nightmares, so she tried to avoid it, drank coffee, picked up a novel, but nothing could distract her. She had lived her whole life with a lie, been blissfully ignorant, been stupid. One minute, she got angry and thought it was insulting and offensive that her mother had wanted to protect her. The next, she felt sympathy for her mother and wondered what she'd have done in the same situation. How could she have explained what happened to a seven-year-old? Exactly when should she have revealed the truth?

Finally, she fell asleep, and when she awoke, her anger and sympathy merged and she decided to compromise. The same principle that applied to Israel and the Palestinians applied to her and her Mom. Each side had to give a little, get less than they wanted. She called Rivka and proposed to work for the clinic over the summer, but go to med school in the fall as planned. She could live with that.

"You've got to start school in the fall," Rivka insisted. "If you put it off, you'll never go. First get your degree. They say that you can defer your admission, but who knows? Next year, they could say there is some problem…."

"I said I'd go, Mom."

"Yes, I know. But it's not just to please me. It's the right thing to do."

"But I'll spend the summer in Israel."

"Oh, Rachel. Why are you doing this? You know how I will worry. Just make sure you are back in plenty of time to get ready for med school."

And so they reached an uneasy truce.

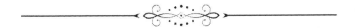

Yusif never drank alcohol or took drugs. He didn't smoke cigarettes or relax in hot baths. He needed to keep his wits about him so as not to confuse the many threads of his identity: Akil loyalist, peaceful poetry professor, Shin Bet mole.

Between him and Ari lay a minefield of twisted loyalties. So, when he took the subway downtown to the park and sat on a bench with Ari beside him, not so close as to be together but close enough to talk, he felt sick with free-floating anxiety.

"Has there been any further activity?" Ari asked.

"We're getting pressure from Akil. He wants this thing to happen. We've let him know that it would be best to wait until the summer but he won't listen. Michael wanted to use Rachel's mother but she's cancelled her latest trip. He's finding all kinds of reasons not to use Rachel."

"Will Akil find someone else?"

"He tried it with someone else once before and it failed. He trusts Michael, so I'd guess that it's him or no one. But then again if he was using someone else, he wouldn't tell me."

"Ah, yes. Only what you need to know."

"That's right," Yusif said, "I'm not hiding anything from you. What would be the point? I'm in this too deep. I…"

"What?"

Without finishing his thought, Yusif got up and started walking down the path.

Michael was on the street just outside of the park. What the fuck was he doing here? Had he followed him? Did he suspect something? If he knew…

He didn't think Michael had seen him, but what if he had? He needed an excuse… He'd say he wanted to buy a gift for Eva. No, maybe a poetry book that he hoped to find at the Strand Bookstore, something he needed for his class. He'd say that he hadn't found it but decided to walk around, explore the area for a little while. That was plausible.

He'd mention it later. Unless that would sound suspect? He'd only mention it if it somehow fit into the conversation. He would bring it up out of nowhere. Shit. What was Michael doing here, anyway? Was he up to something?

Wait, there was Rachel. She was running up to him, giving him a hug. They're going into a restaurant. Perfectly innocent. Unless he'd been seen….

When they were out of sight, he turned back to Ari, but he was gone. A real pro.

Rachel heard shouts through the open window in Michael's apartment and remembered it was Israel 40th Anniversary of Independence Day celebration. Daniel had left her some messages, asking her to help with the preparations, but she'd ignored them. She had considered attending to show her support, but at that moment, she was mesmerized by the movement of Michael's lips up her arm. He was mapping out her body like he'd discovered a new territory, and she was lost in the sensation.

She had found excuses to stay away from him while she'd tried to assimilate what she'd learned about her father. When they finally got together, they couldn't keep their hands off each other. It was easy to forget herself with him; to see him was to touch him. She felt happy despite being sad.

"What's funny?" he asked, nuzzling her neck.

"Can't explain," she said.

"Try."

She leaned back, moving her arm up and down against the sheets. They were soft, a very fine, high-thread-count cotton. For all of his toughness, Michael had a taste for finer things. "Just that I'm here with you and so happy, when according to my mother, I'm only supposed to like nice Jewish boys." She shuddered at the mention of her mother, who didn't belong in bed with them, but continued. "So, I'm thinking that you can't stereotype. And that's what the whole

Middle East conflict is about, isn't it? Everyone is stereotyping. Jews are evil. Arabs are terrorists." She hadn't meant to say that, to conflate Michael with the terrorists. She held her breath for a few seconds, waited for a reaction, but he was silent. "Everyone should just make love and relax and there would be peace."

He smiled. "That's a little simplistic, but I'll vote for it."

The sound of shouts and a recorded voice interrupted her thoughts.

"They're having the Israel Independence Day celebration today," she said.

"Oh?"

"Yes, don't you hear it?"

"Mmm."

"Maybe I should be there."

"Mmm."

"I'm getting up," she said, but she felt like she was glued to the bed. The window faced the side of the adjacent building and let in just a sliver of daylight, not enough to propel her into the day. She was so comfortable. And what would she do when she got there? It sounded like they had plenty of people. It wasn't like they needed her.

"Working on the clinic and the foundation is the best thing you can do," he murmured. "It will bring everyone together. You shouldn't just show blind support for Israel."

"Oh, that's fine for you to say. It's not so simple." It all came crashing back in an instant and she pulled away from him.

He sat up and looked at her closely. "What is it, Rachel? What's wrong?"

She sat up and drew the covers around herself. "My mother told me something at dinner the other night. She told me the truth about something I thought I'd known my whole life, but it turned out I hadn't known anything. I still...I haven't been able to assimilate it."

"What was it? Why didn't you tell me?" he asked with concern.

"It was about my father. You remember I told you that he died in a car accident? My mother didn't like to talk about it, and I had no reason to doubt her. She said it was an accident and no one said otherwise. I was only six when it happened. By the time I was old enough to think analytically, it was already part of my life, like an arm or a leg. It existed. There was no reason to think about it. You don't think about your arm unless you injure it, right?"

"Yes, of course. But, what was it then? Did he run off and leave you?"

"No! Not that." She groaned. "He was in Israel but he wasn't in a car accident. He was killed by terrorists, Michael." She whispered the truth, a sacred revelation meant for hushed voices. "They murdered schoolchildren and the pregnant wife of the man he was staying with and their little child."

Michael moved away from her, just a fraction. His expression changed; the soft loving sensual side of him swallowed by a sober hardness. Of course he knew of such things. His own father was murdered.

"Maybe you've heard of the group," she said. "The People's Revolution Party." She searched his face, but it remained impassive. Still, she thought she saw something in the depths of his blue eyes. "They just murdered people in cold blood. How could they do that?"

"There was terrible hatred, Rachel. People were desperate."

"That's no excuse! Do you know that group?" she asked again. It occurred to her that he might have information, might have even known about the whole incident.

"I've heard of them," he said. "Why did she tell you now, after all these years?"

"I don't think she meant to. She was very upset about me working on the Health Initiative. I think she was looking for a way to stop me and it just came out."

"Such a secret. Why keep it from you?"

"She said she was protecting me when I was little. And then she took the easy way and let it lie. There was no reason to bring it up. Until now."

"Does it change anything? For you, I mean. It was a long time ago."

"That's the thing. I barely remember my father. I don't know what it means. She told me that my father's friend survived. He was a doctor and he tried to keep my dad alive, talking to him so he wouldn't lose consciousness, and my father told him that he loved us and I shouldn't grow up hating. Isn't that amazing? I mean, I think I'm doing what he would have wanted me to do."

"Then you should be proud."

She nodded. Michael was so easy to talk to sometimes.

"So is your mother okay with it, then? Are you going to take the year off?"

"You don't know much about Jewish mothers. She did her best to make me feel guilty about it. She lost her husband...she can't lose her daughter...on and on. I decided to compromise: start med school in the fall, but work on the clinic over the summer."

"Oh."

A look passed between them, a recognition that their relationship was built on fairy dust and couldn't survive a strong wind. The forces that had brought them together—their different backgrounds, medicine, a love of children—would also pull them apart. Sooner or later everything would change. She gave a helpless shrug.

"We still have the next few months," he said, putting his arm around her and pulling her closer. "You know…you can do something very important with this new information."

She could see something brewing in his mind. He had a way of staring when he was thinking out an idea, of looking through her rather than at her.

"Your story is very compelling. Terrorists killed your father, and yet you stand ready to help the children of Palestine to have a better future. You have even more credibility because of this. And your work will honor your father's life, his wish for peace. It's powerful. You should speak about it."

"I've barely begun to understand the whole thing. I was thinking of going to the library to find newspaper accounts of what happened."

"Are you sure? It could be upsetting."

"I want to know! I've been protected my whole life. It's time I knew the truth."

She hadn't thought about her father this intensely in many years. She was accustomed to having just one parent. Comfortable with it. It seemed perfectly normal to her. Once when she was little, she'd written a story about a family with only a mommy and a baby. A small family, she'd written, but happy. Her mother had read it and cried.

This new information changed things. Her father had been murdered in a catastrophic terrorist incident. His death was part of the fabric of Israel's history; it had changed the nature of their response to terrorism. Michael was right. She was in a unique position to argue for forbearance, tolerance, and peace. The next generation need not be defined by the sorrows of the past.

"Dr. Bergman told me what he knows about what happened, but I need to know more. It can't be worse than what I've been imagining. I'm going to the library." She got up and went to shower.

"I'll go with you," Michael said, following.

They were near the Middle Eastern studies center when she heard shouting and saw a giant banner held aloft by six people that said, END U.S. AID TO THE OCCUPATION. Then Rachel noticed SPHR students at tables near the entrance to the center. They were displaying cardboard models of "Palestinian homes," which they crushed at regular intervals, while shouting, "This is what the Israeli army does!" Other people stood at the bottom of the steps with gags in their mouths, their hands bound behind them. Someone held a sign that said: THE SUFFERING OF THE PALESTINIANS.

"What are they doing there? That's where the Israel 40th Anniversary Celebration is being held," Rachel said. She wished they hadn't called it an anniversary celebration. It sounded like a child's birthday party. "We've got to stop this."

"No."

"But it's not fair! It's disrespectful!"

"They have a right to be heard and it's a good time." He stood straight and looked directly into her eyes, the picture of honesty and rationality, but she wasn't convinced.

"You knew about this?" she said.

"Yes."

"Did you organize it?"

"No. I don't get involved in everything." He was starting to sound annoyed with her. He didn't like being questioned, having to defend himself. He was very sure of himself, but this was wrong.

"What are they doing with that banner?" The people holding it started running up the steps.

When Michael didn't respond, she left him without a word, running past the protesters and up to the auditorium, pausing when she caught a glimpse of something familiar crumpled on the ground. She looked more closely and realized it was an Israeli flag that had been torn off the pole and trampled into the dirt. A girl she recognized from SPHR meetings smiled at her and started to hand her a sign that said: ZIONISM IS RACISM, but Rachel pushed her away.

The auditorium was in chaos. The area in front of the stage had been roped off, but the rope and the metal posts supporting it were scattered on the floor and the stage was crowded with people, including the six holding the banner. The speaker, a well-dressed older woman, had backed away from the microphone but was otherwise calmly watching the scene. Rachel saw Daniel's red hair over the crowd and pushed her way through to him.

"Have the campus police been called?" she asked.

He looked at her with surprise. "Yes. So have the regular police. And someone must have contacted the newspapers." He motioned to some photographers who were making their way up the aisle and then crouching by the front of the stage.

"All right, settle down, settle down," a loud, authoritative voice kept repeating. It was a police captain, who was accompanied by four other policemen. "You're going to have to leave this area and come with us," he said, as handcuffs came out of pockets and they quickly and efficiently grabbed the banner and the people holding it. The protesters continued to shout "Zionist criminals!" as they were led away. The audience, who'd been booing them loudly, broke into a cheer as they left the room.

The speaker walked slowly back to the microphone. She was a petite, slim woman with silver-blonde hair, wearing a stylish red suit with a small Israeli ceramic flag pinned to her lapel. "Obviously, some things don't change." She spoke with a slight German accent. There were sympathetic murmurs of agreement from the audience as the room settled into silence.

Something about the woman's elegance reminded Rachel of her mother. They were all descendants of European Jews. If her grandparents had never left Europe, she would likely have been born there. Or never been born. It struck her how close she was to the Holocaust, just one generation away. In the vast timeline of the universe it was the distance of a pinprick.

"This disruption today doesn't surprise me. There are always people who blame the Jewish people for their problems. Now they say that Jews are the root of the Palestinians' suffering. It is not so simple.

"War creates refugees. That's the sad fact. And they are always resettled and move on with their lives. But not the Palestinians. They ask of us what has never in history been asked of a country: to give back territory to a hostile enemy without a peace agreement. After the Six Day War, they declared that there would be 'No peace, no recognition, no negotiation.' Then they complain when we defend ourselves, as if we should allow another massacre of our people."

The speaker went on about how she'd lost her family during the Holocaust and was sent to a displaced persons camp. Eventually, she'd resettled in Israel, married, and had children. "Nothing made up for the loss of my family. I never got back my home or my family's property. But I didn't complain about it for the next fifty years. I moved on. We, as a people, reclaimed our ancient homeland in Palestine. We fought for it and worked the land, drained the swamps and made the desert bloom. We took in refugees from Arab countries, Jews who were forced to leave behind homes and land they had lived on for centuries. They were displaced but found a new home in Israel, a country that has made, and continues to make, an incredible contribution to the democratic, free world.

"If the Palestinians had grabbed the same opportunity to have their own country and worked to make it flourish, we would now be two thriving neighbors. Instead, the Arab governments, with the assistance of the United Nations, have kept the Arab refugees in camps, dangling the promise of

Israel's destruction. They should learn, if I may be so bold, from our example rather than trying to destroy us."

Daniel got up to thank the woman when she finished and introduced the next speaker, a woman whose family was murdered in their home in Netanya in the early 1970s. Four Arab terrorists had come ashore on a boat and captured her husband, parents, and two children who were outside, giving her time to hide in an attic crawl space with her youngest child.

"The terrorists excuse themselves, saying they are driven to kill out of desperation. But these are not desperate acts; they are cold, calculated, well-planned attacks. If they put the same level of planning and thinking into making peace, then we would be living in peace. There is always a choice."

Another speaker, an Iraqi Jew who'd been forced to leave Iraq in the early 1950s, talked about the hundreds of thousands of Jewish refugees who were evicted from Arab countries and absorbed into Israel; they, too, were refugees, no different from the Palestinians, but they had moved on with their lives with the help of the Israeli government.

When the speakers had finished, Daniel went to the podium and announced the other events for the afternoon. With that, people began to file out. Rachel stood by Daniel as people came up to speak with him, and when he was free, he turned his attention to her. "Why are you here? When you didn't return my calls, I figured you weren't interested." His tone was curt.

"I'm sorry, I've been busy."

"We're all busy."

"Well, you did a terrific job of organizing this without me."

"It wasn't just me, it was all of us. We needed everyone."

"All of you, then." She smiled.

He shrugged and gave a half-smile, like it wasn't worth the effort to be mad at her, or maybe he just had trouble staying mad.

"I learned something," she said. "I hadn't thought about how many Jews had been absorbed into Israel since it was created. You'd think the Arabs would do the same and absorb the Palestinians."

"They don't think of themselves as one group," Daniel said. "There have always been a lot of clan rivalries, religious differences among the Christians and Muslims—"

"You know, that's one of the things I heard Michael mention," she told him. "Arab unity. Ending all the rivalries."

"He's Christian, isn't he?"

"Yes, he is. Is that why? Because they're in the minority?"

"It could be. Christian Arabs may feel threatened by the rise of radical Islam. Or maybe he just sees that they will be stronger if they unify. What is his goal, anyway?" He started walking out of the auditorium and she walked alongside him.

"We mostly talk about the healthcare project. I've asked about what they want the *intifada* to achieve, but he never gets too specific. Peace, certainly, but he says it's premature, that the details would have to be worked out after Israel withdraws from the areas occupied in 1967."

"That's convenient. Don't agree to anything until you get everything you want."

"It's so complex. I know you think that, because I'm Jewish, I should support Israel, right or wrong, but I see arguments for both sides. My philosophy is that we are all human beings. Right now, I'm focusing on helping the children. If the children know the goodness of both Jews and Arabs, they will find a way to make peace. Maybe not in this generation but the next."

"You may not think it's political, but it is. Your father was a Zionist. How do you think he'd feel about what you're doing?"

"He'd support it!"

Daniel groaned.

She hesitated but couldn't seem to stop herself. She proceeded to tell him what she'd learned. They stopped walking and stood in the shadow of a giant elm tree as she talked, oblivious to the foot traffic around them and the remnants of the crowd. She was glad to finally have a chance to talk calmly to Daniel. There was no tension, he didn't seem to be pining for her, yearning to hold her. She could just talk.

When she was finished, he tentatively reached out his hand and rested it on her shoulder. When she didn't flinch, he moved in for a hug. She felt his simple, loving comfort and, in that moment, was deeply at peace. "I'm sorry for the way he died and that you never really knew him," Daniel murmured. "He was a great man. The world lost a great person."

He seemed to recognize that she was in delayed mourning, and she was touched. "Thanks, Daniel." Suddenly aware that she'd left Michael abruptly, she looked around but saw no sign of him. "Look, I was on my way to the library to see if I could find any news articles about my dad."

He looked troubled at that idea, as Michael had been.

"It's okay. I think I can handle it," she said.

"You think you can, but it could be hard. I'll come with you. There could be pictures... something you shouldn't see." They began to walk. "So, tell me more about this healthcare initiative you're working on."

She was glad to switch topics. Despite her bravado, she was worried about what she might find at the library; reporters always wanted to shock. "One of the women in our group is an artist and she designed an emblem for us. It has the Palestinian crescent and the Israeli Magen-David and the Red Cross combined into one."

"You sound like you like that part. The symbols together," he said.

"I guess I do. If the symbols can get together, maybe the people can, too."

The microfiche room was in the library basement. When Rachel arrived with Daniel, Michael was peering into the little machine. "What are you doing here?" she asked.

"Come look, Rachel. I found some articles. I wanted to make sure they wouldn't upset you."

"But I told you—"

"I know. Still. Anyway, look at this." He nodded to Daniel as he got up to give Rachel his seat.

Michael had done the initial research for her and she peered into the machine at a newspaper article.

Terrorist Victim, Dr. Mark Weissman. A Brooklyn physician in Israel volunteering his services, Dr. Weissman was one of the eighty-two people killed in a terrorist rampage through an

Israeli town near the Lebanese Border. A group calling itself People's Revolution Party had demanded the release of certain prisoners held in Israeli jails and the return of the territory lost in the 1967 war. When the demands weren't met...

She skimmed until she found her father's name again.

Dr. Weissman leaves behind a wife and a seven-year-old daughter.

There it was in black and white. She looked up at Michael and Daniel. They had the same concerned expression, but somehow it came out differently, like sketches of a flower by two different artists. Michael's had understanding, free of cloying pity. Daniel looked like he wished he could erase it for her, or take it on himself. She felt a surge of warmth toward them both. At that moment, they were the best friends she had in the world.

The two men stepped away to give Rachel some privacy, but she could hear them whispering as she perused the articles, these two men who would never have found themselves in conversation if not for their connection to her.

"Rachel's been telling me about your idea for a multi-national group to study healthcare," Daniel said.

"Yes."

"So this group, the Students for Palestinian Human Rights, did you organize it?"

"No."

"Were you active in politics over there?" Daniel asked.

"It's not like here, Daniel, where you can just go about your business and ignore what goes on around you. Everyone's life is affected by the occupation. Politics is part of daily life."

"But there are different political groups, aren't there? Which one is yours?"

Michael paused. "There are many groups. But in the end, the goal is the same."

"What is the goal?"

"Peace. Democracy. Freedom."

"Alongside Israel? Or instead of it?"

"Come on, Daniel—"

"Well, I'm finished for now," Rachel interrupted. She was reeling from all that she'd seen and didn't have the energy to be with either of them.

"Thanks, both of you. But I kind of feel like I need to be alone for a while, to process all this. I'll see you," she said, looked each in the eye, turned and left.

CHAPTER EIGHTEEN

Ibrahim delivered the news to Akil. "There is new information about the girl in New York."

"The one who's to carry the bomb?"

He nodded. "Turns out she is the daughter of the doctor killed in the 1974 raid from Lebanon."

Akil's eyes widened in surprise. He stood up and began pacing; walking eased his arthritis and helped him think.

"But Yusif says Michael is resisting using her. He wants to find someone else. Says he needs her for his medical work. Shall I send word that it is okay?"

"No! She is ideal. It will show the world that we have not given up on our future, and the struggle will go on from one generation to the next. The press will juxtapose pictures of father and daughter. It's perfect."

"It must be her?"

"Absolutely. This is more important than the clinics."

There was a time when he'd believed in the paramount importance of medicine. He had run a clinic as a young doctor, in the days when he and Michael's father were like brothers. It struck him sometimes how far he'd come from the young doctor he had once been.

His trajectory was reset by the *nakba*. After that, it became obvious to him that their lives were shaped by politics. If they didn't get the politics right, nothing else would matter. The health of the individual required a healthy society, and the

Party was the means to achieve it. Michael's father had accused him of being addicted to revolution, but that wasn't true. He had simply made a commitment and had the will to see it through.

He would never give up because failure was a kind of death. It was truly a zero-sum game. If Israel survived, they would be destroyed. The underpinnings of their society would alter; capitalism and all of its petty values and inequalities would dominate their lives and change their essence, turn them into the *other*. They would call it "peace" but it was just another form of destruction. Compromise would mean the loss of their souls.

"Make sure Michael understands why the girl is to carry the bomb. Tell him to put her in a bundle—he will know what I mean."

Ibrahim nodded and went off to execute the orders. Another prisoner was being released that afternoon and he would make his way to Ramallah and to Yusif's wife. She would get the word out to Yusif.

Akil stood up and approached twenty young prisoners who sat in a large circle. They'd spent the morning in individual study, poring over Marx and Hegel, Sinclair Lewis and Pablo Neruda. They'd eaten a thin soup for lunch and were resting during the heat of the noonday. Soon, he would lead a discussion of the finer points of Soviet versus Chinese Communism.

Rachel managed to avoid Michael for a week, until he showed up at her house. Her mother was in the shower and when Rachel saw him from her window she went outside and closed the front door behind her.

"You're angry with me," he said, leaning against the railing on the porch. "Let's talk about it."

"I don't feel as if I can trust you. I mean, you knew they would be disrupting the conference and you didn't tell me."

"Yes, I knew about it, but I don't tell you everything I know. I don't tell other people what we talk about either. I wouldn't betray your trust and I won't betray theirs."

He had a point, but still, it seemed wrong. "Why didn't you talk them out of it?"

"I had no reason to get involved. I knew they were having a protest, but you're right, it was badly done. I thought they knew better."

She was satisfied that he at least recognized that they'd gone over the top. "It's over. The day was a success, so they didn't accomplish anything. But I've decided not to speak at your conference."

"I'm sorry to hear that. But you do what you think is right."

They stood in silence for a few minutes. "What about Amira?" he said. "You told her you'd dance in her performance. That's art, not politics. I hope you're still planning to dance."

"I don't know. I have to think about it."

He nodded and then surprised her by saying, "I'd like to meet your mother, Rachel."

"My mother?"

"Yes. Let's take her out to dinner. You talk so much about her. Maybe it'll help me figure you out. You're a confusing little thing."

She was standing with her arms crossed in front of her chest, looking up at him. He reached over and gently uncrossed her arms and lifted her by the waist into the air above. She put her hands on his shoulders to steady herself and couldn't help but giggle; it made her feel like a little girl.

Just then the door opened and her mother stood there in her long kimono style robe, her hair in a towel. "Rachel? What's going on?"

Michael put her down and she felt a little dizzy as she tried to gather her thoughts. They all stared at one another for a moment until she said, "Mom, this is Michael. He dropped by to... tell me something. Michael, this is my mother, Rivka Weissman."

"You're Michael?" she said, like she couldn't believe it.

He nodded, "Very nice to meet you."

They stared at one another, sizing each other up.

"I was just telling Rachel that I would love to take you both to dinner sometime soon," he said.

"Oh?"

"Yes. When would be good for you?"

"How about now?" It sounded like a challenge.

"Now? Well... sure, that would be fine. Is that good for you, Rachel?" he asked.

She nodded.

"Just give me ten minutes to dress," Rivka said, brusque and efficient. "Come inside and change, Rachel. You don't mind waiting out here, do you?"

Matters had suddenly been taken out of Rachel's hands—she felt powerless to do anything but follow her mother inside.

"Why does he want to have dinner with me?" Rivka asked her when the door was closed.

"I don't know. Nothing mysterious. I talk about you a lot and he'd just asked me to invite you to dinner with us."

"Us? Are you a couple?"

"I meant the three of us together. Him, me, you. Him and us. I'm the one you both know. You know what I mean…why are you getting me all flustered?"

"Rachel. Are you a couple?"

"We're not *going steady* or engaged or anything. We're just close."

Her mother groaned as if she'd been stabbed.

"Don't worry about it, Mother. If you don't want to have dinner, that's fine."

"No, of course I want to! I wouldn't miss the chance to get to know the wonderful Michael whom I've heard so much about. What mother would?"

"Mom…"

"I'll make a reservation at Dorian's," she said, and went upstairs to get ready.

Michael's eyes widened when Rivka stepped outside fifteen minutes later, dressed and coiffed and made up. He was clearly impressed, and Rachel's pride in her mother's appearance mingled with resentment. Next to her, she felt like an ugly duckling as usual, though she'd changed from jeans into a long skirt.

"We should take our car," Rachel said, just to say something. "Michael's is a two-seater."

"That's fine," Rivka agreed. They piled into her mother's ten-year-old white Mercedes with a tan leather interior. She'd bought it used, it had eighty thousand miles on it, but it was beautiful.

"You have good taste in cars," Michael said, and they discussed the virtues of European versus American automobiles, and various models. Once again, Rachel found herself surprised to discover a new side of Michael. He was an automobile aficionado.

Dorian's was about a twenty-minute drive. It was one of their favorite places, with both great food and ambiance as it was in a renovated carriage house. Old wood beams crossed the ceiling and faded wallpaper with tiny swirls of color decorated the walls. Lanterns kept the lighting nineteenth-century dim. Cozy booths lined the perimeter and heavy wood tables were scattered about. It was nearly full when they got there, and they passed tables crowded with dishes: hearty stews laden with chunky vegetables, juicy chicken dishes, and sizzling steaks.

The maître d' kissed Rachel and her mom on both cheeks in a flurry of turning heads and puckered lips. He tactfully seated them at a round table, saving Rachel the awkwardness of choosing sides.

The three chatted for a while, small talk about the drive, the weather, the lovely old-world atmosphere. Michael and Rivka spoke mostly to each other, feeling each other out through the smokescreen of pleasantries. Then Rivka asked him where exactly he was from.

"Ramallah, a town in the West Bank. But I've been here for nearly two years now."

"Do you want to move here, permanently?"

"No, my fellowship is over in June and I'll return home."

"How did the fellowship come about?"

"Dr. Bergman was already doing research in my area so our interests coincided and his lab was perfect. But I have commitments back home. I must return."

"I don't know if you are aware, but Rachel's father was also a doctor. A pediatrician. She has a lot of his intelligence and drive, and now I see she's interested in politics, as he was. It can be such a magnet, especially when you think you can make a difference."

"Rachel said your husband volunteered in Israel."

"Yes, Mark had several friends there. A lot of them were on kibbutzim organized by a Marxist-Socialist group, Hashomer Ha'tsair." She turned to Rachel. "The same ones that ran that summer camp in the Catskills you went to one summer."

"Camp Shomria," Rachel said.

"Yes, that's why I sent you there that summer. Because of your dad."

Rachel turned to Michael. "It was fun. Kind of wild. A lot of outdoor activity and camping in the woods and farming. I worked in the chicken coops!"

"You?" Michael said, pretending to be shocked.

She laughed, "Yes! They were training us to live off the land."

"Your dad thought we might move to a kibbutz," her mother said.

"You must have hated that idea," Rachel said, surprised and pleased that her mother wanted to share memories of her father.

"No, actually I liked it. Or maybe I just liked *him*, so I would have liked whatever he did."

Her mother looked sweet, at that moment, and Rachel looked at her with new understanding. Rivka would have done anything for Mark because she loved him. Having Michael beside her gave her a greater understanding of the lengths to which a woman might go for the man she loved, and underscored how painful it must have been to lose him.

"Mark was always committed to Israel, and to peace. But his life was cut short."

"I'm very sorry for your loss, Mrs. Weissman. I wish I'd had the privilege of meeting him."

"Do you, Michael? And please call me Rivka."

"Of course I do—Rivka."

His voice was a cello, Rachel thought. *The sound so soothing. How could anyone not love him?*

"Your daughter is special to me."

"I find that odd. Don't your parents object to your dating a Jewish girl?"

"I also lost my parents when I was young."

"You've done very well for a young man with no family." It didn't sound like a compliment, more like an accusation.

"I was lucky."

"And he works very hard," Rachel chimed in.

"Your daughter is a great help in the clinic. You've seen the book she's working on? We'll be implementing a teaching program and using it, this summer."

"Why don't you just take the book, then? She shouldn't risk her life. If you care about her, let her stay behind."

"She'll be safe in Israel," Michael said.

"Why are we even discussing this?" Rachel said. "It's decided."

Her mother looked from one to the other and hesitated. Her mother had adored Josh, and she'd liked Daniel, who had a knack for making Rivka laugh, but Michael was different. He wasn't a boy at all; he was a man with passion, and, Rachel realized that in that sense, he just like her dad. Maybe her mother was remembering what it was like to chosen by a special man to share in their dream. It was an honor not many women could resist. But Rivka clearly didn't want Rachel following after this dream, with all it implied.

"You don't know that," Rivka said. "There is no evidence of that. It's getting worse, not better."

"She'll be fine, Mrs.—Rivka." His voice was deeper, reassuring. "Things happen for a reason. Dr. Bergman, Rachel, me, it's no accident that we've been brought together. And it's obvious that she has a natural rapport with children."

Rivka nodded. "That's true."

"They respond to her, and she to them. It's in her nature to help them. The clinic is an opportunity that a unique convergence of events has made possible, and so she's seizing it. It's not only a career move, it's something she needs to do for herself, for her *spirit*."

Rivka's expression changed a little as he spoke; each word was like a hammer, chiseling her thoughts, chipping away at her skepticism. A slight movement of her head matched the rhythm of his words; she seemed unaware that she was nodding in agreement.

"And Dr. Bergman would never permit her to get involved in anything dangerous. You don't know me but surely you trust him."

"Steven and I don't always see eye to eye. He's tried to get me to Israel many times—"

"You should come!" Michael said, and then, very softly, "*Bevakasha*. Please." His hand, which was resting on the table, moved a fraction toward her and in that moment, Rivka's body arched ever so slightly toward him before she caught herself and leaned away.

Rachel was so astonished that she didn't know what to think. Was Michael seducing her mother? She was disgusted, then offended, and then she got it. He wanted to convince Rivka to support her. He was doing it for her. They were at war for her, and he was using every weapon at his disposal, including his abundant charm and intelligence.

And her mother was falling for it. Perhaps because Michael, with his passion for medicine and children and peace, reminded her of her husband.

"Why don't you come with us to Israel this summer and see for yourself what we're doing," he said. "Or better yet, you could go ahead of us, check it out, assure yourself that it's safe."

"Me? No. I've never wanted to go there. Not after Mark...well, of course, if Rachel is going...but even so, I'm very busy. The New York Accessories show is in June and I always attend, and I have buyers for my fall line coming in after that. I need to be here. I don't know..."

Little by little, Rachel could see that she was relenting. She got the distracted look she got when she was thinking. She seemed to reach a conclusion, then leaned back in her chair, folding her hands neatly on her lap.

"No. I vowed never to go to Israel. Rachel is all grown up, so I can't stop her. I'd rather she stay here, but if this is what she needs to do, she'll do it without me."

Michael seemed about to say something, but then stopped himself.

"Don't worry, Mom. I can handle it."

It was over. She was going to Israel, and Michael had passed his first hurdle in the Rivka challenge.

By the time they got back to the house, Michael felt at ease with Rivka. She'd reached out her hand to say goodnight, but he drew her in for a hug instead, and she hugged him back. After she'd gone inside the house, he said, "Your mother is lovely, Rachel, and smart, too."

"I'm a little shocked to say it, but she seemed to like you."

"That's good. Then the evening was a success."

She nodded and took his hand in hers.

"You're a little like her," he said, "but much prettier." It wasn't true, but a necessary lie.

In fact, Rivka reminded Michael of Leila, the Lebanese model he'd dated in Beirut, but more elegant and refined. Leila was a natural beauty, but she'd used heavy kohl liner around her eyes and dressed in vibrant colors that Rivka would find gauche. Why had he imagined that Rachel's mother would be gray-haired and frumpy, overbearing perhaps, a silly woman? His own prejudices and stereotypes of Jewish mothers were so ridiculous he had to laugh at himself.

He could've just enjoyed the evening sitting between two lovely women, but he was always working, no leisure time for him. He had been hoping to convince Rivka to fly to Israel, the sooner the better—to offer her to Akil as a plausible substitute. But the whole idea was moot, the woman would never go to Israel, not anytime soon, and in a way he was glad. He wasn't sure he could have gone through with it, and his reluctance felt strange. Always before, Akil had been able to push him past his limits and to ease him through the consequences, but this was new territory.

He remembered when his father had been found dead in the street in Ramallah, all those years ago. Akil had stayed up all night with him. He'd shared his cup and served him with his own hands. He had been beside him for days and had never left him since. Akil had no sons of his own, and Michael was his favorite among all the boys orphaned in the wars. It was a new experience to lie to him, and he wasn't sure how to do it.

The car felt lonely without Rachel beside him as he drove back to the city. He almost turned back to get her, to bring her back to his apartment for the night. Instead he fantasized about the two of them living together in a flat in Yaffa, smelling the sea, the languor of long hot nights.

When he got home, Yusif was waiting for him. "The courier is arriving later. We have to get our response together." The courier worked for a UN Relief Agency and her papers enabled her to pass easily through checkpoints. She was sympathetic to the Palestinians and helped them by smuggling messages, sometimes weapons. Michael was glad Rachel was home in Riverdale. It saved him from telling her one more lie.

"Let him know that I can't create the proper device. I've looked into it, and the security protocols have changed. The old methods won't work. There is too great a chance of discovery. I'll need time to come up with something else." It was a poor excuse but he needed to buy time. He wanted nothing to do with this plan. He would find ways to elaborate later, invent problems about detonation, concealment, whatever else he could come up with. Akil understood that airport security personnel weren't complete morons. He was the one who had taught him never to underestimate the enemy.

"What has changed?" Yusif asked.

"It's very technical, Yusif," Michael said with an air of authority that was a touch dismissive. "It's a little different from stringing words together into a poem. You don't need to know."

"I thought I might be able to help, that's all, Michael. Not me, but I could find someone to ask."

"We can't bring anyone else into this. Drop it, Yusif."

"Akil will come up with something else, and he'll still use Rachel."

Michael nodded. Yusif was right, but for now all he could do was buy time. He'd be returning home in June and was counting the days until he would breathe the air of Palestine. He would find a way to talk with Akil directly and explain all he'd learned in the past few years. Akil had been away from medicine for so long, he had no idea how much progress had been made. Michael's work was important; he had to make him understand that. They shouldn't throw it all away by using the conference to make a political statement.

His work was what mattered to him now, and by collaborating with American and Israeli doctors, he had achieved more than he ever could have alone. In that truth lay the seeds of something far more powerful than bombs.

It shouldn't be traitorous to say so.

CHAPTER NINETEEN

Akil had a calm demeanor that set people at ease. It was an anomaly of his character that helped him recruit people and persuade them to engage in dangerous missions. It also masked his feelings, so only an astute observer would have noticed the tightening of his mouth, the slight recoil of his body, as he read Yusif's letter. It wasn't unusual for his men to change or alter plans, but it was difficult to organize a mission across the world from behind barbed wire. Normally he would accept this delay without question and begin to devise a new plan. But something felt wrong. He clutched the note with callused fingers and dead skin flaked off when he brushed them across his pants. "You've known Michael as long as I have," he said to Ibrahim.

"Yes, I have," Ibrahim said. He, too, looked parched, his smile just another crack in the lines of his face.

"Have you ever known him to make up an excuse to try to avoid executing an order?"

Ibrahim frowned, thinking, and shook his head. "He doesn't want to do it? For what reason?"

"He's been away a long time, Ibrahim." The implications hung in the air, but even Akil, a man who suspected everyone, could find no reason to doubt Michael.

"He chose you over his father," Ibrahim said softly. "He belongs to you, heart and soul."

It was true. But he had been a boy then, and now he was a man who had been away for years, living in Beirut and now New York. People change. Michael's own father, George Haddad, the one-time revolutionary, was a case in point.

For many years, he and George had been so alike that people thought they were brothers. They even resembled each other, with the same build and the same rhythm in their walk. From the very beginning, his friendship with George had made him feel more alive: the challenge of his intellect, his often priceless, wry humor.

But then George had lost his way. For a while, they continued to talk, but it was as if they spoke two different languages. His sharp intelligence turned to the service of perverted arguments and there was no getting through to him. Finally, there was no point in them even speaking at all.

The young Michael was like the George he had known as a student. But he was nearing the age that George had been when he had turned from the revolution, and Akil wondered if the pattern would repeat.

He shook his head to ward off the thought. It didn't even make sense. Circumstances had changed George, not age. Maybe it was as simple as Michael said; the plan wouldn't work. It was impossible to judge from a distance. He needed to talk to him face to face, to see his expressions, hear his voice. Michael could question, argue, and be stubborn, but Akil had always found ways into his heart. He loved the boy as he had once loved the boy's father, and it would be painful for him if Michael were to follow in his father's treacherous footsteps.

"We will use the backup plan," he said. "We have contacts at the hotel where the healthcare conference is being held. A crowded hotel will suffice. Tell him to get the girl to Tel-Aviv and the conference," he told Ibrahim. "Others will handle the details."

Yusif delivered Akil's response to Michael.

"He agrees to abort the plan; a failed effort would be worse than nothing at this point."

"That's it?" Michael said, relieved.

"No," Yusif said. "There's a backup plan."

"Oh?"

"Not us. It will be another cell. I'm to send him the details on the conference: times, dates, attendees. He knows the hotel. One of our people works there."

"He's planning something for the conference?"

"That would be my guess. But you know how he operates. He asks for information. He doesn't share any more than necessary." Yusif looked down at the table.

"Yes? Something else?"

"Rachel. She's to be at the conference."

Michael shrugged. "Fine, she'll be there. That shouldn't be a problem." He spoke casually as if it were of little consequence to him, but he was deeply disturbed that Akil would use his conference to make a political statement, and—worse—that he was still insisting on using Rachel. It wasn't enough for him to simply derail the clinic. He wanted Rachel killed.

Even if Michael managed to keep her away, a bomb would lead to an investigation. He might be implicated, although hotels and catering establishments, as well as marketplaces, schools, busses—anywhere people congregated—were all common targets. Even if there were no way to connect him directly, there would be suspicion because he was Palestinian and he'd organized the conference.

If they traced it back to him, all his work in endocrinology would be wasted; he'd be interrogated, probably deported or imprisoned. Even Dr. Bergman and Rachel would be questioned. Her career could be derailed. A cloud of suspicion would follow her throughout her life. But that was the least of his concerns.

There had to be another way, but it would be useless to argue through coded messages; bad enough that he'd backed away from the original plan. Akil must have been terribly disappointed in him. He'd always done just as Akil had ordered, and his refusal must have shaken up his mentor—just as it had shaken him. He felt as if he was losing his footing, in danger of becoming irretrievably lost. His loyalties, once so certain, were muddled.

Michael remained convinced of the importance of the Health Care Initiative and his passion had stirred others: Dr. Bergman, Rachel, the doctors who were to attend the conference. Now it would all be blown up by a bomb. He thought, again, of the bomb that had blown that Israeli soldier to bits when he was a boy. His first real act of commitment to Akil was coming full circle. There was no way to stop it, short of informing the Israeli authorities, and that he would never do.

All he could do was try to keep Rachel out of it.

"Is Rachel set to go?" Yusif asked.

"Yes, Yusif. She's set to go," he said. But he didn't add that he would stop her, drug her so she overslept, misdirect her, or whatever it took.

"He wants her at the conference. He was specific about that," Yusif said.

"Of course. I understand."

Rachel felt dizzy. Everything was moving so fast, the future coming at her like a high-speed train. Four short years ago, graduation had been a pinpoint in the distance, and now it had arrived. There was nothing left to do but gather with her class at their graduation ceremony, listen to the speeches, and pick up her diploma. She welcomed the opportunity to take time out from the rash of activity and reflect.

She stood behind Daniel in the graduation procession because Weissman followed Weiss alphabetically. They'd often sat together in classes and had become better friends because of the serendipitous spelling of their names. It was a kind of a joke to them, but the fun had gone out of it lately.

Rivka and Dr. Bergman sat together near the front. They were an odd couple: one stylish, the other frumpy. He had the pleased expression he often had when her mother was beside him. They were both thrilled to see her graduate—not that there had been any doubt. Her mother wore her father's old watch. It was way too big and heavy for her wrist, but she always wore it to celebrate Rachel's milestones.

"Congratulations honey!" her mother said when it was over, kissing her cheeks one at a time and giving her a hug.

Dr. Bergman kissed her as well, and they both stood fussing over her. Michael was with Yusif and Amira, and they, too, came over and greeted her. Rachel introduced them all and it felt very normal, just friends and family celebrating her graduation. Jill came over with her parents and Daniel with his, all their tensions left behind for this special event, and she felt surrounded by people she loved. She took her mother's left arm, put her hand over the watch, and felt her father with her, too.

Rachel had a million things to do to get ready for her trip. She tried to go about them briskly and efficiently but her mind kept wandering. She'd begin packing and then realize she'd been holding a shirt in her hand for ten minutes, staring out the window. Images of Michael entered her mind and she would start daydreaming about him.

The violence in the West Bank and Gaza had spilled over into Israel and security was ramped up. Her mother was increasingly concerned, but they'd made their deal. Rachel promised to start med school in the fall. In exchange, she could work on the Children's Health Initiative. It reminded her of the deals they'd made when she was younger, where she'd be permitted to watch extra TV if she did the dishes or got her homework done early.

She packed lightly, preparing to travel with only what she could carry, determined to fit everything into one large backpack. She laid all her things out on her bed and the floor and went through everything carefully, taking clothing that had multiple purposes and washed easily. Weight was a factor in choosing books, one of which was an Arabic language manual.

She was absorbed in all these little decisions, so the doorbell startled her. When she opened the door, she felt the same little thrill she always did at the sight of him. Her mother was downtown at work and the house was quiet. As she took Michael's hand to lead him upstairs, he paused to examine the silver-framed photos lined up on the hall table. They were mostly of her and her dad, some from when he was a young man wearing the white coat of a physician, others in which he was holding her in the air as she smiled. They were all from before he was "taken by those animals," as her mother would say.

"You look like him, you know?" Michael said.

"So I'm told. My mom says it means I'm lucky. Some superstition about a girl looking like her father."

"Rivka, superstitious? She seems pretty down to earth."

"We all have our hidden sides, I guess. Come upstairs. I need to finish packing."

He looked at the mess on her bed, then sat in her armchair and picked up the book lying on the side table.

"You're not taking this one?"

"No, too heavy."

"Let me know if you need help," he said, as he opened the book and started leafing through it. It was Michener's *The Haj*, from which she'd learned some Arab history.

"That book treats the Jews who fought for Israel very kindly and the Arabs, well, less so," she told him. "I'm not sure it's quite your thing."

"I'm all for being kind to Jews," he said, with a smile that had a touch of irony and made her feel weak. As much as she wanted to pack and organize herself, she knew that was going to wait. He gave her just the slightest nod. In just a few steps across her childhood room, where she'd grown to be her father's daughter, she was in his arms.

He didn't ask when her mother would be home. He was an improviser and would work with whatever situation arose. But she didn't care anymore, either. She was an adult, could do as she pleased. "It will be quick. That's good too," he murmured, "and then you'll finish your packing."

It wasn't quick. She let herself fall under his spell and forget about time and place and deadlines. They were caught up in a song with endless refrains, and even when they stopped it wasn't over.

"I'll pick you up tomorrow," he said, as he kissed her goodbye. When she closed the door behind him, she collapsed on her bed, right on top of the piles of clothes and fell into a deep sleep.

He picked her up in a taxi the next day and they arrived at the airport at four in the afternoon for their Pan Am flight to Tel-Aviv. The waiting area was crowded with Orthodox men in black hats, their wives in scarves that hid every strand of hair, cooing to babies and scolding the hordes of children. Daniel had once said that the Orthodox were trying to make up for all the people lost in the Holocaust, which sounded depressing, but she found it joyful to be among them.

They finessed their way through the crowd until they found a few seats in a waiting area with other college student types and sat and read for a while, but Rachel found it hard to concentrate. She was glad when he suggested a drink. At the airport bar, they ordered beers.

"I'm going to have to send you into Jerusalem during the first two days," Michael said, taking her hand from the table and holding it in both of his. "I want you to meet with a physician who can't take the time to come to the conference."

"No. I should be there to make sure everything goes smoothly. Can't someone else go?" She wanted to argue more forcefully, but the feel of his hands mellowed her. That's probably why he did it.

"It's not far. You'll only be gone for part of the day if you leave early."

He brought out a map and showed her the distance and then pointed out all the places they would visit together during the summer. That made her lightheaded again, her stomach fluttery, and she wished there was a place they could go to be alone. But there wasn't, and after a while, they boarded the plane. She sat with the window on one side and Michael on the other. She fell asleep with her head on his shoulder and her hand in his. Suspended in the air, in no one's country, on no one's land, next to Michael, it felt like home.

CHAPTER TWENTY

When the announcement came on, her grogginess from the twelve-hour flight evaporated. "Ladies and gentlemen, we have just been cleared to land at Ben Gurion airport. Please make sure one last time your seat belt is securely fastened. The flight attendants are currently passing around the cabin to make a final compliance check, and pick up any remaining cups and glasses. Current local time is 7 pm. Thank you."

"We're here!" she said. It should be morning, but it was evening in Tel Aviv. Her time clock was screwed up, but she was too excited to care. The plane landed with a few bumps that made her squeeze Michael's arm so hard that he protested. Then the aisles filled with passengers all eager to get off, none more than she; she couldn't wait for this adventure to begin.

After what seemed like an hour, they were finally in line to get on the airport van that was waiting to take the passengers to the terminal. But before they could get on, a black van pulled up and a man got out and approached them. He had short, dark hair, black eyes, and a soldier in uniform by his side. Rachel saw a flash of panic in Michael's eyes, and her curiosity turned to confusion and then alarm. "Your passports, please," he said to them in heavily accented English. He glanced at Rachel's passport and Michael's papers and put them in his pocket. "You will come with us for questioning."

Michael was silent, his face devoid of expression, but Rachel expected an explanation. She understood that security was tight at Ben Gurion Airport and random searches were common. She expected some extra questioning when they went through customs, but nothing like this, not pulled away straight off the plane.

"Excuse me, what's this about? We're here to organize a conference. We have meetings arranged."

It was as if she hadn't spoken. The soldier took out a pair of handcuffs and handcuffed Michael with a swift motion and then, to her shock, he pulled her arms roughly behind her and handcuffed her as well. She'd seen it done in movies and on television, but had never felt the hard metal on her small wrists, restricting her arms, locking away her freedom.

"Michael," she turned, appealing to him, "What is this?"

His face was a mask. His familiar, handsome features hard. Under his breath, he whispered, "Be careful, Rachel. Don't trust them."

"No talking," the soldier growled.

The other passengers had formed a line and a woman she'd chatted with while waiting on line for the rest room gave her a shocked, disapproving look. She became aware of the burning heat, so unlike a hot New York summer—a dry, dusty heat that made her feel too far from home—and felt the soldier's hand on her arm, a possessive touch she hadn't authorized. An intrusion. He went about the business of hustling them out of the airport. She was just a piece of equipment being hauled away.

They sat in the back of a van with blacked-out windows but they were blindfolded anyway, one more deprivation that made her even more helpless, leading her little by little to the edge of a desperate fear. Her breathing was shallow and she forced herself to take deep breaths to get control. She told herself she was an American and that these were Israelis, fellow Jews, in a democratic country. She hadn't done anything wrong.

When they arrived wherever it was they were going, the blindfolds were moved. The men led her and Michael through an alley into a stone building. She had a fleeting, frightening thought that these men were impostors, terrorists who were kidnapping them. But when she walked in, what she saw were the trappings of an ordinary bureaucratic building. There were signs in Hebrew, men and women in army uniforms, others who were handcuffed sitting on benches. Michael gave her a parting glance before he was led away from her, and she remembered how she'd thought they would be sitting at a bar along Dizengoff Boulevard in Tel-Aviv by then, shaking off jet lag and soaking in the sights.

A policewoman led her down a hall into a small room with a metal desk and three folding chairs. The barred window let in the shadow of early evening light. The only other light was from a bare bulb in the ceiling. They hadn't removed her handcuffs and her shoulders ached.

"Can you get these off?" she said. It seemed like a reasonable request, but the woman just glanced at the handcuffs as if she'd forgotten something, then clamped them to a chain attached to the table. "I want to speak to the American Consulate," Rachel shouted at her as the door closed.

She wasn't sure how much time passed before a man walked in. "I'm Eitan," he said. He had cropped, light-brown hair, darkly tanned skin, a husky build. His ill-fitting shirt strained, leaving little gaps between the buttons. He stood towering over her, forcing her to look up, straining her already aching shoulders. "I need you to tell me everything you know, Rachel. You're in serious trouble, so don't even think about lying." His voice was gravelly, crackling with disgust.

She still had on the sweater she'd worn on the plane, but it was cool inside the stone building and she shivered; her voice shook when she tried to speak. She couldn't control it. It was as if her insides were coated with a thin layer of ice. "Lie about what? Why am I here? I haven't done anything."

"Don't play innocent. We know all about what you've been up to. Take me through it from the beginning and if your story doesn't add up, if you try to lie, you'll be locked away for a long time."

She tried to remember what she'd been taught to do as a child when she was scared of some bully. She reached way back into her memory and saw her teacher, Mrs. Ryder, telling her second-grade class to pretend that the bully had no pants on, that he was standing in his underwear. All the kids had giggled hysterically. She tried imagining Eitan, all tough and sarcastic, in his underwear. "I'm entitled to a phone call. I want to call the American Consulate."

He shrugged and took out a cigarette. "You don't have any rights now. You're being held under administrative detention because you present a threat to the security of the state."

"That's ridiculous! I'm here to help sick kids."

"Don't give me your bullshit!" he barked.

There were stories, rumors at the SPHR, about Israel's dark underbelly, a place where the veneer of "nice American Jewish girl" offered no protection. And now she'd found it;

she was on a tour none of the guidebooks listed, chained to a table at the mercy of a thuggish stranger, for no apparent reason and with no one to help.

"You've been very active with Students for Palestinian Human Rights. You must have realized that they aren't a simple protest group," he said.

"Whatever they are, they are not terrorists and I'm certainly not one. You've got this all wrong." She wanted to sound firm, but it came out as a plea.

"Stop wasting my time."

There was no way into him, neither through charm nor logic. He wouldn't be giving her the benefit of the doubt, didn't assume she was a person of integrity the way everyone always had since she was a kid—the good girl, smart and reliable. He assumed the opposite and she didn't know how to work with that. She was in the hands of a coarse man and a system whose rules she didn't understand.

"They're not terrorists," she repeated.

"They're not terrorists," he mimicked her. "So what is their purpose?"

"To help people. They hold protests. Legal protests. I wasn't involved with those."

He kept examining her, reminding her of an impatient doctor quizzing an intern, waiting for a better response.

"I worked for a health organization. The Palestinians live in horrible conditions and need better care."

"What are their methods?"

"You mean the mobile clinics?"

"Not that. Their political methods."

"You mean the demonstrations?" she said.

He nodded and crushed his cigarette between his fingers to put it out, then lit another. All the smoke was making her nauseous, and she was confused by his questions. Nothing she said seemed to be good enough for him. She wanted to give him what he wanted so he would leave her alone. She had nothing to hide and wanted to please him, to get him on her side. Did that happen to everyone who was interrogated? She had no experience with this, no training, no preparation, no warning. She tried to pull herself together and give him simple honest answers.

"I was hardly involved with that side of it. I know they wrote articles in the paper. Things like that. Perfectly legal. Not like this arrest."

He ignored that and asked her how she'd met Michael.

"At an endocrinology clinic. He was a fellow there."

"Who were the other members of Students for Palestinian Human Rights?"

She told him names. There was nothing confidential about what he asked.

"Tell me about Michael."

She wanted to protect Michael, to describe him in the best possible light. "He's a respected doctor who was on fellowship at the Center for Pediatric Endocrinology in New York. I told you, that's where I met him. I worked there."

"What else?"

She wondered what would happen if she didn't answer him. But as she looked at his barrel chest, the cigarette hanging from his mouth and the locked door, she didn't want to find out. "I know he cares about children, especially the ones with chronic illnesses like diabetes. He genuinely wants to help them, especially in impoverished communities. He's a good person."

"Okay, right, sure." He looked at the window, as if collecting his thoughts. "You've been very active with Students for Palestinian Human Rights. Was that to impress Michael?"

"Of course not."

"Were you active in politics before you met him?"

"No, but…"

"But what? You were sleeping with Michael. You'd do anything for him, wouldn't you?"

How had he known that? How long had he been keeping track of her? Who had told him these things? Why did they care? "That's none of your business! It has nothing to do with anything!" If only he would tell her what he thought she'd done, so she could explain why he was wrong.

Then his tone changed from disgust to almost friendly. "It's okay. I can understand that. Love makes us do crazy things. Things we never would have imagined."

What did that even mean? "Please tell me what this is this all about." She attempted to appeal to him with her innocence; it was in her voice, in her expression, in the way her head cocked to one side as she looked up at him, her lips slightly parted.

He didn't respond. Instead, he leaned against the wall, drew in smoke from the cigarette, and blew it out. "Tell me what you did for him, Rachel. There is no point in trying to keep secrets. It's over."

"Over? We haven't even begun. We're here to help the Palestinian children. It's very bad for them and I want to help."

"I see. That's very admirable. A bombing would help them. I understand." He'd moved behind her and his voice echoed eerily off the walls. She strained to turn around.

"*A bombing?* What are you talking about?"

"You were lovers. You were devoted to him. So you did whatever he asked, didn't you, to help him and the Palestinian children."

He said *children* with disdain. He thought she was making it up, that they were an excuse.

"Tell me how you helped them."

She was going to correct him, to insist that she hadn't done everything Michael asked. And then she remembered how she'd walked around campus putting up posters, danced at the rally, and dropped things off for him at SPHR headquarters. There was a kernel of truth in Eitan's accusations, but she wouldn't admit it. He was twisting things around, making innocent activities sound evil.

"I didn't do everything he asked," she said. "He wanted me to speak at their conference and I refused."

"He wanted you to speak out as the daughter of a victim of Palestinian terrorists?"

Her stomach turned. How did he know so much about her? Dr. Bergman had warned her that it was different in Israel; they couldn't afford to take any chances, here; there was no room for error. Not with terrorism. If they were lax, men like her father, kids like those schoolchildren, were killed.

"To say what?" he continued. "That you were in favor of returning the land, of giving in to the hostage takers' demands, even years later? That your father had been killed and yet you would sleep with his murderers?"

"No! They weren't his murderers!" Now she could prove he was wrong. She was desperate to correct him, to find a way out, through a logical train of thought. "That was a fringe group. Students for Palestinian Human Rights wants the same as my father wanted, peace in the region—independence for the Palestinians. You obviously don't agree with that, but that's politics, not terrorism."

He looked at her carefully, his eyes roaming over her face and body as if searching for clues in her posture or the way she tapped her foot restlessly against the floor. "You're lying. Michael wasn't just organizing peaceful demonstrations and you were closer to him than anyone in New York. You need to tell me exactly what you know, from the beginning, and what you've done. Everything. If you help us and if you're the innocent pawn you claim to be, then we'll see about working something out and sending you home. But don't make the mistake of thinking that being an American will protect you. You're on our soil; we control things here. You better think about that. Your little romance has gotten you in serious trouble. And right now, I don't believe your act."

He got up and walked out.

Left alone, Rachel felt herself collapse inside. All she wanted was to be at the conference, to make this all go away and to start her visit again. And where were her belongings? The storyboards for the children's books that showed children learning about diabetes and doctors explaining how to care for themselves? All that work and all that planning. The thought that it would all go to waste was devastating. Everything was slipping away from her. She might never get into med school; her whole life might go awry if this wasn't straightened out. How could he think she had anything to do with a bomb?

The cuffs hurt her wrists but moving her hands around just made them tighter, like those Chinese handcuffs she played with as a child. She willed her body to loosen up, but couldn't get comfortable and finally let her head drop to the side and closed her eyes. She didn't sleep, just drifted in and out, wondering where Michael was and what exactly they thought he'd been involved with. Daniel and Jill had been suspicious of him all along, had warned her to stay away. Had they been right?

She kept trying to work it out, but nothing made sense. The stupor induced by the Mediterranean summer heat and jet lag got hold of her. The faint smell of Michael's cologne was still in her clothes, her hair. She still felt his energy like an aura, distracting her from rational thought.

Her eyes were watery but she was unable to properly wipe them. She was a mess and knew she had to regain control, to figure this out, to get it right.

Eitan seemed convinced that she knew something important. He wanted something from her, a confession or something tying Michael and SPHR to terrorism. It was such a stereotype, assuming anyone who supported Palestinians was a terrorist. She could just imagine Amira's disgust and disappointment at such a charge. *Or was Amira complicit in something nefarious as well?* Eitan had her doubting everything and everyone she knew. It didn't help to know that she had been deceived for her whole life by her mother. And by Dr. Bergman. Was she the only honest person on the planet?

No. Eitan was wrong. It was all wrong. Nevertheless, she searched her memory as if hunting through files for a misplaced paper. *Had she seen something in Michael's expression when he was engaged in discussions with Yusif and she walked in unexpectedly? What about the way he kept certain papers in a locked drawer? Why hadn't she listened more closely when he'd talked about the group he'd belonged to as a kid?* Michael had always spoken of his childhood antics with amusement, reminding her of when she and her friends went punk for a while and dyed their hair purple. A passing phase. Kid stuff. Then she remembered how he'd intimidated those punks in the car, slamming the door shut. He was so capable in the face of potential violence. *Had she ignored the signs of something because she was so besotted, so thrilled at the thought that he liked her?*

When Eitan returned, he immediately banged his fist on the metal table, startling her. "What was your role, Rachel? What did he tell you to do?"

She waited a beat. Gathered her thoughts. She felt shaky, but would not give him the satisfaction of seeing her cry,. "I told you, I only worked on the Children's Health Initiative, and I was part of a Palestinian dance troupe that performed a few times. I went to their meetings and learned their side of the conflict. They were outspoken and sometimes over-the-top in their accusations, but that was the worst of it, and they made some good points. I don't know what you're talking about. What are you talking about?"

"That's all you know?"

She nodded. It sounded as if he were starting to believe her.

"Then why weren't you going to be at the conference?"

He kept coming up with new accusations. "Michael said he needed me elsewhere."

"You wanted to be out of harm's way, didn't you?"

"No, I wanted to go to the conference, but—"

"Rachel, the group you were involved with has used violent means to bring attention to their causes in the past. They haven't given up. Tell me about their plans."

"There's nothing."

"Yes, there is. Bombs, murder of Jewish civilians."

"That's ridiculous. I would have known," she said with more conviction than she felt. She knew Michael kept things from her. But this?

"Have you ever heard of a Dr. Waseem?"

Rachel remembered the picture in Michael's apartment of the gentle looking man who had bought Michael a drum. She nodded.

"He runs an organization in the territories," Eitan said.

"Yes, I know of it. Michael mentioned him a few times."

"It is called the People's Revolution Party."

"No, that's not it. That's the name of the group that murdered my father."

He nodded.

"That's not possible. You're making that up to confuse me." She began to sob, the strain suddenly too much. He observed her like she was an insect that he couldn't decide whether to crush or let live. His expression made her angry, and she managed to pull herself together. His timeline didn't work. "Even if it were true, Michael was just a kid then. He wouldn't have been involved."

"These kids start young."

"*These kids?* Don't group them together; they are individuals. People! Michael—a respected doctor—wasn't involved with anything like that!"

"He was. And he is."

She shook her head.

"You're saying you didn't know? You're not too bright, are you? Or did you never talk, just spent all your time fucking? Was he good in bed? Was it worth it?"

She cringed.

"Think hard. You need to remember everything that happened in the past few months. We've arranged a *suite* for you here at our *hotel*. We'll talk more tomorrow. And the next day, and the day after. As long as it takes."

"My mother," she said. "I'm supposed to call her to let her know I've arrived."

"We'll call her. Come on."

The "suite" was a room just large enough for a cot, a sink, a squat toilet, and a door that locked from the outside. She was too tired to protest and knew it would be useless anyway. They finally removed the handcuffs and she massaged her wrists and moved her head in circles to unkink her neck and shoulders. They gave her some bread and fried chicken so greasy it soaked through the cardboard box, and a Coke with Hebrew writing on the outside. It reminded her of the poster at Henry's, the first time they went there. Michael saying, "Have a Coke?" She smiled to herself at the memory, but then tears welled up and her smiled faded. She'd never felt so powerless, so abandoned, in her life. And when she thought about what Eitan had said about Michael, she wanted to crawl out of her skin. If it were even remotely true, she wasn't sure she could live with herself. She certainly couldn't face her mother. *Could Michael have been involved with her father's murderers?* She pictured him huddled over the news stories in the library, his concern for her. It wasn't possible. She had to find a way to talk to him. He would explain it. They'd gotten it all wrong. It was a massive mistake.

She couldn't sleep, just sat on the cot, her knees drawn up, her arms wrapped around them, glad, at least, to be free of the handcuffs. She thought about all that Eitan had said. From everything she knew, Israeli intelligence was among the best in the world.

Could their accusations be true?

The next day, they brought Rachel back to the same interrogation room. She was dizzy with hunger, having left the greasy chicken dinner untouched, as well as the hardboiled egg and cheese breakfast.

"We just arrested another member of Michael's group who worked at the hotel where the conference was scheduled to take place," Eitan told her. "We found parts that would've been assembled to make a bomb. We believe Michael would've supplied the rest of the parts or had the know-how to put them together and detonate it."

"No." Her voice was hoarse, her throat dry. "He's a doctor. A healer. He doesn't blow things up." But a fragment of uncertainty had lodged in her mind overnight. *They'd found a bomb?*

"He must love you, alright," Eitan said almost to himself. "I've seen your type before, women who get all hot and bothered by Arab men."

"You sound jealous."

He bit his lower lip. "That's good, Rachel. Show some spunk. Defend your lover."

"I want to see him. You're trying to wear me out so I'll say anything, agree to anything. Where is he? I want to talk to Michael. He'll set it all straight."

"Maybe we'll allow you to talk to him, eventually. First, tell me how he communicated."

She looked at him blankly.

"With the doctor. How did he communicate with him?"

She shook her head, baffled.

"He works for the doctor. He always did and still does. You're telling me that you never put it together?"

"Put what together? Are you talking about Dr. Waseem?"

Eitan's eyes narrowed and then rolled upwards as if seeking help.

"You're saying that Dr. Waseem is a terrorist, not a human rights activist, and Michael follows his orders?"

"Yes Rachel. That's it. Now you've got it. But you already knew that."

She shook her head. "Even if that were true, why would they plant a bomb at a conference? What would be the point in destroying an organization of people who want to help their sick children?"

"You tell me, Rachel. Why would they do that?"

"They wouldn't. It makes no sense." She wasn't a fool. She knew there was terrorism. It existed. But not Michael.

"*Sense?* You think this is logical? These are people with a mission and they're not above killing to make a point." He let out a breath and sat back. "So, you say you knew nothing of any of this. Your boyfriend led you along like a trusting puppy and you just barked and wagged your ass? Are you sure you want to admit to being so foolish? It's not a defense. It might lighten you sentence, but—"

"*Sentence?* What am I accused of?"

"Conspiracy in a terrorist plot."

"No! I'm working on a children's health clinic! I'm going to med school! Michael was working on important medical research. He's a brilliant doctor."

Eitan softened his tone, as if finally taking pity on her. Good cop and bad cop all rolled into one. "Yes, Michael's very bright. In another life, he might have cured diabetes, who knows?" He sounded almost wistful. "But he took a different path. His whole life has been the revolution. He picked that path when he was too young to know what he was doing, but that doesn't excuse him. He's made some terrible choices."

"What terrible choices?"

"Has he told you about his father? Has he told you how he treated his own father?"

That didn't make any sense. Michael had spoken of his father with love and respect. Hadn't he? Or was it the doctor that he spoke of with reverence? But even if Dr. Waseem was extreme, it didn't mean Michael was involved. He wasn't a cold-blooded monster. He would have an explanation for all this and the culprit would be Israel. They put Palestinians in prison all the time, and now she was here because she helped

Palestinians. Someday she and Michael would be together, away from all this, closer because of it—

"Rachel! Pay attention!"

She looked at him.

"Waseem is head of the People's Revolution Party. They call him Akil. I've been following the group for years. You might say they're my specialty. Waseem's in prison now and he'll be there for a long time. I allowed Michael to operate only because we were keeping track of him and, frankly, his involvement was limited until recently. But he's active again. The original plan was to plant a bomb in your luggage and send you ahead."

Now she knew that his accusations were preposterous! Michael would never risk her life.

"I can believe he didn't tell you about that. Even your great love for him might have its limits, and you wouldn't voluntarily carry a bomb that would kill you. But that plan was aborted in favor of a bomb at the conference, and I think you did know about that plan and that's why you were going to stay away. Were there other plans? We need details. It's time for you to do the right thing."

Her face was blank, puzzled, pale.

"Answer me! Or are you committed to their cause?"

She didn't answer.

"Let me show you some pictures of what they do in the name of their cause." He opened a folder and brought out a photograph of the body of a young woman. It was difficult to tell how old she was because a bomb had mangled her body. "This was the result of a terrorist act we weren't able to stop. The People's Revolution Party took credit. It happened eight years ago and this young woman was about to go to university. She wanted to be a doctor. Like you, Rachel. Twenty people were killed when a bomb exploded on a bus in Jerusalem. Ten others were seriously injured. These are their pictures."

He laid them out on the table. She stared at them, picked up each one individually, tried to give each person the proper respect. Much of her sympathy had flowed toward the Palestinians these past months. She'd almost forgotten why Israel had to enforce strict security measures; the same measures she'd protested because they were so hard on the innocent. And yet, how many lives had they saved? She imagined thousands of Israelis marching in grotesque formation—people who would also be dead or injured but for those measures.

All of Michael's arguments were built on a fragile foundation. She'd been intrigued by them, by the whole package: his apartment, his parties, his meetings, his attentions. She thought she loved him. But if this was true, then he'd left her out of what mattered most to him. She'd only scratched the surface of his life and hadn't recognized what she'd found there.

All of her romantic dreams of getting to know Michael better in Israel over the summer were a stupid fantasy. She was a stupid girl; there was no other way to see it. She'd been so thrilled that a man like Michael would fall in love with her. She'd thought of herself as so mature and morally upright and unprejudiced—unlike her unenlightened friends and former boyfriend.

What a joke. If it were true.

She tottered back and forth, believing and disbelieving Eitan. She had to hear it from Michael. She had become accustomed to his counsel; he was mentor and confidant and friend as well as lover. She needed to hear his side.

"We take these things very seriously. We need to know in advance, not after the fact," Eitan said, his voice soothing now, as if he wanted her bent but not broken.

"These are terrible pictures. But there are pictures of Palestinians that are just as bad. I only wanted to help the children. Michael's little sister died. Did you know that? We were naming the clinic in her honor." She was attempting to appeal to Eitan's humanity, get him to recognize that there was another side, but he was like a block of steel, impervious to anything but his own beliefs.

So she answered his questions the best she could. She got dizzy, closed her eyes and rested her forehead in her hand, and he kept on questioning her, steady and relentless: Who made their reservations, who packed her luggage, who reserved the hotel, the list of attendees, their plans to travel in the country, the names of any people Michael had mentioned. So many questions. When he had exhausted her completely, she pleaded with him to see Michael, holding tight to a tiny shred of hope that there was another explanation.

He must have thought it would help them, because he said yes.

The Jews pride themselves on being intellectual, Michael thought, yet they send thugs to control the Palestinians, to interrogate them with threats and taunts and abuse. He'd told them nothing and yet he could tell by their questions that they knew everything. How was it possible? He wracked his brain, tormenting himself with possibilities as they'd questioned him. *Was it Rachel? Was she planted there all along—the perfect spy? Had he been duped by her?* Or had she become involved unintentionally? Had she gotten up in the middle of the night and found something on his desk and figured it out? But he'd been very careful and there was almost nothing in writing. They knew things about his past that she had no way of knowing.

No, it wasn't her. But now she would know. She would believe he was a monster, twist everything around so it appeared he was using her the whole time. He had been, but not for that purpose. It was all for a good purpose, a goal they shared. And if wanting her to love him was using her, then so he had done.

If it wasn't Rachel, then who? These men knew more about the plan than he did. He hadn't even received any final instructions about the bomb, had been hoping Akil would use someone else, and yet his interrogators knew all about it. They understood his status in the Party, his history, but they wanted more: names of other members, other cells, meeting places, safe houses. He hadn't told them anything except some things he'd made up in an attempt to send them on a wild goose chase and waste their time. But they'd somehow known he was lying, so even that had failed.

Eitan told him that after his arrest, they'd raided safe houses and arrested others. Men and women who'd operated under the radar for years had been exposed. The damage to Akil's inner circle was heavy. His plans to disrupt the peace talks were derailed. He was finished. The moderates would take over the Party and lead the Palestinians to the negotiating table.

It was a devastating failure caused by a traitor and the harm to Akil was likely irrevocable. There was only one thing left for Akil to do. He would identify the traitor and get retribution. Someone would have to pay and Michael realized, at first with amazement and then with certainty, that it would be him.

He was a dead man. Because if Rachel wasn't the informer, that left only one other possibility. Someone who knew both his background in Palestine and his activities in New York and used his knowledge to set Michael up.

Yusif.

But why? Was Yusif jealous of him? Desperate for money? Had the Israelis blackmailed him? Such a betrayal from a man he'd known and trusted almost his entire life. It was inconceivable, yet there was no other explanation. Yusif had betrayed him.

Yusif was playing a dangerous game and if Akil and the others figured it out, it would cost Yusif his life. The Israelis couldn't afford to lose Yusif. They did their best to protect their informants. One thought followed another in inexorable progression to the only possible conclusion: *The Israelis would frame him to protect Yusif.*

The only question remaining in Michael's mind was how they would manage it.

Eitan solved that riddle when he mentioned that Yusif had discovered large deposits into Michael's bank account in New York and reported them to Akil. It was all a fabrication, of course, but Michael had given Yusif the keys to his apartment when he left, so it was plausible. Forged paperwork was easy.

Michael guessed that Yusif also told Akil that Michael was planning to keep Rachel away from the hotel—contravening Akil's instructions—as further proof that Michael was working against them. Michael's desire to protect Rachel had unwittingly given him that minor betrayal.

It was Yusif all along. How had he not guessed?

It was Akil's mistake, having him work with Yusif, using Eva as a conduit for messages. It was Akil's mistake but he would pay. He'd been dead the moment the plan was put in motion. Whatever plan they'd decided upon, Yusif would have stopped it and the Israelis would have found a way to implicate him.

CHAPTER TWENTY-ONE

The discordant sounds of the metal chairs against the linoleum floor provided a welcome distraction from the sight before her. Rachel had never seen this man before, though he'd been so close to her she still had a scratch from the stubble of his beard on her cheek.

Now his beard was just long enough to cast a sinister shadow. It didn't suit him, made him look evil, or perhaps that was just her mind playing tricks on her. It was shocking how he had changed in two days. She saw no bruises, but he looked beaten. His eyes were glazed, like they'd been in a kiln and hardened against the appeal of her emotions. She couldn't find the Michael she knew in them.

"Rachel. You've come at last." He spoke with the same seductive voice, the one that always got to her. It made her want to fall in love with him again, to forget where they were and all the Israelis claimed he'd done.

She sat opposite him across a small table. His hands and feet were chained. "You look awful," she said.

"They're not very nice to me, your Israeli friends."

"Nor to me. But they're doing their job. They said that you were going to get me killed."

"That's what they told you?"

She nodded.

"I wouldn't have let anything happen to you, Rachel. I would've protected you."

He spoke clearly, enunciating every word, and Rachel felt his voice reverberate inside her. She believed him and felt weak with relief—until she understood. He would have protected her, but only her. "You would have let them kill others?"

He looked tired, as if he didn't want to answer any more questions. "What have they told you?"

"That the Children's Health Initiative was established to give your Dr. Waseem a chance to commit a terrorist act and murder innocent people."

"That's a lie."

She felt a glimmer of hope when he said that. But she had grown up in that little cell overnight, so it didn't last. "What's the truth?"

"The truth? There are so many truths. Which one do you want? Akil's truth? That children are suffering because the Zionists have taken what doesn't belong to them, first our land, then our dignity. That because we have no armies to fight them, we must use the only weapons available: explosives, airline schedules. That though lives may be lost in the short run, in the long run, many more will be saved. That's the truth I grew up with."

"You told me you wanted peace."

"My father wanted peace. I wanted victory. Revolution."

"That was when you were very young, just a child. You grew into a different man. You aren't some fanatic, Michael! You're a respected doctor, a brilliant researcher. You help people, cure them. *You aren't a murderer.*"

He gave a sad smile. "Ah, Rachel… it's true that I'd hoped to... do so many things."

"So, why this plan? If you knew there would be a bomb at the hotel, why didn't you stop it? This wasn't some campus protest... all those people...doctors who wanted to help ... I invited them and helped convince Dr. Bergman to give his approval. They think I'm involved."

"They're not the ones you have to worry about."

"What do you mean?"

"You should be careful."

"Because your friends are dangerous?"

"They are not my friends anymore. But yes."

"What are they to you if not friends? Colleagues? Is that what you call them?" she said, almost as sarcastic as Eitan.

He didn't respond.

"Not even that? What then? Did they buy you? Your first-class education, the beautiful apartment, the car?"

Michael held her gaze, said nothing.

"You do what that doctor commands *because he pays for everything?*"

"Don't be ridiculous, Rachel," he scoffed. "Akil doesn't buy anyone. He invites loyalty and is careful whom he trusts. I chose him as much as he chose me. I make my own decisions." He paused. "I fell in love with you, Rachel, all on my own."

He'd never said he loved her before. She closed her eyes as a feeling of warmth flooded through her. For a moment, she wasn't in a prison with a terrorist. She was with the man she loved and felt weak with tenderness. She edged her chair closer and reached out to him. He enclosed her hand in his.

"But it could never happen. It was doomed before it started."

She pulled her hand back.

"I chose when I was young and I don't get to change my mind. This isn't America, where you can reinvent yourself. There is no turning back or veering onto another path."

"Michael," she said, still uncomprehending, "Why would Akil kill doctors who want to help your people? Why destroy clinics that would benefit your children?"

He raised his voice, as if volume would lend reason to his argument. "It was a question of priorities. The clinics would have addressed the symptoms, not the root of the problem. The whole paradigm must change. Children will suffer as long as there is an occupation, no matter how many clinics we build."

There was something essentially wrong with the logic. Yet, she remembered how frustrated she'd felt when she learned of all the roadblocks, literal and bureaucratic, the seemingly unnecessary obstacles Israelis place in the way of helping Palestinians in need. She'd argued about it with Daniel, making the case for easing restrictions, letting people travel without checkpoints and searches.

But, for her it had always been an intellectual discussion over strong coffee in a warm cafe, surrounded by normalcy. She could afford to congratulate herself on her good intentions. What about the Israelis who lived with actual threats, day after day after day? People who feared for their children?

The inconveniences and indignities borne by the Palestinians were life-saving for the Israelis. The occupation was necessary because of people like Akil, who chose violence over peace. He wanted to obliterate Israel, but only succeeded in keeping his own people mired in misery. Yet, somehow he was the one who carried on his work, while her father's life was cut short.

The whole region was filled with grief and loss and tragedy, but she had thought that only a few crazy radicals reacted by intentionally killing innocent people. Now she knew that Michael was a part of this. How could he believe such things? How could he go along with them?

"That's Akil, speaking. Not you. You're a doctor, a healer. You respect life."

She sat back in her chair. Flies buzzed around the room and one landed on the table. The bars crossing the open window cast faint shadows across the floor. She heard a loud cough outside the door and a woman's voice—high-pitched, speaking very fast in a language she didn't understand.

Michael fingered the rough stubble of his beard. He was always so meticulous, but now he looked dirty. Troubled. She saw defeat in his eyes, heard it in his voice. It broke her heart to see him this way. She knew now that Eitan was right about him and that she would not see him again for a very long time. She needed answers and this might be her only chance to get them.

"You said your father was working with the Israelis. Didn't you feel any responsibility to him? You told me how both our fathers—"

"My father…"

"What happened to him?"

"I've told you."

"No, there's more," she said, surprised by the resonance in her own voice. 'I know that now."

He looked at her carefully. "It had to happen," he said.

"What did?"

"It had to be done, so I helped them."

"You helped whom?"

He'd told her about his past before, back in the diner and when they were in bed. She wondered if any of it had been true. Or even if he was now telling the truth.

"The Party. My father was working against us. He was trying to make peace with Israel. I tried to make him stop. I begged him to keep fighting the Zionists, not to give up. He would have traded away our land, our pride, our very identity. My mother hated what he was doing. She'd always been so proud of him, but she was ashamed. I wanted her to be proud, at least, of me.

"I remember how he would say that we should have accepted the partition when they offered it to us, like we should have taken their scraps. He was wrong and had to be stopped, a message sent to others who would have followed him. You had to hear Akil when he explained it. He had a vision for our future. He was the only one who made sense."

"That's what you believe?" she asked. "That there could never be—*can* never be--coexistence with Israel?"

He stopped and looked at her, his eyes roaming over her face as if searching for an opening into her mind. "I believe in a better world for my people."

"But so did your father!"

"No, no....You don't understand because you have always been proud of your father, of his memory, of the fact that he was a respected physician. It was different for me. No one respected my father. Even the stupidest, the lowest of the *fedayeen* felt superior to me because I was the son of a traitor. I tried to distance myself from him, but it wasn't enough. There was only one way to redeem myself."

He'd only been a child at the time. Even now, his words sounded like hollow echoes of a litany that must have been drummed into him years earlier. They flowed through him, but didn't come from the man she knew.

"He knew that what he was doing was dangerous, so he kept moving around and they couldn't find him. No one knew where he was except me and my mother. I had to distance myself from him in the eyes of my comrades. To show them that I was committed."

"You were only a child! They used you!"

"No, I knew what I was doing. I wanted to live a courageous life. And I loved Akil. *Wadih.*"

"Wadih?"

"It means *peaceful*, like a glassy river on a calm day. It was his name, my friend…"

For a few seconds his eyes filled with what she recognized unquestionably as grief, and that sign of humanity gave her hope for him. It was inconceivable that he'd had to live with this burden his whole life. She wanted to reach out to him, to comfort the child in him, but he reversed the course of his emotion on his own, an exercise of self-control he'd mastered over the years, his only means of coping. She looked at him with pity and his lips twisted in disgust.

"Don't look at me like that. You don't know what it's like to work for something bigger than your own life, to commit yourself to a greater cause. How could you know? You act on whims and sexual attraction."

She realized he was mocking her.

The shock on her face seemed to wake him from his dazed confession. He smiled his old smile, so appealing, even now. "Forget about it, Rachel. There's no reason for you to understand this. You were only working on the clinic. You're not responsible."

"But the clinic was a sham."

"It didn't start out that way. You are absolved," he said, making a motion with his hand as if wiping away the stain.

"They said that Dr. Waseem is the leader of the People's Revolution Party."

"That's true."

"But you said you'd barely known of them."

"I couldn't tell you the truth about that, Rachel. You would never have understood."

"Did you know about the massacre—when my father was killed? *Did you know about my father?"*

He seemed to consider the question, then, for whatever reason, maybe because there was no point in lying anymore, or maybe because he wanted her to hate him—or perhaps because truth was the only gift he could give—he said, "I never made the connection until you told me. It was a long time ago. I was just a kid, and there were so many actions, so many killings. I just remember that at the time, we celebrated the whole thing as a success. Everyone was so proud. There was dancing in the streets when we heard. The Israelis had imposed a curfew but there was nothing they could do to diminish the joy and celebration."

Rachel felt numb. "You were proud of the murder of schoolchildren? A pregnant woman and a small child? My father?" The intense yearning she'd felt in Michael's presence had completely vanished now. There were some things that could never be forgiven or understood. *He'd celebrated her father's death.* It was a highlight in the "struggles" of his people. His "political statement," meaningless in the end, had inflicted a wound she'd suffered her whole life. She wanted him to apologize, to be ashamed, to beg forgiveness.

"It wasn't personal, Rachel. It brought attention to the cause. It showed them that they were not infallible, that they would never be safe. That's why Akil wanted you at the conference, because you were your father's daughter. But I was sending you away. Don't you see? I went against him to protect you."

He reached for her hand but she drew it away. "I lied to him. I'd never done that before. It was the only way to make up for… for what I've done."

"No, Michael…it doesn't excuse…"

"I would have protected you, but I couldn't stop the others. I wasn't even involved in what was going to happen at the hotel. All I could have done was warn the Israelis and that I could never do."

"Why not?"

"Because… I hoped to talk to him, to Akil, to turn his ideas around. I couldn't destroy him. I don't know how to explain this to you, but I am committed to him. That can never change."

"Yes it can. You can work for the Israelis. If you show them you've changed, they will let you stay here. Maybe you can go back to New York, continue with your research—"

He shook his head, put up his hand as far as the chain would allow. "Stop. It's not going to *all work out*. There's no way to fix this. I'll never work for Israel." He paused and looked at her thoughtfully, almost kindly, so unlike himself, more like her. "But you can. When I met you, your concerns were so simple. Med school and a little pediatric practice. Marriage and a few kids. I gave you a taste for politics and commitment. Don't go back to an irrelevant life. Let your life mean something."

"Mean something?"

"Make the clinics a reality. It'll be harder, but you can still make it happen. Help the children. They don't have to suffer. Do it for me. For us. For your father and for mine. For Hanna."

In that moment, he sounded like the Michael she knew, a man with a purpose who found ways around obstacles. If only he could find his way out of this mess.

"It will be our legacy," he continued, his voice gaining in strength. "Something good can still come of us. It was our creation, but you must make it real on your own. Bergman will help. Find others. Promise me." His voice was alive with urgency. "It will make what's to come bearable."

"What's to come…" she repeated.

"Tell me you will do it. Say it." He looked in her eyes— the brilliant, harsh, demanding, complicated man she had loved. At that moment, she would say anything he needed to hear.

"Yes, of course I will."

He closed his eyes and his features relaxed. "Good. Now go, Rachel. Leave me." He turned away from her.

The door opened and Eitan came in. He motioned to her with his hand. "Out."

She didn't move.

"Now!" he barked. Michael was looking at the floor. She got up, went around the table and put her arms around him and whispered, "I will," before Eitan pulled her away.

"You have a visitor," said Eitan, and there was Rivka. The sight of her mother made her weak with relief. She took a few steps toward her when Eitan grabbed her shoulder. "You have two minutes. I have more questions."

Rivka ignored him and wrapped her arms around her daughter. Rachel heard herself sob, but it sounded oddly distant, as if it came from someone else. She knew Eitan was standing close; she smelled the odor of cigarette smoke emanating from his clothing.

Rivka pulled back first, looked her in the eyes. "You idiot," she said, stroking Rachel's hair.

Her mother was pale and wore no makeup or jewelry, evidence of just how distraught she was. Rachel saw her concern in the lines that etched her eyes and lips. "I'm sorry."

"I tried to stop you. I told you not to come here. But I never thought—"

"None of us did. Not even Uncle Steven."

"Bergman! It's his fault. Why did he have to hire that man? He couldn't hire a Jewish boy? An Israeli, if he wanted to be international?" She looked at Eitan, as if he'd understand, but he just made a sound like a snort and pulled at Rachel's arm. "That's enough. *Yalla.*" He motioned to the door leading back to the interrogation room. "I have more questions."

"What about Michael? What's going to happen to him?" Rachel said.

Eitan shrugged.

"Forget about him!" Rivka cried. "Erase him from your memory! All my life, I tried to protect you from something like this, from anything remotely like this, and even now you ask about *that man*? What about me? What about my life? I thought I'd lost you, I..."

"Mom," Rachel whispered. "You're right. I'm sorry. I wasn't thinking. It's all so strange, I thought..."

"The important thing is that you're safe," Rivka said, recovering herself, the shrillness gone, or at least under control.

"Go back to your hotel," Eitan ordered Rivka. "I'll call you when, or if, we're ready to let her go." He pushed Rachel ahead of him into the hallway, which led to the interrogation rooms, and directed her inside one of them.

This one had no windows. It was airless, the gray paint was peeling and the metal chair was hard, but Rachel couldn't have relaxed in the finest feather bed. She was tired in a way she'd never experienced before, inside her bones, in the recesses of her brain. She was drained of the force that once gave her vitality. She didn't need sleep. She needed hope.

Eitan began again, as if they'd never spoken of it before. He quizzed her about Yusif and Amira, showed her pictures of people she didn't recognize, made her recall every detail of Michael's apartment and SPHR headquarters. He asked her what she knew of Michael's finances, how he paid for things.

"You didn't suspect anything?" he asked for what seemed like the thousandth time. "He had money for an apartment, dinners, a car, and you thought that was normal for a boy from the Palestinian territories?"

"He was working. He had a fellowship and I knew that a doctor had helped him after his father died..."

"You disgust me."

She stared at him, shocked.

"You live in New York, with every opportunity, a mother who would do anything for you, a father who was killed by these animals, and this is who you fuck?"

She didn't respond. He was right, and he was wrong. He kept talking, repeating how she'd been in bed with her father's murderer, making sure she knew how low she had fallen. Then he left the room for what seemed like forever, but with no watch or clock or even a window, she had no way of knowing. When he came back, he held the door open. "Up. Move. *Kol Tov*. We're done"

"I can go?"

"You want to stay?"

She didn't argue.

She was free.

Michael's hands were tied when they put him into the back of the Army Jeep. He was weak from the long days of interrogation. Listless. He knew where they were taking him and what would happen there. After all these years, what he'd worked so hard to avoid was coming to pass as if it were pre-ordained. Akil would abandon him and the Party would reject him because despite all he'd done to disprove it, they would believe that he was his father's son after all. A traitor.

The road leading to Ramallah meandered through the hills. Its unpaved edges merged with the dirt. It was so narrow that the Jeep had to pull aside to make room for the occasional passing truck. Around them, rocky hills were softened by clusters of olive trees. A lone goat wandered nearby, reminding him of a homeless man on the streets of New York. The sky was blue and endless. The driver kept a steady pace.

"Are you planning to drive me right into the middle of town?" Michael said to the soldier next to him.

"Whatever is most convenient for you. It's your home, right? I'm sure your friends will be glad to see you." The Israeli spoke as if they were two buddies out for a ride. Michael wondered what his game was.

"Fine," he said defiantly, "take me right into the middle of Ramallah. Let them all see how well you treat me. Let them think we are the best of friends."

The soldier turned to him. "They're your people, no? Won't they at least give you a chance to defend yourself? A chance to be heard? A trial? They complain enough about how our trials don't meet their high standards."

Michael's eyes burned into him.

"No, of course not, the soldier continued. "They don't hold trials, do they? Except after the fact, sometimes. Maybe they'll declare you a martyr someday."

The driver pulled the Jeep over and turned to Michael, his eyes hidden by sunglasses. "Look, it's not too late, Haddad. We can drive you back. You can still make a deal. We'll protect you. You can still do something with your life. If you help us, we'll help you."

He didn't bother to respond. The Israelis were no better. Their laws and courts and democratic society favored some and discriminated against others. In any case, he could never live as a stranger in Palestine. He just wished he could die a respected man, remembered for loving and sacrificing for his people.

Despite the heat, he felt cold and shivered, more from sorrow than fear. He would never finish his research or establish his clinics. He had denied himself life's simple joys because of some greater goal that he could hardly remember. He struggled to recall what had mattered so much to him for all those years, but his thoughts were no longer ordered, just disconnected fragments.

As the Jeep bumped over the rocky road and Ramallah came into view, a sensation of peace came over him. The image of Akil faded and was replaced by the lined, worried face of his father. Michael had come to resemble his father more with each passing year. He was nearly the same age now as when his father was killed. He remembered his father's warnings.

"Stay away from Akil. He is high on revolution; it is his drug. He didn't start that way, but now he is addicted. He doesn't care about you. He pays you attention because you are my son. It's his way of mocking me."

"No, it's not! He cares about me and will avenge Hanna."

"Don't sacrifice yourself to his lunacy. He will give you a moment of mad joy and a lifetime of misery. You must listen to me."

The image of his father, so real for a few moments, disintegrated into nothingness and a moan escaped him, a sound of mourning from deep inside, for his father and for the sons he would never have. There was no one to carry on. *But carry on what?*

It came to him as an image: thriving cities, peaceful towns and placid farms, hills empty of settlements, roads free of checkpoints, ancient mosques and temples restored. A vision of Palestine as a beautiful realm with many strange and exotic creatures all blending together in harmony: *keffiyas* among black hats and colorful scarves, long robes and skimpy bathing suits. A place where young Rachels and Hannas played together and danced together and then went home to dream. And when they awoke, they got to live out those dreams. Rachel had always seemed so absurdly innocent. But he wanted, just for a moment, to share in her belief—in the belief their fathers had shared—that Jew and Arab could live together in peace.

The soldier untied his hands and let him out at a café.

It didn't take them long to find him. Outside the café, a strong arm pulled him into an alley. "Are you Michael Haddad?" a man asked, his *keffiya* pulled across his face in defiance of Israeli regulations. Michael nodded and the man acted swiftly and efficiently. Two bullets to the heart. Without another sound, the man disappeared into the crowded marketplace.

CHAPTER TWENTY-TWO

Rachel was in the hotel dining room having tea with her mother the day after her release. A security detail had been assigned to them, shadowing their every move. Eitan came in and sat down without asking permission. "There is news," he said, "We let Michael out of prison and took him home. And then, well, here, read it for yourself." He took a *Jerusalem Post* from his backpack and pointed to an article on the first page:

Israel Law Center condemns Tuesday night's brutal murder of a suspected Israeli agent in Ramallah. The body of Dr. Michael Haddad, 29, a former resident of Ramallah, was delivered to a Palestinian hospital late last evening. The People's Revolution Army claimed responsibility for the gangland-style execution. A masked spokesman for the group accused Haddad of assisting the IDF in identifying and arresting fugitive Palestinians. "We shot him dead because he was a collaborator who has helped Israel kill and detain many Palestinians."

She read it with disbelief. Killed by his own group? That made no sense. "He wasn't an Israeli agent." She looked at Eitan with suspicion. "What have you done!"

Eitan rolled his eyes and brushed a piece of lint off his sleeve.

Rivka turned to Eitan. "Stop looking at her with that condescending expression. Her father gave his life for this country, she deserves some respect."

Eitan looked almost amused at Rivka's outburst, but didn't respond.

"Why did you let him go?" Rachel asked. "That makes no sense."

"We let him go so that he would lead us to others. Only it turns out that his people thought he'd betrayed them. We've made some arrests and they blamed him. It doesn't take much these days. They're killing collaborators right and left over there. Your friends."

Rivka's eyes widened. "What about Rachel? Is she safe?"

"She should leave the country. We're working on it."

Rivka bolted up. "Well finish making the arrangements! Rachel, come with me to the room."

But Rachel didn't move.

Nothing made sense. Not Eitan's explanation, not Michael, not the Palestinians. She needed space to think, to move around, to be on her own. She pushed her chair back. "I'm going for a walk."

"What are you talking about? You're in danger! We have to leave."

She looked hard at her mother. She'd been so relieved to see Rivka, but now she felt smothered. "No, Mom. I can't breathe right now. I need to be alone."

"Eitan, talk to her."

"You can't go walking around by yourself."

"Right, I guess not, but I don't want to go home with you, Mom. I want to go home alone. I have to deal with this myself."

"It's not the worst idea, actually," Eitan said. "I can get Rachel out of here this afternoon and Steven Bergman is arriving tonight. He agreed to be questioned, and we'd like to talk to you, too, Mrs. Weissman. Stay another day. We have a secure house where you and Dr. Bergman can both stay, and you'll be safe there."

"I'm not staying here. I can't get out of here soon enough."

"That's the problem, Mom." Her mother looked surprised at her tone. She was speaking with authority, coolly certain. "You've always avoided facing Daddy's death. You lied to me about it and you lied to yourself. Stay and face it. Get in touch with the man who survived and was with Daddy at the end. Yaakov."

"They build a memorial to the victims of the massacre in the town. Your husband's name is listed," Eitan said.

"You see, Mom? You didn't know that, did you?"

"No."

"Do it, Mom. It's the right thing. They'll make sure I get back alright."

"I can't believe this. Fine. If that's what it takes to get you to leave, Rachel, I'll stay. You make sure she stays safe!" she told Eitan.

It all happened quickly after that. She threw her stuff in her bag and Eitan drove her to the airport. As they made their way through the streets of Tel-Aviv she drifted off, forgetting everything for minutes at a time, awash in the colors and sounds around her, the shouts in Hebrew through the open window, young men and women in dark-green uniforms with guns slung carelessly over their shoulders, the smell of the ocean, the laughter from the cafes, the rush, rush, rush. And then she'd remember: the prison, the feel of handcuffs restraining her movements, the relentless questions—a swelling of memories that climaxed with the horror of Michael's betrayal and his death.

She was glad to be leaving. She would remember her promise to Michael, later. For now, she wanted nothing to do with this country. It took her father. It took Michael. She'd had enough.

Yusif arrived at the Kennedy Airport an hour early, anxious to see his wife. He was as nervous as if it was their first date. When he saw her moving through the crowd, her hips swaying slightly, he smiled. She walked into his arms and he held her for a long time, oblivious to the other passengers moving past them.

"It was horrible, Yusif," she told him as they made their way through the terminal. "They've arrested everyone. Even friends and relatives who had nothing to do with it! Anyone who was ever associated with the Party during the seventies, their parents, their spouses, everyone is being questioned and jailed."

She spoke very fast, the words tumbling out in a rush. Yusif averted his eyes.

"Why can't we get rid of them?" she said, swatting the air, as if the Israelis were invisible bugs.

"They are impossible to destroy. They were reduced to ashes and still they go on. It's like trying to take away half a number until you reach zero. It doesn't happen; something always remains."

"What are you talking about?" she said, irritation creeping into her voice.

He shook his head. "Nothing. Just that we must keep fighting."

"Yes! They arrested two sons of our neighbor, the Khalids. They are still in their teens! And the grandmother, too."

"At least you are here, now. Safe with me. At last. I missed you terribly."

"Me too," she said with a smile, but it faded in an instant. "I got out, but I worry for my parents. What will they do? I am here and our friends are arrested. They have no one."

"Your parents will be fine. We will bring them here."

"Here? How will they live here? They are too old to move."

"They can start again! They must learn to adapt!"

Eva swiveled around so she was facing him. "Yusif?" Her eyes were large and round and framed by long dark lashes. He'd felt them brush his cheek when he kissed her. "We're not living here forever. This is just temporary. Until things change."

"I have a life here, Eva. I teach, I run the Palestinian student organization. There are many ways you can help from here."

She frowned. "No—"

He pulled her in for a kiss and she was briefly distracted. They continued walking through the airport with their arms around each other. He felt her warmth through her thin dress. She told him, in hurried half-whispered sentences, how Michael had betrayed them and was killed in reprisal. "The same Michael we've known all our lives! Did you have any idea? Did you suspect anything over the last year?"

"Nothing. Michael was a loner. We only worked together. We haven't been friends since we were children."

"My parents were astonished. Everyone was. It's because of him that so many of our friends were arrested. Such a traitor, after all these years!" Her voice was bitter, her lips curled with distaste.

"They have ways of turning people, with bribes or threats," he said. "Who knows what they had on Michael?"

She nodded. "The people they turn are weak. Susceptible. I never thought of Michael like that. But he's been away a long time. Beirut, New York. He forgot what was important." She grasped Yusif's hand. "Why is your hand so cold and clammy? Are you feeling alright?"

"Yes, I'm fine."

She stared at him. "You look pale."

"I'm fine! It's been difficult for me, too. Just because I'm here doesn't mean I don't feel horrible for what is going on at home. I feel responsible..."

"You had no way of knowing," she said, "You're not responsible for their soldiers. But it's gotten much worse since the *intifada* started." Eva continued describing the country he'd left behind, the soldiers patrolling the streets and walking into homes unannounced, stopping men on the street, making Palestinians wait on lines at checkpoints.

"Yusif? Are you alright?" she asked.

"Maybe I am coming down with something. A bug of some kind. But you are right. The Israelis are intent on keeping us under control, but they have no vision for our future. They use...people...force them underground, make them into outcasts and traitors...like Michael...many others..." He trembled and leaned against the wall to steady himself. Eva stood beside him, watching him, puzzled.

And then she looked away.

Rachel climbed the metal stairway leading into the plane and walked down the narrow aisle with small, awkward steps, as if her ankles were bound with chains as Michael's had been. She'd glimpsed them under the table as she left the room but it hadn't registered at the time. Now, it appeared like an image from another galaxy that coalesced before her eyes light years later.

She sat in the middle seat, in the middle of the plane, crowded and uncomfortable. A week earlier, she would have been annoyed and claustrophobic, but now she felt lucky to be free. Lucky that stupidity wasn't a crime.

She never thought that she and Michael would last forever as they were: intimate, lovers. But the future had unfolded gracefully in her imagination, one thing leading to another. She'd thought that in the generous space of time, the energy of their physical attraction would be redirected into their work. They would transform from lovers into colleagues, working together over distance and years. During visits, they would update each other and look back with a melancholy, sweet nostalgia at what they'd once shared. They would be forever entwined by their shared passion to improve the conditions of the Palestinian children. They would be models of mutual acceptance.

Rachel took a sip of vodka. She'd had to show her ID to get served and the stewardess looked suspicious anyway. The man next to her kept asking her what was wrong and telling her to smile. Finally, she said, "My best friend just died," and that shut him up. She wondered if it were true and thought about what they'd shared, not just the physical attraction but something else, something more spiritual, something that made her breath catch in her throat and tears well up in her eyes.

They'd loved each other.

He'd said it only that once, at the end, but she'd known it all along, felt it inside her, and it had made her crazy with joy. She'd believed everything he told her and would have followed him into hell. She almost did. If the Israelis hadn't uncovered the plot, men and women whom she'd cajoled and persuaded to attend the conference would be dead.

Maybe growing up without a father had damaged her, made her susceptible to charlatans like Michael. Even Josh had deceived her, in his own way. So had her mother. Whom could she trust?

She could start by recognizing that evil exists. It had been right in front of her, but she'd refused to see it, had softened the stark edges of the truth and reshaped it to her liking. Michael had admitted that he'd spent time in an Israeli prison. He'd told her how he'd disagreed with his peace-seeking father. Sometimes he'd said "Zionist" as if it were a dirty word. But she'd convinced herself that it was just a stage of his life, youthful rebellion, in the past. The facts of his life told a different story: his close relationship with Dr. Bergman, his prestigious fellowship, his passion for helping children, his openness to a relationship with her. Would a rabid Jew-hater fall in love with her?

She still believed that, at his core, Michael was a man who cared about other people—but the damage had been done early and well. He'd been taught that his survival depended on destroying the Jews, a zero-sum game, a song whose rhythm was drummed into his soul. He didn't understand that the enemy was never the Jews; it was men who would foster such hatred.

It was clear to her now that Michael's leader, his Party, had never wanted two states, side by side. They had steadfastly refused to recognize Israel's right to exist because they wanted it destroyed, wiped off the map. She had heard platitudes like that before, but it was a mindset more hateful and intractable than she'd grasped. Their goals were not aligned with Israel's in any way. They were two circles in a Venn diagram with no point of intersection.

And yet, his Party didn't represent all Palestinians, much as they tried to dominate. Their whole plan was meant to derail the peace talks, which other Palestinians were willing to consider. There were men like Michael's father, who had lost his life working for peace. There was Amira, who sometimes had seemed to recognize the complexity of the competing claims to the land and prayed for peace.

A little boy was in the seat in front of hers, maybe four or five years old. He stood and turned around and peeked over the top of the seat, an invitation to play peek-a-boo. He knew his customer, as her mother might say. She smiled at him and he laughed and hid, then slowly brought his head back up. She played along for a while, until his mother apologized and stopped him, but it was enough to remind her that she needed to see the kids. If there was any hope, it was in the children. They had to be taught differently. Her desire to help them was not a mistake. She had to hold onto that. Her own father had guessed that she would face this moment, and his last words warned her against turning to stone.

She finally fell asleep and woke up when the stewardess announced they were starting their descent. The whole plane erupted in applause as they touched down on American soil.

As Rachel emerged from customs and baggage claim, she saw a tall, redheaded man leaning against one of the concrete columns and was startled to realize it was Daniel. His eyes flickered over her as if searching for something.

"Why are you here?" she said.

"I got the information from your mother. She told me what happened." He kept talking, explaining. She didn't pay attention to the words but the sound of his voice, representing all that was familiar and loving and *normal*, was comforting. She thanked him for being there and asked him to drop her off at the clinic.

"Sure, if that's what you want." He led her to the car without asking any questions. They settled in and he concentrated on navigating out of the airport. After a while she said, "Michael is dead."

"I know. I'm sorry, Rachel."

"You were right. I was in over my head."

"I didn't want to be right. And besides," he said, speaking slowly, as if trying to find just the right words, "The conference and clinic were good ideas. You were right to support them."

"Yes, but…"

"You're a good person, Rachel. You care about children and knew they were suffering and you wanted to help. That's who you are and your instincts are…admirable. Don't let this define you and make you bitter. You can still do a lot of good."

It was the same message her father had left her. Even Michael had begged her to continue their work. All of them so different, and yet they shared this common goal.

She glanced over at Daniel. He was clutching the wheel awkwardly, his body hunched over it, so unlike the way Michael had filled the car seat as if it had been built around him. But, for the first time, she found it attractive, because she realized his awkwardness was a function of his struggle.

When they arrived at the hospital, he dropped her off in front and told her to call him when she was finished, that he could drive her up to Riverdale.

Walking the hallway to the clinic, her shoes tapped out a familiar rhythm. She opened the door to the waiting room. It was a good day. A busy day. Lots of children, different ages, different colors, a range of nationalities. All of them getting along because they were too young to worry about property rights and killing each other. They just wanted to be healthy, to have fun and play games and laugh.

She could deal with that.

Sean, her favorite, was playing solitaire and she remembered how Michael had sat with them once, and they'd teased her. Sean was happy to see her. She pulled up a chair and sat next to him, and he moved his chair a fraction closer to hers. She leaned over the table to see the cards but couldn't, because tears began to spill from her eyes.

Sean looked up, troubled, and awkwardly patted her back, and the room got quiet. One by one, the kids walked over, curious, troubled. The little ones put their arms around Rachel, leaning against her, until she was at the center of an ever-widening circle, a cornucopia of children united around her, trying to make things better.

THE END

OTHER WORK BY SUSAN LERNER

A Suitable Husband, a novel

In 1930s Poland, the economy is crumbling, the government is in chaos, and Jewish groups argue over how best to deal with the increasing anti-Semitism. Among them are the Guardsmen, daring and organized young Zionists, determined to start a new life in Palestine.

A Suitable Husband brings this vibrant period alive with the story of Bianca Lieber, caught between the pressure to marry Alex, the intelligent but staid doctor presented by the matchmaker, and Wolf, the intrepid Zionist leader who can help her get to Palestine.

"...A compelling and superbly written page-turner...with engaging characters, appealing subplots and a fascinating historical background..." Long Island Woman Magazine

The Journal Project, Capturing the Magic of Family Life through Stories

"You are a storyteller. We are all storytellers. Give your family the gift of your stories."

Everyone loves a great story and tales of family life have a special resonance. Keeping a journal of family stories will bring you joy, benefit your children, and leave an invaluable record of your unique family for future generations.

This book discusses why you should keep a family journal, ways of incorporating journaling into your routine, and how and where to journal. It will encourage you to take the first step and the rest will follow.

Visit the author's website at: http://www.sblerner.com to learn more.

And thank you for reading!

Made in the USA
Columbia, SC
14 April 2017